Fool Me Once

by

Deany Ray

Copyright © 2023 Deany Ray
All rights reserved.

This is a work of fiction. All names, characters, places, events, and incidents are either the product of the author's imagination or are used fictitiously. Any resemblance to real names, characters, places, events, and incidents is purely coincidental.
No part of this work may be used or reproduced in any format, by any means, electronic or otherwise without prior consent from the author.

Chapter One

My name is Piper Harris and, together with my grandmother, I was relocated to Florida as part of the witness protection program. Harris isn't even our real last name. I thought witness protection would involve more dark sunglasses and fake mustaches, but it turns out it's just a lot of paperwork.

If anyone had asked me what I thought was more probable, me moving to Florida or an asteroid hitting the earth, I would have tipped for the latter.

I never understood how anyone could live in this humidity at one thousand degrees outside for the most part of the year. Not to mention that when it rained, it didn't get much cooler either.

To top things off, the town we were relocated to was named Bitter End. Yes, exactly. We now lived in Bitter End, Florida. The people working in the witness protection program really had a weird sense of humor.

My home had been in Oregon, where I lived with my grandmother in the same house. Just me and Gran. My only family. Well, to be fair, we were part of a bigger family as well. I'd only known life as part of the Oregon Falcons, an exclusive motorcycle club, the most successful branch of the Falcons network. Some might say they operated like the mob; I would say they were much cooler than that. I mean, we rode Harleys, for crying out loud. We wore denim jeans, leather jackets and biker boots. I always felt like the coolest chick in that outfit.

Fast forward to my current situation: khaki shorts, a constantly sweaty T-shirt, and flip-flops with a flowery pattern on them. Every time I looked in the mirror, I had to hold down the nausea.

It was exactly in this outfit that I stood, hands on hips, in a barely furnished two-hundred-and-fifteen-square-foot apartment with a window the size of a matchbox that was broken and didn't open, with the smell of rotten eggs wafting from every inch of the gray carpet.

"It's not that bad," Edie said, wincing.

Edie Donovan, whose actual first name was Edith, was a resident at the Bitter End retirement community where Gran got her new house. Edie was Gran's next-door neighbor. She had a thing for polka-dot dresses that kind of hurt my corneas. Today, she wore a pink-and-yellow polka-dot dress and chunky sandals.

"Not that bad?" I asked. "We're standing in the same apartment, aren't we?"

Edie looked around and held her nose. "It does smell pretty bad."

"You don't say," I said, shuddering.

"Well, at least the bathroom looked clean," Edie said.

"The bathroom is in the hallway. I would have to share it with four other people." I paused. "Four freaking strangers!"

Edie waved her hand in dismissal. "Big whoop. You can close the door from the inside, can't you?"

I stared at Edie.

She looked away. "Yeah, okay, this place is a dump."

"Thank you." I pulled out a piece of paper I got from Edie from my back pocket and crossed out the fifth apartment we visited in the last three days.

It's been three weeks since Gran moved into the retirement community in Bitter End, Florida. And I moved in with her. That was the genius move behind the whole witness protection thing, because nobody would ever think to look for us here. Every person from our former lives knew we hated the beach and loved the mountains. We hated the heat and loved the chilly. Some days we really thought this was our absolute bitter end. But I guess that's normal when your life goes up in flames and you have to put all the remaining pieces together.

Nobody in Bitter End knew about Gran's and my real identities, and we had to make sure it stayed that way. The WITSEC—witness protection program—had extremely strict rules, and sticking to those rules was the only way to gain maximum success and to survive this new life. Emphasis on surviving. The Oregon Falcons were out for revenge. Revenge on Gran and me. The reason being that Gran testified against them. So it was actually Gran's fault we were in this predicament.

She got busted for tax evasion and money laundering, and that was something the government didn't take lightly. On the contrary, they used Gran's illegal activities to propose a way out for her. Testify against your own members, against your own family who was also involved in nefarious activities, and the government would protect you by providing a new identity for you and a new life for you. There wouldn't be any jail time if you did what the government wanted.

So Gran testified against the Oregon Falcons, put a couple of people that were high up in the organization in prison. And the US marshals, the emotionally. And the aftermath we were *still* dealing with. Some people would pop happy pills; Gran's and my way of coping was drinking a lot of rum and beer. At least you didn't need a prescription for that.

I wouldn't be able to live with Gran in her house forever, so here I was apartment hunting and hating it. Edie immediately wanted to come with me as my personal consultant, which was more than fine with Gran. This wasn't exactly up her alley. But it was definitely up Edie's alley. A lot of things were up Edie's alley.

The other apartments we saw were only a tad better than the dump we were currently standing in. But still no places any human should live in. If I were owning this, I would set the place on fire and cash in on the insurance. That people actually paid money to live just above rat-life level was a mystery to me. On the other hand, if I didn't change something with my own financial situation, I would have to live a life just above rat level.

"I wish you could stay at Dorothy's, and not just temporarily," Edie said as we exited the building. "It's working out fine this way."

I laughed. "I don't know. You bringing us over a peach pie almost daily has me worrying, size-wise."

authority in charge of relocating witnesses, found a new place for Gran and for myself. I had to go with, because of the risk of the Falcons hurting me to get to Gran.

After the marshals whisked me out of my home, Gran and I spent the next thirteen months in hiding, waiting for the trial against the Oregon Falcons. They knew Gran was about to spill everything she knew, thus making us enemy number one with the Falcons. For the first couple of months, I couldn't get over the fact that the people I grew up with, the people that protected me, the people I learned so much from—yes, handling guns and knives counts too—were now after us. It does something to your mind when you're the traitor who ratted out your family in order to save your own butt, and was now on their hit list. Technically, Gran was the rat, but I didn't feel that much better. I knew deep down inside that I could have easily been the one caught doing, let's just say, undesirable stuff. I was no innocent lamb either, and law enforcement had their eyes on us for a long time, just waiting to gather solid proof against us. But as it was, Gran had the pleasure of becoming the testifying witness.

There aren't enough therapists at WITSEC to help you deal with what Gran and I have dealt with

FOOL ME ONCE

"I wouldn't worry that much," Edie said. "You're young; you're burning off calories while breathing. Besides, there's nothing like some good fun in the dirt to raise your appetite for real food." She moved her eyebrows up and down.

I inwardly cringed. I knew what she meant. The residents of the retirement community were going on a field trip the day after tomorrow. To a paintball field. Yes, that's right. They were going to play paintball. Seventy-year-olds and eighty-year-olds with cataracts and artificial hips were going to put on their combat clothes and shoot at each other with balls of paint. If that didn't have hip dislocation written all over it, I didn't know what did.

Outside, the air felt hotter than before. We headed over to the car I shared with Gran, a silver Ford Taurus, and I already felt pearls of sweat forming on my forehead. I looked over at Edie and she seemed to be way fitter than I was. Then again, she'd lived in Bitter End for five years already. And she loved this climate. Her short white hair was perfectly arched, making me wonder what kind of product she was using to avoid frizz.

My once beautiful, long, wavy, dark-brown hair, probably good enough to star in a shampoo commercial, was now all frizz and looked like an undefined blob on my head. Most days I wore a ponytail, seeing as that was my only option.

Edie saw me fiddling with my hair. "Are you sure you don't want to work at a hair salon here in town? Isn't that the easiest option for you?"

Funnily enough, being a hairdresser was one of the lies I told here in Florida. It wasn't a super thought-out plan—actually, it was no kind of plan; it was just something I blurted out when I got asked what I did for a living. And it wasn't the smartest thing that came out of my mouth either. As it turned out, the female residents of the retirement community were in dire need of a hairstylist and thought I was their knight in shining armor. *Way to disappoint.* After a relative unfortunate incident with one of the residents, where she got purple hair instead of silver because she wanted me to dye her hair, I kind of exited this business and declined further invitations from the community residents.

Now, if I could only find a *real* job, that would be awesome.

"I got sick of being a hairdresser," I told Edie. "I want to do something else. Something more exciting. Besides, I wasn't very good at my job either."

"I highly doubt that," Edie said. "I can't imagine you not being good at anything, especially if you really put your mind and heart into it."

A warmth flooded my chest. Having someone believe in me this much after meeting me for the first time only a couple of weeks ago was beyond my own comprehension limit. Granted, I was in a complete opposite state of mind in my current life. The word "trust" had gotten a whole different meaning in the last year. But that was the thing with Edie. Sometimes, she came off totally naïve, other times incredibly stubborn, oftentimes the heart of the party, too often too brazen, and then there was this. She threw out these checkmate, deep and profound statements, prompting me to take a closer look at my own life and my own decisions.

As was the case right now. I had zero idea what to do with my life, but the universe kept pushing for me to find some answers soon. I spent most of my adult life working behind the bar at Choppers, back in Oregon, back when I had my life. In the last few years there, I ran the books as well, a skill no one would ever learn with an official education. Unless they come up with Money Laundering 101 as an economics major.

Edie and I got back to the car and, as soon as she closed the door, I turned on the AC.

"Okay, where to now?" I asked.

It was midmorning on a Monday at the end of September, and I promised Edie I would join her for her errands in downtown Bitter End after we visited the potential apartment for me. I didn't actually know where exactly the trade-off was, since Edie liked both activities and I wasn't a fan of either one. But it was hard saying no to Edie.

"The bank," Edie said. "I need to retrieve some dough." She rubbed her hands together.

"Don't you use the ATM for that?" I asked. "Or just pay with your card?"

"No." She blinked at me like I had asked her if she planned to fly to the moon soon. "I want to be able to go out somewhere, out of my house, talk to a person, look a person in the eye and get the transaction done. You forget us older folks don't have any jobs anymore. The day gets long and lonely if you minimize your humanly interactions."

Right. I kept forgetting that part. The generational gap was never an issue with Gran. That was because Gran was just . . . different. She used to go to the driving range purely for fun. She used to hang out at Choppers and could drink the younger guys under the table any day of the week. But now Gran also had a new life here in Florida, one with fewer activities. Zero activities, actually. She had to quit her former job as a manager of a trucking company, and now her days suddenly became as empty as any other retiree living in the Bitter End retirement community. If I'd see the day Gran would rather put on clothes, get into her car and drive to a brick-and-mortar building only to get cash, I would have to use her own gun against her.

"Okay, the bank it is," I said and pulled out of the parking spot.

Bitter End was about thirty miles from the Atlantic Ocean. Not a village, but not a metropolis either. The architecture was a mix of styles, with a blend of old, low buildings and some new ones. The downtown was heavily populated. There were palm trees scattered on the sides of almost every street. Flip-flops were the footwear of choice, and the clothes were colorful. The buildings were colorful. The cobblestone streets were colorful. Pastel colors were the way to go around here.

Barf.

All in all, the atmosphere seemed to be laid-back and relaxed. That was at least the impression I got from the few times I got out of the retirement complex.

One hour later, we finished Edie's business at the bank and at the post office. We were sitting at Gélato, an ice cream place at Liberty Square in downtown, people-watching, Edie with her vanilla-vanilla-vanilla cone and me with two scoops of dark chocolate mocha.

"So what now?" Edie asked, working on her cone from every angle so that ice cream wouldn't melt over the edge.

"What do you mean?" I asked.

"I mean what are you going to do apartment-wise?" Edie asked. "Don't you need a job before being able to rent an apartment?"

"That's usually the way things go, yes," I said. "I'm just..."

Edie turned to me. "You're lost." That wasn't a question, it was a statement.

There was a pause before I said, "Yes, I am. And I don't know how to get out of this funk."

Edie got back to her ice cream. "You'll figure it out."

"You sound so sure of it," I said.

"I already told you; you can do whatever you put your mind to."

"How can you say that?" I asked, taking a spoonful of chocolatey heaven. "You barely know me."

Edie shrugged. "I dunno. Call it a sixth sense. Call it experience. But I just know."

I still had a very hard time grasping Edie's so-called sixth sense.

If there was anything the last thirteen months had taught me, it was that you couldn't trust anybody. Even the family I belonged to trusted us—me and Gran—and look what they got. They landed in jail, that's what they got. And considering Edie didn't know the real me, I also had a hard time trusting her trusting me.

Nonetheless, her faith in me was kind of . . . adorable.

"Anyway, I need to figure out what to do soon, or else I won't have a roof over my head," I said.

"Well, you can stay with me," Edie said. "Or you can just switch it up and stay with every resident for a couple of weeks."

I laughed. "Yeah sure, that's what I'll do. I bet everyone would be happy to take me in."

Edie laughed as well. "Maybe Lucretia would have a problem taking you in."

Lucretia was Lucretia Barnett, whom I endearingly dubbed Sourpuss. She was one of the residents that was always spreading a toxic vibe. No, she was the only one with the toxic vibe. I still didn't know what her problem was, but she was the least of my problems right now.

We were finished with our ice cream and Edie said we had one last stop.

"Where's the last stop?" I asked.

"To the Feldmans," Edie said.

She said that as if I was supposed to know who the Feldmans were and what they did. Edie saw me looking questioningly at her, so she said, "The Feldmans are financial managers. I need to make my monthly deposit with them."

"What is that?" I asked. "Some kind of investment type of thing?"

For some unknown reason, my spidey senses were tingling.

"Yeah, something like that. I heard about it around six months ago from Marilyn Strobe—you know the one; she lives on the north-east side of the complex, and she heard it from Burt Vernieu and he heard it from Earnest Reed."

"Oh, okay," I said, not knowing one whit who this Marilyn and those other guys were, "if you heard it from Marilyn who heard it from Burt who heard it from Earnest whatever, then it has to be legit."

Edie rolled her eyes. "You really have trust issues, don't you?"

If she only knew.

"Did you even research these Feldmans?" I asked. "Do they have a solid track record? How long have they been in this business? What investments are they using? Are they sending you a regular tracking sheet of your personal investment?"

Edie blinked at me. "Wow, you sure know a lot. But yes, I've researched them. They have an online presence, and trust me, it was hard for someone with minimal computer skills to click myself through all that bull that's out there on the Internet. I've used one of the computers at the community center. The Feldmans have been here in Bitter End for over a year now, they have a storefront office right on Grant Avenue, and Marilyn said she got her first payout just last month. She said she paid a lot into it but needed a payout now for her great-grandson's knee surgery. And that was in her contract too. Premature payouts. So it's all legit."

"If you say so," I said.

I tried to convince myself I was just overreacting, that I just saw unfounded danger at every step; it was just that hearing about so-called financial managers who promised wealth to the elderly was too clichéd. Most of them turned out to be scammers. I never understood how anyone could ever fall for such obvious and ludicrous promises. Then again, that was probably that generational gap again. I sensed the baby-boomer generation was just so much more trusting than my millennial generation. And given my background of working around the edges of the law, my antenna went up every time someone mentioned a "financial manager." Heck, I could have been a "financial manager."

Fifteen minutes later, Edie and I got out of the car on Grant Avenue and headed to the Feldmans' office. I decided I shouldn't care about this whole financial manager thing. It was not my business. It was not my money, and it was not Gran's money. Edie could do whatever she wanted with her money, and the rest of the residents as well.

"Does their business even have a name?" I asked Edie. *Way to not care.*

"Feldman Financial Services," Edie said. "Stop being so skeptical, would you? I just retrieved a good chunk of money from the bank, and I plan on putting it to good use here."

Oh Lordy. She was giving them cash too. It was like an invitation for illegal activities.

Edie continued. "You could do the same." She paused. "After you get a job, of course."

I thought about that. I could be my own personal financial manager, but that would probably be against the terms of service of the witness protection program.

Grant Avenue was busy with people rushing to and fro. There were various shops with storefront windows, boasting clothes, jewelry, insurance services, a laundromat, and a couple of food places.

The Feldman Financial Services office was in a four-story building and had floor-to-ceiling windows. Despite the sun glare, I could see a room with a small desk inside and a leatherlike chair in front of it, and something that looked like a mobile AC device on wheels right next to the desk. There was a black couch on the right wall with a glass coffee table in front of it on a small carpet, and some books on the table. A painting hung over the couch, and I could see a coffee corner in the back.

There was a huge leatherlike chair behind the desk and a woman was sitting in it. Her head was thrown back and her arms were dangling by her side.

Edie frowned. "Way to take a nap," she said. "That's real professional. Tammy should know better."

"Hmm."

"What?" Edie asked. "What is it now?"

"I don't know," I said. "That's an odd position to be taking a nap."

"Then let's wake her up, shall we?"

Edie yanked the door open, and I followed her inside. We took a few steps toward the desk then Edie let out a yelp, covering her mouth with her hands.

The woman had dirty-blonde hair, and curls that looked to be from the nineties. Which was weird because she seemed to be in her forties. She had on a light-purple sweater and a chunky golden necklace. Her mouth hung at an odd angle and her eyes were wide open, staring at the ceiling.

Oh, and there was also the hole in her forehead. Oozing blood. My obvious guess? Gunshot. Close range.

Maybe I didn't want to become a financial manager after all.

Chapter Two

AW CRAP.

Not another dead body. This was so not good.

I slightly hyperventilated. When you're in the witness protection program and you're supposed to lay low, finding dead bodies was, like, the last thing on the list of things you should be doing. No, actually, it was not even on the list. If Edie weren't here, I would have bailed. Let someone else find the body and go through the whole process of calling the cops, giving statements, blah blah blah. Just getting this near to law enforcement gave me the heebie-jeebies.

One fingerprint background check through the system and they would know something is up with me. While the marshals made sure Gran and I got new last names, new birth certificates, new driver's licenses, and social security cards, they also made it clear they couldn't just fake a whole new past for us. Meaning, if someone started digging around, they would find out we didn't have any financial documentation. No prior banking records, no credit reports, no nothing. That spelled fishy.

I needed to give my statement to the cops and put this behind me. And hope Edie wouldn't find another dead body. This was the second one in three weeks. What was up with that? Shortly after Gran and I moved to Bitter End, Edie had found Edgar, who lived in Gran's house before her and was Edie herself's former lover, stabbed in her front yard. I tried not to get involved, but somehow I got pulled in and Edie and I managed to solve the murder mystery. But there were so many close-call moments where my real identity was almost exposed, and I intended to avoid that this time.

Edie half fainted in my arms.

"Whoa there," I said, trying to prop her back up. "Come on, let's get you on the couch."

"Is she . . . ?" Edie asked, her eyes popping out. "Is she dead?"

"I'm afraid she is," I said and took another look at the woman. "Clean work. One shot. She was instantly dead."

Edie stared at me. "What the heck are you talking about?" Her voice got one octave higher. "You sound like a hired killer."

Oops. I still hadn't gotten used to just shutting my mouth and trying not to give myself away with my knowledge of these sort of things.

"You're right, sorry," I said. "Is this Tammy Feldman?"

Edie glanced in the direction of the body. She nodded.

I looked around and saw an open door to a room in the back.

"Call nine-one-one," I said to Edie and stood. "I want to check out the back."

"I don't have my cell phone with me," she said.

I turned back around and sighed. I forgot I had to deal with a septuagenarian, who owned a cell but never carried it with her. What was even the point of owning one, then?

I pulled my own phone out of the back pocket of my shorts and threw it at Edie. "Knock yourself out."

I knew there was no other way, but I even dreaded using my own phone to call the cops. It was the phone I shared with Gran, and we used a prepaid card. There were no strings attached this way, we weren't in the system with the telephone providers, and there was less chance of being tracked. Even with our new lives and our new last names, there were just some things I couldn't shake off. Which kind of made sense, considering the Oregon Falcons probably had killers looking for us throughout the whole country. So you could never be too careful.

DEANY RAY

I headed for the room in the back and, while I was slowly approaching, I made the move to pull my knife out of my boots. *Mental forehead smack.* I didn't wear boots and I didn't have my knife with me. It was moments like this that were making my heart beat faster. And not out of enjoyment, but out of frustration and anger. It felt like missing a limb.

I shook it off and slowly pushed the door all the way open. Hoping I wouldn't find another body in there, I peeked in. The room was small and looked to be a storage area. There were boxes everywhere, some shelves containing hardware stuff, and some brooms and cleaning supplies were jammed in a corner. There was a stamp-sized dirty window on the opposite wall, barely letting some light in, and a back door was next to it. Deciding there was nothing here of interest, I returned to the front room, where Edie was sitting on the couch, staring down at the floor. She handed me my phone back.

"Why are you so relaxed?" Edie asked. "Why aren't you freaking out? You reacted the same way when I found Edgar."

I would have loved to tell Edie this wasn't my first rodeo with a dead person. Neither was the Edgar thing my first go-round with a corpse. Instead,

I had to lie to her again. But hey, lying kind of became my second nature since I got to Florida.

"Why would I be freaking out?" I asked. "I don't know this person. It's a shame all right, but I'm not going to break down and cry because of it."

Edie rolled her eyes. "I swear your generation is too unemotional. I'd rather have it this way. At least I feel something."

I felt something, all right. Dread. Dread that I was there in the first place.

Edie sighed. "Should I be worried about me finding another dead person? Am I dreaming? Is this a nightmare?"

Okay, it was starting to sink in for her.

I scratched the back of my neck. "I don't know what to tell you. It's weird indeed."

Edie stared at me. "What are you doing? You're supposed to comfort me!"

I threw my hands up in the air and sat next to her on the couch. "I'm just being honest. I can't just lie and say everything is fine. This is the second dead body in what? Three weeks?"

Edie put her hands over her ears. "No, I don't want to hear it. This is making me sick."

Sometimes I wished I'd be like a normal human being. Polite and comforting and all. It was just that I didn't see the point to it. Why lie to each other to make us feel better? How was that better? I just didn't get it. Should I have lied that there is no dead body in front of us, like literally a couple of feet in front of us? And the fact that Edie found her former neighbor dead in her front yard a couple of weeks ago, was that only our imagination? No, it wasn't. It was real. So there you go.

Maybe I should have also reminded Edie that she'd gotten me involved in solving that Edgar murder, and that almost got my and Gran's cover blown. But of course I couldn't say that to her, because she had no idea about our real identities and the fact that we were kind of in hiding here in Bitter End.

"You don't suppose this was suicide?" Edie asked, sounding downright hopeful.

"It wasn't suicide," I said. "First, nobody shoots themselves straight in the forehead, and second, there's no gun around."

Edie glanced around the desk, around Tammy's chair and around that mobile AC device. Then she let out a breath in disappointment.

Five minutes later, we heard the sirens. The cops came bursting in, but then stopped short. They were probably thrown by the picture before them.

To their left was a woman with a gunshot in her forehead, her eyes staring at the ceiling, her arms dangling beside her, and to their right was Edie, sitting on the couch, her head on the headrest and her eyes closed, breathing in and out in long sighs and me sitting next to her, with my elbows on my knees, staring at the floor.

One officer came forward and frowned. "Aren't you . . ." He cleared his throat. "Wasn't there a dead body at your house a couple of weeks ago?"

Edie threw her hands up in the air. "Yes! Okay? Yes, there was!"

The cop raised an eyebrow. "Hmph. That's weird."

I had to hold a laugh in. Poor Edie.

The cops did their thing, and we gave our statements. I heard them say the murder must have happened in the early hours of the morning. It was funny that either nobody else on the street heard the shot or they heard it and figured it was a car backfire or something, since nobody reported anything.

Edie looked away as the crime scene investigators examined the body. Finally, the EMTs covered up the body and took it away. I watched them roll the gurney out the door when Ryker came striding in, with a grim look on his face.

Ryker Donovan was Edie's grandson. He was in his thirties, and he looked like he'd stepped out of a male model magazine. He was six foot two, had short dark hair, and sparkling dark eyes. With his strong build and broad shoulders, he commanded authority when he entered a room. Just like he did now. That was kind of hot and totally annoying at the same time.

Ryker and his associate owned Donovan's Security and Investigations. In layman's terms, Ryker was a PI. And I wasn't very fond of PIs, to put it mildly.

We'd bumped heads a couple of times when Edie and I were interfering with his investigation of Edgar's death, and I realized this guy was cleverer than I had expected. He immediately realized I was different than your ordinary hairdresser and he made it very clear he had his suspicions about me, and about Gran, so I tried to stay away from him as much as possible.

Ryker's gaze zeroed in on Edie and me and he headed over to us. His eyebrows furrowed when he looked in my direction.

Oh, goody. Just what I needed. A scowl from the local private eye.

"Grams, are you okay?" Ryker said and gave Edie a long hug. The sleeve of his black T-shirt went up and I could see his tattoo on his left arm. A skull with a bike helmet on, nestled between two pistols that crossed each other.

That reminded me of my own former tattoo, that I had to laser away because of the risk of recognition. Another WITSEC policy I had to abide by. Although now, in retrospect, to be honest I had mixed feelings about removing my ankle tattoo featuring the shape of a falcon with the word Oregon etched beneath it. At first, it felt like something was missing, like an integral part of my identity was just gone, but then . . . being that I was now the enemy of the Falcons, the enemy of my own family that I grew up with, it wouldn't have felt right to parade the tattoo around. I just wished everything was back the way it was. My current state of mind was extremely confusing, and it went from sadness to anger to resignation to nostalgia in merely a few seconds. How could I ever come out of my funk this way?

I pushed these thoughts away and decided to focus on the present. We had another dead body on our hands. Sort of. Only this time, we didn't have any emotional connection to it, so we would just give our statements and be on our way home. No snooping around. No asking questions. No nothing.

I looked over at Edie. I really hoped she would go the no-nothing route.

"Ryker, it was horrible," Edie said. "We came in so I could make my monthly deposit, and there she was." Edie shuddered. "Poor Tammy. Who would do such a thing?"

Ryker scanned the room, then looked back at Edie. "You found another dead body?"

"Yeah, so?" Edie said and I could see her chest getting wider.

"Hmph," Ryker said. "That's weird."

Edie's eyes turned into slits and Ryker blushed. Now that *was* funny.

Ryker cleared his throat. "Anyway, my contact from the PD called it in and I rushed here immediately." He turned to me. "Why am I not surprised to see you here?"

"What's that supposed to mean?" I said, crossing my arms.

"It's just weird," Ryker said.

"So be it," I said and held his look.

Edie waved a hand between us. "Okay, I don't have time for your banter. Tammy Feldman is dead. I really can't believe it. Did someone call Lloyd?"

Ryker and I blinked twice.

Edie sighed. "Lloyd. Lloyd Feldman. He's Tammy's husband. They run the company together."

"What kind of company is this?" Ryker asked. "I saw the sign outside just now, but I didn't know you had these kinds of financial arrangements. Did you research them thoroughly? Are they legit?"

Edie's eyes went ping-pong from Ryker's to mine. "Wow. She asked the exact same thing."

Ryker looked at me and nodded. "That, I agree with."

"Gee, thanks a lot, glad you do," I said and Ryker slightly grinned.

"Of course they're legit," Edie said. "Marilyn Strobe is in. And she already got a payout. And they have their own website. And they're . . . you know," Edie gestured around herself, "here. They have an office and all. I came here once a month and talked to them. It's not like one of those online scammers sort of thing. Although now that Tammy has been . . . murdered, I'm guessing we'll all get our investments back. Now that's a shame."

Ryker and I exchanged looks. Despite Edie's arguments, I could tell something didn't sit right with him. And that was exactly how I felt. But hey, let Ryker and the cops solve this one. I was out.

"Okay, if we're done here, I'd like to drive back to the house," I said.

Ryker walked over to an officer, and they talked to each other, looking at us. Then Ryker strode back to us.

"You're free to go," he said. "I'm going to stick around and see what I can find out." He looked at me. "Could you take Grams back safely?"

"Of course," I said.

Edie gave Ryker one last hug, then she said, "When you get ahold of Lloyd, tell him to call me. I want to express my condolences to him."

"Will do," Ryker said.

Edie and I headed for the car. We jumped in and Edie let out a sigh. "What a day," she said, as I turned on the ignition. "Tammy is dead. I still can't believe it."

"Murdered, no less," I said as I stepped on the gas.

"No, I can't wrap my mind around it," Edie said. "I can't be as detached as you are. I just hope they'll catch whoever did it soon and I hope Lloyd is able to get over this in time."

I didn't say anything. I resisted the urge to point out that in most cases, it was the spouse who was the guilty party.

Chapter Three

EDIE AND I DROVE IN silence back to the retirement complex. Edie sighed for the millionth time as the car rolled by the sign that read *Welcome to Till the Bitter End Independent Living. Where your tropical dreams come true.* Well, no tropical dream of mine has come true here yet.

I parked the car at the curb, turned off the ignition and looked over at Edie. She seemed to be lost deep in thoughts.

"We're here," I said.

She shook her head and came back to reality. "Oh, already?"

We both got out of the car, and I asked Edie if she'd be all right. She nodded and said she felt so drained, she might just take a nap. A nap sounded good right about now. Not like I had anything else to do or anywhere else to be.

I opened the door to Gran's house and immediately cringed. That was nowadays the norm, considering the nauseating décor of the house. From the light-yellow carpeting to the brown couch to the CRT television set screaming seventies' design, it made you want to turn around and run for the hills.

FOOL ME ONCE

The layout of the house was simple, yet efficient, I had to admit that. Living room and dining nook in the front, kitchenette to the side, bedroom and bathroom in the back. Gran slept in her bedroom, and I took the couch every single night. I was this close to burning down that couch, it was so uncomfortable. Yet, I was still here, weeks later, living in Gran's house. What did that say about me? Ugh, better not to think about it.

Gran was sitting at the table in the dining nook, playing solitaire with a deck of cards. I plopped down on the chair next to her and stretched my back. Without looking up, Gran asked, "How was the apartment?"

"It bombed," I said.

"Bummer," she said.

"But we did find another dead body."

Gran stopped with her hand in midair and looked up. "You found another dead body? What do you mean? Like in the apartment?"

"Nope." I said and rubbed my face. "At some financial services company where Edie is their customer. We went in and found a woman shot in the forehead."

"Well, that's a shame," Gran said and got back to her cards.

And Edie was worried about *my* nonemotional reaction.

But what did I expect? Gran was seventy-three years old, and you don't change your inner self anymore at that age. You're done. And actually, any change that occurs in your life at that point was probably going to feel much more burdensome than if you were a few years younger.

I glanced at Gran. While I tried at least to adapt to our new life and often gave up wearing my normal clothes—biker boots, leather jacket, the works—Gran was stubborn and still wearing her usual outfit. Real denim jeans, her biker boots, and a white top. She turned some heads when we first walked through the streets of the retirement complex—okay, she turned *all* heads—but now the others seemed to have been getting used to Gran and her unusual ways. Well, at least some of them.

There was one crucial change Gran had needed to make. From fiery orange hair, she had to go to a short honey-blonde bob with bouncing bangs. The orangey hair was too much of a trademark for a witness protection member. She also had the same ankle tattoo I had and had to remove it as well.

"You're not getting involved in this one, are you?" Gran asked, eyes on her cards.

FOOL ME ONCE

I shook my head. "Hell, no. I don't have anything to do with it."

"Yeah, that's what you said last time," Gran said. Then she asked, "What about Edie?" How does she feel about it? She found another dead body in like, what? Three weeks?"

"Yeah, that seems to be the standing joke around here," I said then looked over at the window facing Edie's house. "She's upset, that's how she is. This isn't normally part of her world."

Gran let out a snort. "You got that right. So who died exactly?"

I reported to Gran everything I knew.

She leaned back in her seat. "It's going to be mayhem."

"What is?"

"Getting the money back," Gran said and turned her attention back to her game.

"Could you be more specific?" I asked, feeling my patience running out. Apparently, I was getting way edgier way faster in my new life then I'd been before in my old one.

"Those were scammers," Gran said. "No way was that legit."

"How do you know?" I asked.

"Because I know," Gran said. "Let's just call it experience. Or a sixth sense."

I rolled my eyes. I kind of had it with that so-called sixth sense from the septuagenarian women in my life.

"Remember Tiny Timmy?" Gran asked. "He was gone for a couple of years, going from state to state, pretending to be some financial guru and wiping away the wealth of divorced fifty-year-old women? Those suckers never knew what hit them. Timmy was just that good."

I thought about it. "That's what he did? I never knew about that."

"You were a child back then, that's why," Gran said.

"I remember him going away, and then when he came back, he bought that mansion down Sumter Road. I think he even put in gold-rimmed window frames."

Gran nodded. "See? It's because he was so good. A good con artist can do anything. Especially if you have older people involved. Good con artists can sweet-talk, and they make it seem they're your buddy, your pal, your ultimate love, whatever their intention is. And thinking about the people who live around here, I'm pretty sure that's easy enough to pull off."

I thought about it some more. My first thought was exactly the same, yet I hoped I was wrong. My heart went out to Edie. I hoped Gran was wrong as well, although with her life experience and her line of work, I tended to believe her. Funnily enough, I tried to force myself not to feel this much empathy. I mean we'd only been here for a couple of weeks, for crying out loud. I couldn't be walking around caring so much about, basically, strangers. Yes, these were still strangers. Gran always tried to remind me of that fact and she was right. Three weeks ago I only cared about what happened to me and Gran. That fact hadn't changed, but somehow I found myself slightly caring for our next door neighbor and the other residents.

Gran was eyeing me. "Please don't do it."

"What do you mean?" I asked.

"I see it in your face. You're thinking about them. And you're thinking about her. But it's none of your business. You remember what happened last time you got involved in their business?"

I sighed. As mentioned, Gran always reminded me of the harsh reality.

"Well, you can't expect me to do a happy dance if these people here were getting scammed," I said. "Especially since now one of them is dead. I wonder what will happen to their investments."

"That's up to the cops to find out," Gran said.

"I guess it is," I said.

I decided not to think about it anymore. Gran was right. It was not my problem. Edie would get over the shock of seeing another dead body, and life would take its normal course again.

I watched Gran. "So what is this? You just can't leave those cards alone, can you? What happened to your buddies? No more poker playing?"

Gran was an excellent poker player. So excellent in fact, that I worried what she would do here at the community complex. They shouldn't be worried about some fake financial manager; they should be worried about Gran. She could wipe out all their money in one fell swoop. Gran was just that good. At first, I didn't like her playing poker at all. It was not exactly the best way to lay low when you were in the witness protection program. But I knew how much it hurt her to stop playing. How she'd managed to stay away from a deck of cards for the thirteen months we were in hiding, I had no idea.

But as soon as we landed in Bitter End, she started all over again.

The residents here got sweet on it and now they had regular meetings where Gran showed them how to play poker. I didn't know what her ultimate goal was, but I didn't like it at all. Unfortunately, I couldn't force her to quit, and I also knew this was all she had now.

She was managing a trucking company back in Oregon and she was hanging out at Choppers. She had meetings, she had a full life, and in a second it was taken away from her. She literally had nothing now. Except for poker. So I kind of understood that this was the one thing she wouldn't give up, no matter what. I just hoped she knew about the fine line between having fun and keeping busy and ending up in hot water with an illegal hustle of some sort.

"We're taking a break today," Gran said. "If it were up to me, we would be playing all day long."

I laughed. "That I know."

"So what's your plan for the rest of the day?" Gran asked.

"I have zero plans," I said.

Just like every single day.

DEANY RAY

It was almost two in the afternoon. And I had absolutely nothing to do. This came to be my normal day-to-day life in the last couple of weeks, dragging my morale even further down. On the one hand, I kind of went with the flow of just doing nothing. Just lying on the couch watching daytime TV. But at the same time, it was also unnerving because I had to get my life straight.

Doing nothing is what I'd been doing in the last thirteen months when we were hiding out at motels, waiting for the trial against the Falcons. We changed motels every couple of weeks, went from state to state, were babysat by the marshals, and were being watched twenty-four-seven. There literally wasn't anything else to do except watch TV.

And now here in Florida, starting a new life, with barely any skills for jobs, still trying to wrap my mind around everything that happened—my life taking such a turn—I figured it was only natural to sink into a big hole of depression.

I took a cold beer from the fridge and sat on the couch turning on the TV. Ten minutes later Gran finished her solitaire game and she joined me on the couch with her own bottle of beer. We clinked the bottles and just sat there watching *Seinfeld* reruns.

About two hours later there was a knock at the door. Gran and I looked at each other then looked at the door. I shook my head at how relaxed we were. Three weeks ago, a knock on the door sent Gran straight for her gun, and me for the knife. Her illegally purchased gun, of course. It was not like she could get legally fingerprinted for a gun permit. Another stupid WITSEC rule. So Gran was already in hot water for carrying a concealed firearm.

But now after learning who we dealt with here, aka the residents of the retirement complex, who were not exactly the kind of hit men the Falcons would hire, Gran and I got really chill. Besides, it got tiresome to be in that state of alert every time we had a visitor. And we often had visitors.

Gran groaned. "Do you realize there hasn't been a single day since we moved here that someone didn't come over for whatever unimportant reason?"

"It's probably Edie coming over to talk about what happened today," I said.

Gran got up, walked the few feet to the door, looked through the peephole, and sighed. She opened the door wide and put one hand on her hip. From the couch I could see Theodore standing outside, smiling wide.

DEANY RAY

Theodore was one of the residents at the retirement complex and he had a crush on Gran. He was six feet tall and had thinning gray hair. He had broad shoulders and a sturdy build, and if he were a couple of decades younger, I would definitely make a move on him. He reminded me of those actors in the sixties, well-dressed and a gentleman through and through. But the most admirable quality in Theodore was that he was self-confident enough to hold his own with Gran.

Gran wasn't at all happy with her pursuer, although I was sure she kind of liked it deep down inside. Deep, deep down inside. She just didn't show it, and I was curious to know if she would ever let her guard down. I was also curious to know how patient Theodore would be. Gran was never married, and she had no regrets about that. She'd had a long relationship with my grandfather until he died twenty years ago. My father came out of that relationship but he—along with my mother—died in an airplane crash shortly after I was born. If Gran had any other semiserious partners or affairs or whatever, then I didn't get any wind of that. She always said she was self-sufficient, and she didn't see the point in sharing her life with someone romantically. She shared her house with me, but she rejected sharing it with a man.

"Hello, Dorothy," Theodore said, then he looked in my direction. "How's it going, Piper?"

I smiled and told him I was okay. I assumed he didn't hear about Tammy Feldman yet, and I wasn't the one to tell him about it.

Gran still stood in the doorway. "Can I help you with something?"

Theodore wiped away some sweat from his forehead with a handkerchief. "I came by to ask you if you want to drive together to the paintball game on Wednesday. It would be my pleasure to have you two ladies accompany me there."

"To the what?" Gran asked.

"The paintball game," Theodore said. "We're all leaving at seven in the morning and we should get back by noon."

"At seven in the morning?" Gran asked. "Are you insane?"

Theodore laughed. "No, I am not insane. We're leaving that early because it gets hotter later in the day."

"You know, I'm not really the type to—"

I jumped off the couch and walked to the door.

"Actually," I said, "we'd be happy to ride with you there."

From the corner of my eye, I saw Gran giving me her signature death stare. But I didn't care. It was not like we had anything else to do, so we might as well just go and play paintball. If Theodore wouldn't convince us, then I was sure Edie would have taken us by force.

"I'm happy you're coming with," Theodore said. "I'll be here on Wednesday morning at seven, then." He winked at Gran then turned and left.

Gran closed the door and put both hands on her hips. "What the hell? We're going to a paintball place? Do you really think that's wise? We can shoot everybody off in five minutes straight."

"Yes, but you're not going to bring your gun there, so you'll have to hold off on the pleasure of really shooting anybody."

"You think I can't do any damage with a paintball gun?" Gran asked.

"I'm sure you can, but you're going to restrain yourself," I said. "Just try to enjoy yourself for crying out loud."

"Like you're enjoying yourself so much," Gran mumbled.

Yeah, okay, she had a point there, but it was so much more fun throwing Gran into the focus of attention while I could remain on the sidelines.

We returned to the couch and finished our beers. Just as expected, I felt sleepy and closed my eyes. When I opened them again, almost three hours had passed. This was really a sad way to live life. But hey, at least we had AC inside the house.

I turned and saw Gran was slouched and snoring with her mouth wide open.

There was a loud knock on the door and Gran jumped up. "What? Who's there?" She looked frantically around her. I was glad the gun stayed in place at the small of her back. How she could take a nap with that thing poking her in the ribs, I'd never understand.

"Relax, it's just someone at the door," I said.

"Christ, we really have to move," Gran said.

I saw lots of white curls through the peephole. It was Edie. I'd expected her to come over sooner, as a matter of fact. I opened the door and saw the concern in her eyes. She marched straight in and nodded a hello at Gran.

"What's up?" I asked. "Did you find out anything new about what happened today?"

"I sure as hell did," Edie said. "They couldn't find Lloyd anywhere. His cell is turned off and he wasn't home either. And get this. Ryker did some research into the Feldmans' company. He has some fancy search programs at his office, you know." Edie paused and looked at the floor. "He found the Feldmans' company on the blacklist of some official government institution, and he also found previous financial fraud charges against them." She paused. "You were right. Their business was a fraud. They scammed us."

Chapter Four

CURSE WORDS WERE the first thing that came to mind. I wanted to believe I was wrong, and Gran was wrong, and Ryker was wrong. But we were all right.

"Edie, I'm so sorry," I said.

There was a pause while both of us looked over at Gran. Her face didn't move a muscle, then finally, probably feeling the pressure, she said, "I'm sorry too."

Way to be empathetic.

"So much sentiment, Dorothy," Edie said and rolled her eyes. "Well then. What's done is done. Now it's time to counterattack." Edie put her fist in the air.

"Um . . . what does that mean?" I asked and already dreaded the answer.

"Come on, let's go," Edie said, "We have an emergency meeting at the rec hall."

Gran and I exchanged looks.

"So?" I asked. "We don't have anything to do with it."

"Nonsense," Edie said. "You're part of this community. I know you want to act like you don't belong here but you do, even if you don't see it now."

"Whoa, whoa, whoa," Gran said, "not so fast. She may have something to do with it"—Gran pointed at me—"because she was with you today at that office, but I'm the last one here who has anything to do with it and so I'm staying put."

Way to throw me under the bus, Gran.

Edie crossed her hands and narrowed her eyes at Gran. "Dorothy, we need you. You are an accountant, and you could help us figure this out. I already told the others you two were coming. How does that make me look if I can't get you there?"

Ouch, checkmate again. Edie really had a way with that.

I looked at Gran and grinned. She made the mistake of telling people her former job was as an accountant, and now she had to live with the consequences. Which was kind of funny, because she *was* a kind of an accountant, only not the legal kind the others thought she was.

I could see Gran was weighing her options. She could still say no and stay in the house, but then again, that would have meant almost going to war with Edie and the others. And she probably figured the latter was not really the best decision, so she sighed and said, "Fine."

It was almost dark outside. We jumped in Gran's golf cart and took off. That was another thing we'd had to get used to, and we still needed to get used to. In our old lives we owned Harley Davidson bikes. We drove our bikes so often up in the mountains and we felt so free. Obviously, we had to give up our bikes just like we had to give up our house and our belongings and basically everything we owned in our former lives. The golf cart came automatically with the house here in Florida. Every resident owned one, and it was the easiest way to get around the retirement complex. Which was so spread out, they were giving out maps for it.

But going from a Harley bike to driving a golf cart in flip-flops felt just like a slap in the face.

"Would you step on it already?" Edie said from the passenger seat. Gran sat in the back and mumbled something along the lines of shoot me now.

"Jesus Edie, you're stressing me out," I said. "Getting into an accident before we even get there is not the best idea, is it?"

The Bitter End retirement community was like a village. It took about ten minutes to drive from Gran's house to the rec hall, officially named

Community Hall. There were diamond lanes on the streets, meaning there were more golf carts driving around than cars. One thing about the golf cart wasn't that bad, and that was the headwind. That is until you parked the cart. Then you started cursing at the heat again.

I parked the cart, and we walked on the path between the perfectly manicured lawns of the retirement community, past the swimming pool, past the mini-golf course, past the dining hall, and into the rec hall. I found it suspicious that there wasn't a single soul outside besides us. I then knew why. The rec hall was packed. All the tables were taken, people were standing along the walls, and everybody was talking among themselves producing a noise level that was hurting my ears.

I scanned the crowd and spotted Beatrice waving at us. Edie motioned for Gran and me to head over to her while she walked to the front. Why did she walk to the front?

Beatrice was the woman whose hair I dyed purple by accident. At first, I was worried she might have a heart attack, but Gran convinced her it was a good thing to stand out. So she kept the purple hair.

We approached Beatrice's table and I saw she held two chairs free for us. She said, "Don't even bother" to a man and a woman making their way to the chairs. I had to smile. For only just getting here three weeks ago, we'd gotten pretty popular. Edie liked us. Beatrice liked us. Theodore liked us. And a couple of others as well. I still had to figure out why. We stuck out like a sore thumb in this crowd. Then again, maybe that was exactly the reason.

"There you two are," Beatrice said, looking at us through her thick glasses. I didn't know where to look first: her shiny purple hair or her lipstick that was outside the lines, as it always was. "I've been saving these seats for you, and I almost got lynched for it. What took you so long?"

"So you were so sure we were coming?" I asked as we took our seats.

"Of course I was," Beatrice said. "You're part of the community. Everybody's here. We would never keep you out of the loop."

That was kind of . . . sweet. Even if it was just saving seats. It reminded me of my former family, the Oregon Falcons. We would always have each other's backs no matter what. When Gran and I left our former lives, I didn't think I would ever feel this way. I never would have thought that saving seats for us at a retirement complex would spark warm feelings in my chest.

DEANY RAY

I covered my ears and looked around me. Belly Man and Raspy were sitting at the table next to ours and smiled in my direction. Those two were inseparable. I didn't remember their names, but one of them obviously had a predominant beer belly and the other had a distinguishing raspy voice.

I saw some poker-playing buddies of Gran's making their way through the crowd, walking past us and each giving Gran a fist bump. I shook my head.

Lucretia Barnett, aka Sourpuss, was standing in the back corner of the room and was surrounded by her own group, that was looking similarly sour faced. Sourpuss had her hair up in a tight bun, like she always did. It really matched her personality.

Theodore entered the rec hall. Our eyes met and we both nodded to each other. His glance moved to Gran who pretended she didn't see him. Theodore looked back at me, smiled, shook his head, then made his way to the back where he greeted some other residents.

As I was waiting for whatever to happen, I asked Beatrice if she'd also invested through the Feldmans.

"Unfortunately, yes," Beatrice said and pushed her glasses further up her nose. "Those bastards took advantage of almost all of us." There was an anger in her voice. That made Gran smile.

"How did you all find out about it?" I asked. It was just this morning that Edie and I found Tammy Feldman dead, and now twelve hours later the whole retirement complex was in rebellion mode.

"Marilyn's granddaughter works at the insurance office a couple of doors down from the Feldmans' office and she told us about the murder. Then about one hour ago, Edie called."

Okay, I guessed that made sense; if almost everybody here had invested with the Feldmans, then they had the right to know. It was their money.

"Is Marilyn here tonight?" I asked Beatrice.

She looked around. "I just saw her before. Don't know where she is in this crowd. But look, there's Burt and Earnest at that table. Marilyn heard from them about the Feldmans."

I turned and saw a man wearing a flat cap with an orange and a lime pictured on the front, eating a weird-looking fruit. He was handing the other man—who was wearing a green T-shirt and green shorts, probably disappearing when being outside on the lawn—the same kind of fruit. Green Man bit into it and scrunched up his nose, mouthing "eww."

I raised my eyebrow at Beatrice.

She waved her hand in dismissal. "Earnest has been looking to cross-pollinate an orange with a lime since forever. Says nobody has done it before and he'd be rich when he succeeds. But as you can see, only garbage comes out of it."

"You tried the orange-lime fruit?" I asked her.

She nodded. "Unfortunately, yes. It tastes like sour feet. I'm not even sure they're edible."

Apparently, seniors around here had a thing for fruit. A lot of them were fans of fruity-looking patterns on their clothes, and now they even tried their hand at playing God by manipulating botany. Retiree life must be really boring to give you such ideas.

I leaned in my chair and looked over at Gran. She looked just as miserable as I felt. She kept looking toward the door and I expected her to bolt out of the building any second now.

Suddenly, there was a loud, sharp noise and everybody groaned, holding their ears.

"Oops, I'm sorry," Edie said. She was standing in the middle of the room, holding a mic, with her shoulders pulled back and her chin high as if she were starting the halftime show for the Superbowl. She cleared her throat. "Good evening, everybody."

Everybody greeted back.

Gran turned to me and mumbled, "It's like a cult."

Edie walked back and forth as she spoke. Man, she took every chance she got to be in the spotlight. She would have been perfect working in showbiz.

"A gathering like this is usually a reason to be happy," Edie continued. "But not tonight. Tonight, it's about strategizing and getting back what's ours."

Everybody clapped and whistled.

No, I took it back. Not showbiz. Edie would have been perfect for politics.

"We all know what happened today," Edie said. "Today, we—"

"Today, you found another dead person!" A voice from the back said.

There was silence and everybody turned to look.

Sourpuss. Who else could it have been?

"What's your problem now, Lucretia?" Edie asked over the mic.

"You are *our* problem," Sourpuss shouted. "This is the second dead person you found in what? Three weeks?"

I saw Edie's grip on the mic getting tighter. "Yeah, so?" she said between her teeth.

"We should be aware of *you*," Sourpuss continued. "You're bringing bad luck upon us. Who's the next dead person you'll find? Maybe one of us?"

There was an agitated hum through the crowd, and I saw Edie trying to find words to defend herself.

Come on, Edie, you can do it. Don't let Sourpuss win this round. Any round, for that matter.

"Do you really think—" Edie started, but the crowd got restless and weren't listening to her anymore.

I saw Sourpuss smirking. She was totally enjoying this. She was enjoying putting Edie down for nothing.

"Wait, um . . ." Edie tried to get a word in, but the people were talking to each other, giving Edie some confused looks and also some not very nice looks.

"Didn't they know Edie and I found Tammy Feldman today?" I asked Beatrice.

"They know," Beatrice said, "But apparently Lucretia has a way of highlighting the bad stuff. What a shrew."

I agreed with that.

The agitation rose as Edie was trying to calm everybody down, but I could see on her face she knew she was losing this battle. She was losing the people. That had to hurt her. Being a leader was Edie's thing.

"Look, I just wanted to—" Edie spoke louder into the mic. But still nothing.

I was wondering if this shindig tonight was going to be over before it began, but then I saw Gran getting up and heading over to Edie.

Crap. What was she up to? Was she going to shoot everybody?

With my eyes wide, I saw Gran in her calm demeanor, oozing authority, snatching the mic from Edie's hand and saying, "Now listen up, you cowards."

Silence.

All eyes swished to Gran.

All jaws were on the floor.

Nobody blinked.

I wished I could have looked away, but it was like a car wreck.

"Where I come from, we don't have patience for this," Gran said. "We don't have patience for immature and childish games, mind games played by an obnoxious and stupid and transparently hateful person." Gran fixed her gaze on Sourpuss. "A person was shot, a person who took your money away and now you're seriously sitting here throwing shade at the one person who got you all together here, who is willing to do something about it so you get your money back that you so stupidly gave away. I was asked to come here today but if I'd known what kind of nonsense you are choosing to believe, then I might as well use my energy for knitting or something. No wonder those people got your money if this is the way you act. Like fools. Have fun getting it back." Gran did a mic drop, then she traipsed back to her seat.

It was so eerily silent you could almost hear the grasshoppers outside on the lawn. I was almost sure Gran just set herself up to be lynched. Any second now they would all throw themselves and their walkers on top of Gran and take her apart.

But the opposite happened. A wave of loud clapping and woo-hooing erupted. I had to cover my ears again. What the hell just happened here? What did Gran do?

"That's the way to do it, folks," Edie said into the mic cheerily.

Gran just sat there in her chair with no emotion on her face whatsoever and rolled her eyes. So she basically insulted the whole crowd and they started clapping for her. Was this some kind of parallel universe?

"Dorothy Harris, everybody," Edie said. People turned to Gran and clapped again. Gran's face looked like, *Lord, can we get this over with?*

I couldn't help laughing. Gran was acting all tough, like she didn't care about anybody, but deep inside her, there was a softy. She just had a special way of showing it.

I turned around and saw Sourpuss was pissed. She knew she'd lost this round. She stomped out of the building, probably plotting her revenge on Gran. I wished I could warn Sourpuss not to mess with Gran, but that wouldn't be possible without me divulging our real identities to her.

"Do you know if Lucretia invested with the Feldmans?" I asked Beatrice.

She shrugged. "No idea. Even if she did, it's not like we care about it, right?" I laughed and gave Beatrice a pat on the back.

Edie was back to herself. This felt more like a party, with Edie the leading emcee.

"Dorothy is right, everybody," Edie said. "Tammy and Lloyd Feldman were our consultants. Our financial consultants. Some would say they were our friends. And now to find out they've scammed us out of our money is just unacceptable. I know not every one of you invested with them, but I know you've heard about them and I know you are supporting this community."

Clap clap.

"Tammy Feldman has died with a gunshot to her forehead," Edie said. "Piper Harris and I found her this morning; you know this to be true already."

People turned and stared at me. *Awesome.*

"The police don't know who did it but I hope they find out soon. At this point, I don't know what connection there is between Tammy being dead and our money. They couldn't find Lloyd. His cell phone is turned off. But after finding out what they did to us, anything is possible now. Maybe Lloyd is the guilty one and maybe he killed his wife."

Everybody sucked in a breath.

"Maybe Lloyd took all of our money and wants to leave the country," Edie continued. "We need to find Lloyd and we need to get our money back." The people were nodding in agreement. "Everybody who invested with the Feldmans needs to file a police report. That's the way you can make it official. That way, the police will have enough incentive to start digging around and see where our money is. Right now, their main priority is finding out who shot Tammy." Edie paused and shuddered. A few people to my left and right were shaking their heads in disgust. That was kind of cute. I've dealt with this my whole life and was absolutely emotionless. But normal people fell into a stupor.

"So I want everybody to file the report tomorrow at the police station and make some pressure for the cause," Edie said. "There are other departments and other law enforcement entities out there who are dealing with scams like this. We need to get them to move their butts." I could hear a few yeses and woo-hoos from the crowd.

"And like Dorothy already said: she, as a former accountant, is here to help us," Edie said and nodded toward Dorothy.

Gran closed her eyes and rubbed her temples. I knew she regretted her appearance before the crowd.

"If anybody needs a consultation, you know Dorothy lives right next to my house and she is almost always home," Edie continued.

Gran turned to me. "We're moving to another house."

"Or you could catch her at one of her poker-playing meetings here at the rec hall," Edie added one more.

I busted out laughing. This really made my day. Gran went white as a ghost. She pinched the bridge of her nose with her thumb and index finger, then leaned in. "Piper, we're moving to the other side of the country tomorrow before sunrise."

I had a second wave of laughter. "Too late, Gran. You're already so deep into this, they won't let you leave."

Gran mumbled something about shooting her way free and I ignored her. This was way too much fun.

Chapter Five

The next day, Gran and I were silently sipping coffee at our kitchen table. It was about nine in the morning and the sun had already cast its hot rays over the house. I took another sip and smiled at the memory of last night.

"Stop that," Gran said.

"Sorry, I can't help it," I replied.

The gathering yesterday was so not what I had expected. Sure, with Edie being the mover and shaker, it could only get exciting, but Gran's little improv production sent it right through the roof.

"You know they're all going to come over now, don't you?" Gran said. "I'm never going to have some peace and quiet."

I raised an eyebrow. "Do you *want* peace and quiet?"

Gran looked at me but didn't say anything.

"I thought so," I said.

I knew what Gran meant by that. She wanted action when *she* felt like it and she wanted downtime when she felt like it. Well, she could kiss that timeline goodbye, now that we were living here.

Gran leaned in her chair and looked at the cell phone.

"What is it?" I asked.

"I'm just timing the first knock on the door," she said.

"You're kidding, right?" I said, rolling my eyes.

"There should be one knock in five, four, three—"

There was a loud knock at the door.

My jaw dropped on the table.

Gran wickedly grinned at me. "Told you so."

That was frightening and amazing at the same time.

Huffing, Gran opened the door to Edie. She was holding a basket in her arms.

"Why am I not surprised to see you here?" Gran asked as Edie marched in, went straight to the kitchen counter, put the basket down, and poured herself a cup of coffee. Then she pulled out muffins and put them on a plate and served them to us. Then she took a seat at the table. She felt so comfortable, it was like she was living here at Gran's.

"Hey, I've at least waited until nine to come over, okay?" Edie said. "Since I know you're not super early risers. So you should appreciate that instead of giving me a hard time."

"Oh yes," Gran said. "Silly me. *I* should be appreciative."

I was appreciative for the freshly baked muffins, so I dug in. It was our luck—or our bad luck girthwise—that Edie used to be a top-notch chef. She still loved baking and she loved sharing her creations.

"So how are you today?" I asked her.

"I really don't know how I am," Edie said. "We found Tammy dead yesterday, someone had shot her—and by the way, I still think it's weird you're not freaking out—then I find out her company and her investments are all a scam and she tricked us all. And now nobody can find Lloyd and I don't know how to get my money back and everybody else's money back."

"What do you know about the Feldmans?" I asked.

Edie took a sip of coffee. "As far as I know they moved here about a year ago but I don't know where they're from. They rent that office we were in yesterday and they live in the apartment above it. About six months ago I heard about them from Marilyn, and they seemed totally legit. You know how I like face-to-face interactions, especially with this type of thing. And so I went there and they seemed totally nice and totally competent."

"That's part of their hustle," Gran said. "They know your weak spot. They know you probably wouldn't fall for a scheme if it were online or if they called by phone. It's actually genius. They know retirees—especially baby boomers—are more gullible; they're not as burnt and cynical as the generations after them, and good con artists take advantage of that."

Edie looked at Gran in disbelief. "Con artists? Good Lord. Are you always this brutally honest?"

"Yes," Gran deadpanned.

Edie shoved a whole muffin in her mouth.

"Look, burying your head in the sand won't make it better," Gran said. "It will only make it worse. You have to smarten up, see the truth for what it is, then make your move."

"Oh my god, you're right," Edie said. "I *should* make a move. I should take this whole thing into my own hands." She paused then looked at her watch. "Okay, then let's finish up these muffins, and let's go."

"Um . . . go where?" I asked.

"To the Feldmans. We'll start with their office. I'm sure we can find out something there."

I looked at Gran in a *Gee, thanks for that* way. She put her hands up in defense and said, "Hey, it's not my fault. You know her. She would have come up with it herself."

"Listen, Edie," I said, "we're not going anywhere. We're not going to snoop around. The cops will take care of it and we're not going to meddle in their investigation."

I almost let out a snort. Who was this person talking? "The cops will take care of it"? "Not meddle in their investigation"? Sheesh. I must be getting soft. I had never let the cops handle anything in my whole life. They were a nuisance, if anything.

"So you're saying you don't care that those people took my money away?" Edie asked. "That those people took everybody's money away? You're really just going to sit here and not do anything about it?"

Oh, she was good. Extremely transparent but also good. Did she think I couldn't see through her emotional manipulation? It was so not my fault that Edie fell for the scam and that all the residents who invested with the Feldmans fell for it too.

Gran grinned at me and said, "Oh, she's got you now."

Edie turned to Gran. "You think you're off the hook? You're part of this community whether you like it or not, and you have experience in the field. You're coming with."

Gran's grin instantly disappeared. I almost pointed a finger at her and laughed.

Gran and I just sat there, like a couple of kids in school with Edie the teacher scolding us. A naïve retiree, with zero connections and knowledge about the bad stuff in life, about the illicit stuff in life, was scolding *us*! A money-launderer and a book-cooker! It was like a scene from a sitcom.

But despite Edie's see-through attempt to use guilt to get her way, it worked.

I sighed. "I'm so going to regret this, but fine," I said. "I guess it wouldn't hurt to just drive by there."

Gran whipped her head in my direction. "You're not serious. You're getting involved?"

"*You* are already involved," I said. "Remember your speech last night in front of everybody?"

Edie laughed then clapped her hand over her mouth when Gran gave her a death stare.

"Then it's settled," Edie said with a content look on her face. "We're taking your car."

Shoot me now. What have I done?

Of course we were taking our car, our plain old boring car, since you could spot Edie's car from another galaxy. She owned a shiny candy-apple-red

1967 Chevrolet Impala. While the car was absolutely gorgeous, it was the last car you wanted to drive if you wanted to remain inconspicuous.

We finished our muffin-and-coffee breakfast, and I snatched a couple pairs of latex cleaning gloves from the counter drawer, because I knew where this was heading. We jumped in the Ford Taurus and headed for downtown Bitter End.

The streets at the retirement complex were again suspiciously empty, and I asked Edie if there was another gathering that she wasn't taking part in? Which I highly doubted. Edie said of course there was no gathering, because she didn't call it in, and the residents were most likely at the police station filing a report against the Feldmans.

Gran was sitting in the back seat and chilling against the AC stream. Stubborn as she was, she wore her biker boots and her denim jeans, but I was glad she at least didn't wear her black leather jacket anymore.

"So what exactly did those people tell to you?" Gran asked Edie. "What was their pitch?"

"They said they had investments specifically tailored for retirees and that we could supplement our retirement funds. Now that I think about it, I couldn't tell you what the investment was, really. It was some fund or some stocks or some bonds that they managed, I think. In their brochures there were testimonials of other retirees who were really happy about the payout." Edie paused. "But I'm guessing now that the brochure was fake, and so were those testimonials."

"Of course they were fake," Gran said. "Anyone can print whatever they want."

I swerved to the right then turned my head to Edie. Heartache showed in her face. I guessed it was very easy for an outsider to judge others. Like how come she didn't know it was all a scam? How come she hadn't immediately sniffed them out? It was easy for someone not emotionally involved to just not understand how anyone could fall for a scam like this. But just like Gran, I also knew that good con artists would make you feel emotionally involved so that you didn't ask too many questions and research them to the bone.

And there was also Edie being Edie. She tended to believe the best in people, not the worst. That was the difference between Edie and us. Now that I thought about it, maybe it was Edie who got it right all along, despite the scamming. Because Gran and I always lived our lives knowing to be suspicious of people in general, and especially now—with our new lives—our trust issues had gone through the roof. That really took a toll on us. It got to be mentally and emotionally tiresome. Edie, on the other hand, saw the good in people. Her life was happier than ours.

"How much was your monthly deposit?" Gran asked Edie.

I felt Edie hesitating. Then she said, "Five thousand every month."

I stepped on the brakes so hard we were all thrown forward. "Dollars?"

Gran mumbled something about Jesus Christ.

Edie waved her hands in the air. "I know how stupid it is now! But again, Marilyn Strobe got a payout. It was all so very believable."

"How do you even have five thousand dollars a month to spare?" Gran asked.

Edie turned to face her. "I'm seventy-five years old. I've worked all my life and I know how to handle money well." She paused. "Well except for this thing. Anyway, I had saved a monthly amount that I put away for over fifty years. That amounts to a really good sum. After meeting the Feldmans, I thought that was such a sweet deal what they presented, especially since all the money I have will belong to my daughter someday, and in the end, to Ryker."

Oh. I didn't even think of that. But of course. Edie was thinking about her heritage, about her family being taken care of. Which made sense at her age. Wow. I had never thought of what would happen when I left this world, if I would ever have my own family and some fortune to my name that I would want to leave to my descendants.

"So you paid five thousand a month for how long now?" Gran asked.

"For four months," Edie said.

"Wow," Gran said. "That's twenty g's."

Edie put her head in her hands. "I don't even want to think about it. Because the more I think about it, the more I just want to cry. How could I have been so stupid? How could I have not seen through it? It's all so clear now."

Gran and I were silent. It was hard to comfort someone who fell for a money scheme like this. I mean, it was not like someone put a gun to her head.

"I had no idea scammers were this good," Edie said. "I've only seen this in movies."

"Unfortunately, this is also real life," Gran said. "Really good con artists make it all seem legitimate and they will blind you with blah-blahs. I'm sure you had good and long conversations with them, right? Some semi-personal ones, right?"

"Yes!" Edie said. "Every time I went in to give them my deposit, we talked for over an hour."

"Then I'm guessing you were the one to talk more and disclose more about yourself than they were about themselves," Gran said. "And if they talked about their own personal stuff, then it was probably just superficial stuff and it doesn't take a rocket scientist now to realize it was most probably a big fat lie."

"Yes," Edie said and it seemed to just keep further dawning on her. "Oh my god, the signs were all there. You are so right. I barely know anything about them. They didn't mention kids, they didn't mention parents or friends or where they moved from. God, they were good."

"You can't be even sure they're husband and wife," Gran said. "They could just be business partners venturing out against the elderly and taking them for a sleigh ride."

Edie rubbed her forehead. "You are so right. I have to question everything now. Everything I thought I knew about them, everything they told me about themselves, I have to question just everything now."

"What kind of return on profit did they promise or guarantee?" I asked Edie.

"About thirty percent," Edie said.

Gran and I whistled at the same time.

"What? What?" Edie asked. "It's not like they said one hundred. That *would* be suspicious."

Edie was so naïve, it was almost cute. Sad and cute at the same time.

"Thirty percent is huge," Gran said. "The average stock market return is about ten percent per year for nearly the last century, at least measured by the S&P 500 index, which is one of the most commonly followed equity indices."

"Oh," Edie said.

"Yeah," Gran said. "Those people were good. They didn't promise so much as to raise alarms, but they still promised enough to make you want to fork over your money. Genius move."

"You keep saying they were good, and it was a genius move," Edie said. "Like you're jealous or something."

I had to hold in laughter. Edie had no idea how right she was.

"Sorry, I just have to respect their hustle," Gran said.

Edie rolled her eyes next to me. "So do you have any other opinion on the Feldmans besides that they were geniuses?" she asked.

"I'm guessing they took half of your money and really invested in something, so that they could show that they did something, and they probably stashed the other half for themselves. They've been probably doing this a long time and they're using their previous hustles to convince people of their new ones. Meaning that, for example, the payout that Marilyn broad got was more than likely legit. Most probably they used money from previous hustles for it."

"So they would be more believable this way," Edie said.

"Exactly," Gran said.

We drove in silence the rest of the way. Gran knew a lot about this stuff, more than me; however, I was guessing she wouldn't spill the beans on everything without getting herself into trouble over her knowledge.

Downtown, I parked one block away from the Feldmans' office. When we got out, I smelled a light sea breeze. I found it very odd, considering Bitter End was about thirty miles from the ocean, but I figured the wind just blew that way sometimes.

It was eleven a.m. when the three of us walked over to the Feldmans' office. We were standing on the sidewalk staring at the crime scene tape in front of us. Five minutes later, we were still staring.

"So what exactly are we doing here?" I asked. "Standing in front of their office and staring at it?"

"I don't know," Edie said. "I just know I have to do something, and going to the office where everything bad happened, kind of like, you know, makes me feel closer to it and then maybe I'll get an idea."

The office was empty, and it looked exactly like the day before minus the dead body.

Another five minutes later, Gran said, "Okay, we've seen it. Can we go back to the house now?"

"Hmm," Edie said. She looked to her left and her right. I didn't like this at all.

"Come on, let's go," Edie said. She started walking and we rushed behind her.

"Where are we going?" I asked.

"To see if there's a back door," Edie said.

Crap. I knew there was a back door from when I'd peeked inside the back room at the Feldmans' office.

"You said we won't be snooping around," Gran said. "This is not our business. This is not our problem. If you want to get into trouble, then by all means. It's your money and I get that you want to get it back. But getting yourself arrested is really not the way to go.

Whoa. Was this really Gran talking? "Getting yourself arrested is not the way to go?" I raised an eyebrow at Gran and she shrugged.

"Fine," Edie said. "You don't have to snoop around. You can be the lookout."

I laughed. Gran had zero escape.

There was a back alley behind the building. Nobody was there, just some dumpsters and some rats scurrying around. Edie screeched while Gran and I remained impassive.

"This must be the back door," Edie said. Then she turned to me. "I just realized, you were in that back room after we found Tammy. You must have seen the back door, right?"

I nodded.

Edie sighed. "Well, you could have just said that there's a back door."

"No," I said. "I didn't want to encourage this bad behavior."

Edie rolled her eyes then moved closer to the door. Then she turned to Gran. "Okay, Dorothy, you stay right here and give us a sign if somebody comes."

Gran gave her a look like, *Are you serious?*

This was like a child's game for Gran and me, considering the surveillance jobs we'd done in our former lives. But Gran played along, and she just nodded. Then she moved to the side of the door and put her hands in her jeans pockets.

Edie said, "Wait. What's the sign if somebody comes?"

"How about 'somebody is coming'?" Gran said.

"Don't be silly, Dorothy; that's too obvious," Edie said.

Gran stared at Edie. "Yes, clearly, *I* am the silly one."

"How about a frog sound?" Edie said. "Or a bird chirping? That sounds more natural, considering you're outside."

Gran stared at Edie some more. "Sure, because it wouldn't be at all suspicious if a person mimics a bird chirping."

Apparently, that went totally over Edie's head. She said, "Awesome, you can also cup your hands around your mouth like this and—"

Gran put her hand up. "Please stop. You'll get a bird sound, let's just leave it at that."

I laughed and gave Gran a thumbs-up.

FOOL ME ONCE

Edie rubbed her hands together and said they were sweaty. I pulled out the cleaning gloves from my back pocket and handed one pair to Edie.

"Good thinking, Piper," she said, as she put them on. "This is why I couldn't do this without you."

Some more emotional manipulation. I gave her a stare and she grinned at me.

I put on the other pair of gloves while Edie looked to her left and right, then tried the door handle. It opened straight away. She gave me a fist bump.

"Now's not the time, Edie," I whispered. "We can fist-bump later."

Edie peeked her head in. "It's dark inside." She whirled around to face me. "You go first."

"Why me?" I whispered.

"Because you're younger and more agile than me," Edie said.

"Fine," I said.

I switched places with Edie and slowly pushed the door open. I peeked my head in, but it was so dark I could only see the shapes of the shelves and the boxes. There was barely any light going in from the stamp-sized dirty window next to the door. The other door to the main room was closed. I felt for a light switch and found one on the left side of the wall. I flipped it on, but nothing happened. *Awesome.*

I pushed the door wide open and stepped inside. I turned back to Edie and told her the coast was clear. Edie stepped inside as well as I crossed the room to open the door to the main office.

"So what do you want to do now?" I asked Edie.

"I kinda hoped you had some good suggestions," Edie said. "I remember the last time we went snooping, you seemed to know what you were doing."

I thought about it. Then I said to Edie, "Go to the front and see what you can find around the desk. I'm going to look around these boxes here and then I'm coming to the front too. Please be careful so that nobody sees you from the street."

"You mean I have to fumble around that chair at the desk that Tammy was in?" Edie said.

"Are you serious?" I asked.

"I don't want to touch that chair," Edie said. "It most probably has murder cooties on it. And that mobile AC device is still there next to the chair, blocking that part of the desk."

"Edie, forget about the chair," I said. "It doesn't have any Feldman cooties on it, okay? This was your idea, remember? Now suck it up and do it."

"Fine," Edie grimaced and slowly moved to the front office.

I left the door open between the office and the storage room. This way it wasn't super dark inside. We left the back door slightly ajar. Gran was outside probably counting to ten and then leaving for the car without us.

I moved to the first box to my right and looked inside. There was all sorts of hardware stuff in it: power tools, plumbing supplies, cleaning products. Totally not interesting. I figured these didn't belong to the Feldmans, because, why would they? They probably belonged to the owner of this building. The second box contained paint and painting tools, but they were dry, so who knows how long they'd been here. In the corner of the room there were a few boxes on top of each other, and as I approached them, I heard a scuffling. I stopped in my tracks. I made the move of reaching down my boot for my knife, when of course I realized I didn't have my boots on, and I didn't have my knife with me. What kind of world was this where you couldn't have your knife on you?

I could hear Edie in the office room sifting through some papers, but I focused and kept my ears open for that scuffling I heard. It came from the corner, behind that pyramid of boxes. I was sure that it was just a rat. Maybe a big fat rat. I slowly approached the boxes and, just as I was about to look behind them, a black shadow leaped up and jumped at me.

It wasn't a rat. It was a person.

Chapter Six

I GAVE OUT AN involuntarily yelp and fell on my butt.

Damn it. I was so unprepared.

The black shadow was bolting for the back door, and I yelled to Gran, "Get him!"

In a second, Edie came running to the storage room, asking in a high-pitched voice, "What's going on in here?" She turned her gaze to the back door just as the person was sprinting out. "Lloyd, is that you?"

I jumped up and ran outside. Only to see this presumably Lloyd person—a slim man about six feet tall, short sandy-blond hair, wearing a disheveled gray suit—on top of Gran, both on the ground. I was just about to grab him when he jumped up and started running down the alley. Man, he was fast.

Gran also jumped, and just as I was about to take off after him, Gran quickly pulled her gun from the small of her back. In rapid succession, she shot three rounds but missed him. Then he disappeared around the corner, and he was gone.

"What the hell are you doing?" Edie shouted. "Are you shooting at him? Are you crazy?"

Crap and double crap.

That was a huge mistake.

I gave Gran a look. "You did not just shoot, did you? Do you know how much trouble that can lead us to?"

Gran blew off the end of her gun barrel. "I don't understand where the problem is. He was getting away."

"So the solution is to kill him?!" Edie started hyperventilating. "Why do you even have a gun? And why do you carry it with you like it's ChapStick?"

"You're acting like I pulled out a chunk of plutonium," Gran said. "It's a gun. Doesn't everybody carry a gun around here? And you weren't so strict against it a couple of weeks ago, when we saved your butt from that nutjob who held you hostage."

Ouch. Gran was letting Edie have it. That was what you got for rude comments about her gun. Gran was referring to our first interaction with Edie here in Bitter End, when we solved the murder of her former neighbor.

Okay, this was not how it was supposed to go down. This was starting to get out of hand.

"You know what?" I said. "We don't have time for this right now. We need to get out of here. Pronto."

"But . . . but . . ." Edie started, but I grabbed her arm and we all power-walked back to the car, got in, and sped away.

The atmosphere in the car was so tense, you could cut it with a knife. That only reminded me of my own knife. Ugh.

As I made my way back through downtown Bitter End, we were all looking out the windows, trying to see if there were any cop cars following us. But we didn't hear any sirens either.

I swerved on a side street, found a free parking space, and I screeched into the spot, cutting the engine.

I whirled around, putting my arm over the headrest. "What the hell were you thinking?" I asked Gran. "I don't think I have to tell you what you have just done. You've gotten us into trouble we don't need right now. I said get him, not shoot him!"

"That guy pushed me to the ground, so it was self-defense," Gran said.

"How was that self-defense?" Edie asked. "That's never going to hold up in a courtroom. I may not know much about stuff like that, but I'm certain about this."

"In a courtroom?" Gran asked. "Why would you assume this will go to a courtroom? Nothing happened. And I didn't plan on really shooting him. Okay, maybe only in the foot. To get him immobilized. How's that an offence?"

Gran was really incorrigible. I had the feeling that she sometimes forgot we were in the witness protection program, and we couldn't just go shooting people. Especially with her illegally purchased gun.

"What if he pulled his gun on you?" I asked Gran. "If he killed his wife or partner or whatever she was, he must still have the gun."

"But he didn't pull out any gun, did he?" Gran asked. "So either he got rid of it or he's a wuss."

I turned back around and let out a breath.

"So what now?" Edie asked.

"Let's just hope nobody saw us there and nobody can identify us," I said. I just realized then, Edie and I were still wearing the gloves. We both took them off and I pocketed them. I was probably going to burn them when we got back to the house.

"There wasn't anybody there to identify us," Gran said. "I made sure of that. We were in a back alley, not on a busy street. Then there was nobody in the alley, and chances that someone from the surrounding buildings looking out the window at exactly that moment are slim to none. And we got out of there pretty fast. Besides, I could see the windows from those buildings were totally smudged, so you can probably barely see through them."

Edie looked just as stunned as I felt. Even after living my whole life with Gran, she still managed to amaze me. She really thought this through. And as much as I didn't agree with Gran and her whipping out her gun and opening fire, if she says there were no witnesses in that back alley, then there were no witnesses in that back alley.

"But someone would have called the police, right?" Edie asked. "Someone had to hear the shots."

Gran nodded. "Unfortunately, that is correct. Somebody must have heard. But they didn't see us."

We all thought about that for a few moments.

Then I asked Edie, "So that was Lloyd?"

"Yes, it was," Edie said. "I recognized him from behind. What was Lloyd doing there?"

"That's a good question," I said. "He was already there when we arrived. He didn't get in past Gran."

From the back seat, Gran mumbled, "He sure as hell didn't."

"Anyway, as I was saying, he was already in there when we arrived. And he hid behind those boxes in the corner when he heard us come in. So actually, someone is able to identify us."

"Oh my god, you're right," Edie said. "Lloyd knows we were there."

"So what if he does?" Gran asked. "He can't say anything without giving himself away. He's probably the killer. He's probably more preoccupied with running and hiding than we should be about him identifying us."

"But when he gets caught, he's going to tell on us," Edie said.

"And do you think that's going to matter when they get the killer?" Gran asked. "If they have the killer then nothing else matters."

Edie covered her ears. "Could you stop saying killer? It really creeps me out."

"Fine, the culprit," Gran said. "We could say we were just concerned citizens. I mean it's your money he stole, right?"

Edie seemed to think about it. "Yeah, I guess you're right."

"Damn straight," Gran said.

Okay, so let's just assume Lloyd wouldn't tell on us; let's not worry about him seeing us. He doesn't even know Gran and me, although it wouldn't be hard to find out that it was us and you who were here. The question I ask myself is, what was he doing there?"

FOOL ME ONCE

"He was looking for something," Gran said. "Or he has unfinished business."

"What do you mean?" Edie asked. "Maybe he was just in hiding. You know, his apartment is right above the office."

Oh.

"He lives right above the office?" Gran asked. "Interesting."

"Why is that so interesting?" Edie asked.

"Because now we don't know if he has unfinished business at his home or at his office," Gran said. "Must be really desperate to stick around here, knowing the cops are after you."

"Dorothy, I have no idea what you're talking about with the unfinished business," Edie said.

"What Gran is saying is that Lloyd most probably has some loose ends here, but they could be in his apartment or his office—or both, for that matter," I said. "He hid in that storage room, but he might have easily come down from his apartment. And we caught him just as he was about to leave, so he scurried into that corner behind the boxes. He probably knows he's suspect number one in the shooting of his wife."

I thought some more about that. The gunshot was close range. Very close range. I didn't need a police report to know that. It reeked of an execution-style murder. Not a murder of passion. Rather cold-blooded. And Lloyd didn't pull out any gun when he escaped us. He seemed desperate to get away from us. He was zero confrontational. Not like I would picture a cold-blooded killer.

"He definitely has something to hide," I continued. "I mean, besides the obvious. If you're guilty, you're looking to run away and be as far as possible from the crime scene. But he wasn't as far as possible. He was right there at the crime scene."

"I see," Edie said. "I know I shouldn't defend him, but what if he didn't do it? What if he isn't the killer? What if he's in hiding because he wants to prove his innocence?"

Gran let out a snort. "No way. Whoever is able to scam elderly people and feel nothing, is not innocent. And if he really is, and by that, I mean he didn't shoot the woman—because he's guilty of everything else—then it's still suspicious he was there."

"Well, we were there and we're innocent," Edie said. "We were also looking for some clues so maybe that's what he was doing."

Gran and I didn't have a reply for that.

"Edie, even if you're right, it still doesn't look good for him," I said. "I know the system says you're innocent until proven otherwise, but for me this guy is guilty until proven otherwise. And I'm talking about the murder here. He's *already* guilty for scamming you out of your money."

Edie sighed. "I know he is. And I struggled within myself when I saw him just now. I was thinking about all those times I was in their office, and I talked to him and Tammy about whatever and he was so nice and accommodating, and now to know he's actually the bad guy . . . it just doesn't compute in my head."

Yeah, that was the thing. Edie had this great impression of Tammy and Lloyd Feldman, and now her world was crashing down. My guess was Lloyd shot Tammy to get his hands on all the money.

After a while, I asked, "Did you find anything useful in their office?"

Edie shook her head. "No. I mean, I don't know. I shuffled through some papers, but I don't actually understand what they mean."

"Jesus," Gran said.

Edie turned to face her. "Well excuse me for not knowing how these things work. I didn't work in the field, remember? *You* worked in the field, but you were the lookout, instead of being there and shuffling through the papers yourself."

I grinned. Edie knew how to eviscerate Gran when needed.

"Because I said I didn't want to be any part of this," Gran said.

"Yeah, better to go shooting people," Edie said.

"Okay, okay," I said. "Let's not blame each other. "Let's just agree this Lloyd person took us all by surprise." I paused. "So what now?"

"Let's just go back home," Edie said. "I think I'm done with snooping for today."

Nobody said another word on the drive back to the retirement complex. I was just pulling out on our street, when I saw a black Fat Boy V-twin softail cruiser with solid-cast disc wheels parked in front of Edie's house. I think I just drooled a little. That was one fine bike. I wondered if I could ever afford a bike like that again. Someday maybe when the marshals let the strings a bit loose, maybe when enough time had passed, and the Falcons forgot about us. If that day ever came.

"Uh-oh," Edie said, when she spotted Ryker standing on her porch.

"Oh man," I said. "This can't be happening. No way is he here about the shooting. It literally just happened." I turned to Gran. "And you said nobody could identify us."

"And I'm right," Gran said. "I don't know why he's here, but it's not about that."

I parked the car in Gran's driveway, and we all got out, just as Ryker sauntered over.

"Hey, Ryker, what's up?" Edie asked in her innocent voice.

"Grams, what did you tell the others?" he asked, taking off his black aviator glasses.

"The others? What do you mean?" Edie asked.

"What did you tell the other residents?" Ryker asked. "I just drove by the police station, and they got hit by an angry mob of people. You could see the crowd from the street. The station can't even accommodate that many people!"

I let out a laugh just picturing the three-hundred residents bursting into the building with torches and pitchforks.

Ryker gave me a dirty look and I made the motion of zipping my mouth shut.

"Well, they're filing a complaint, that's what they're doing," Edie said sheepishly.

I bet she didn't really think it through last night when she urged every one of them to go to the cops today.

"Grams, it looks like a riot," Ryker said. "I would say call the cops, but they are the cops who are under attack, kind of."

Now Gran was the one holding in the laughter, and I elbowed her.

Edie crossed her arms. "Well, what can I tell you? It's their right to file a complaint and it's their right to have someone look into the matter. It's not just about Tammy dying, it's also about our money."

"Yes, I get that, Grams," Ryker said. "But assailing the police station is really not the way to go, and I think you should—" Ryker pulled his cell from his jeans pocket. "Just a sec, I have to take this."

Ryker moved away from us and took the call. During which I whispered to Edie, "They should have gone to file their reports in shifts or something."

Edie waved it away. "Nonsense. The more pressure we put on the authorities, the more likely it is they'll handle the scam. Especially if the Feldmans' firm is already blacklisted. I want my twenty thousand dollars back."

Ryker ended the call and came back to us. He sighed and rubbed his forehead, then asked Edie, "Grams, did you break into the Feldmans' office just now?"

My eyebrows shot up involuntarily. His question totally took me by surprise, and I hated how unprepared I was.

"Did I . . .?" Edie's hand flew to her chest. "Did I what . . .?" She asked in the most innocent voice, and I had to give her props, she seemed way more prepared than I was.

"Were you just now at the Feldmans' office?" Ryker asked.

"What kind of a question is that?" Edie asked. "How do you even figure?"

"I just got a call from my contact at the PD," Ryker said. "He said there were some gunshots reported around the area of the Feldmans' office and someone has been seen through the glass window facing Grant Avenue. A little old lady with white curls, twerking on the desk."

Okay, this was too much. Gran and I both burst out laughing. We bent over and held our stomachs. I saw Edie blushing a bit.

"Why is that so funny?" Ryker asked.

It was so obvious why that was funny. The images Ryker put in my head were priceless. I can just imagine what that one witness had seen through the glass window. And I bet I know that Edie was in fact looking like she was twerking because she didn't want to touch the chair Tammy was in—because of the cooties—and the one side of the desk was blocked by the AC device, so she just climbed onto the desk.

Edie cleared her throat. "Why do you assume that was me?"

"Let's just call it intuition," Ryker said. He put his hand on his hips and shook his head. "You know what? Actually, I don't want to know. It's enough what I know and that I'm going to have nightmares about it. I should have known you would get involved. Grams, I am begging you to leave this to the police and leave this to me." Ryker looked me in the eye. "Every time Grams gets into trouble, you're there too and your grandmother also. I'm assuming the reported gunshots have nothing to do with you?"

Gran and I shook our heads.

"Good," he said. "Because if they are, then you're in big trouble. So I'm asking you to leave this alone."

I looked Ryker in the eye as well. "We're not doing anything. And besides, you can't really tell me what to do. Maybe if *you* would do a better job in solving this, then we wouldn't have to."

Ryker went white as a ghost and Gran said, "Oh, burn."

Ryker recovered fast. "Unlike you, I am following the law when investigating and I intend to keep it that way."

"Don't you need a client to be on this case?" I asked.

"I have a client." He looked at Edie. "My grandmother."

I rolled my eyes. That was a clever little spin, actually.

Edie flashed him a wide smile and said in a proud voice, "My grandson."

"Very well," I said. "Then I'll leave you to your investigation. Now if we're done here, I'd like to get back to the house and get on with my day."

I turned on my heel and, with Gran beside me, we stomped to the house and I slammed the door behind me. I made a beeline for the window facing Edie's house and peered from behind the hideous greenish curtain. Edie and Ryker headed for her house and, just before they went in, Ryker turned and glanced my way. I quickly moved from the curtain. Damn it. I felt like a freaking teenager.

Gran was taking off her boots and she was grinning.

"Why are you smiling so wickedly?" I asked.

"You're so intent on setting me up with Theodore, while you are pushing *him* away."

"Pushing him away? Who are you talking about? Him?" I pointed toward Edie's house.

"Of course him," Gran said. "He's totally into you. And you're totally into him."

I covered up my ears. "I don't want to hear it. Let me know when you're not talking nonsense."

Gran laughed. "Whatever you say. I'm gonna take a shower."

"Be sure not to shoot anybody on your way there," I said.

Gran laughed even harder as she headed to the bathroom. "Only if they piss me off."

I inhaled a deep breath of air and looked at my cell phone. It was shortly after noon. I was guessing Edie would come over as soon as Ryker left. So that gave me a few hours to do . . . nothing. Which wasn't all that bad, actually. I imagined Edie would pitch the next wild idea to us, so better to get some rest now.

Chapter Seven

As expected, Edie showed up later in the afternoon. Gran almost bolted through her bedroom window just to get out. "I'm done for the day," she had said. "You can't make me come with you on a reconnaissance mission, then have a problem with me doing what I do best."

"Shoot at people?" I asked.

Gran pursed her lips. And went to hide in her bedroom.

I let Edie in, and she made herself comfortable on her designated chair at the kitchen table. I found it fascinating and terrifying at the same time, how cozy Edie felt at Gran's after only a couple of weeks of knowing us.

"So how was it with Ryker?" I asked her, while I took a seat next to her. "Did you tell him about Lloyd being there?"

Edie put her head in her hands. "No, I didn't. I hate lying to him but I have to save myself, you know?"

I laughed. "Yeah, I get what you're saying."

In the end, everybody thought about themselves. All this talk about being a good person, whatever that meant, about thinking about other people and putting the people you love first; that was all bull. People had, like, a built-in survival chip, and in a time of crisis they thought about themselves first. That's how the survival mechanism worked.

"I wanted to tell him about Lloyd at first," Edie said. "Especially since me not telling him or the police about it probably means I am messing with their investigation, and I feel a bit guilty about that." She paused and seemed to think about it. "Which means now we only have to be more decisive in finding out how to get our money back. Also, we have to find out who killed Tammy, because if it was Lloyd, and Lloyd is the only one who can give us our money back, then they're interconnected."

I sat there and thought about how I could have let this happen. Again. Let Edie pull me in into her affairs, twice in three weeks now. Or, I was so bored out of my mind, that I *wanted* Edie to pull me in. Which was kind of sad if it came to this. I decided to push those thoughts away.

"So Ryker didn't know about you investing with the Feldmans, right?" I asked.

Edie shook her head. "No, he didn't know. I didn't think it was necessary to tell my grandson what I do with my money. But now"—a sadness crossed her eyes—"I wish I had told him. It took him only about twenty minutes to search the Feldmans through his programs and find out they were scammers, that something wasn't right with them."

"That's rough," I said. "I'm guessing the Feldmans, if that's their real names even, moved from state to state and did their thing. I wonder how long they would have stayed here in Bitter End."

"Yeah, I don't want to even think about it," Edie said. "I know it sounds weird, but if this murder thing didn't happen, then the fraud thing may have never surfaced, at least not as long as the Feldmans were here."

I tried for a smile. "So you could say we got lucky with the murder?"

Edie stared at me. "I swear, your humor is sometimes really sick."

"At least I can see the humor in it," I said. "It's not like we can change something now and bring her back alive. Besides, if she scammed you, I wouldn't take that much pity on her."

"Anyway," Edie said, "Marilyn Strobe is expecting us now."

"Huh?" I asked. "Did I just miss something? Why is Marilyn Strobe expecting us?"

"Her granddaughter is with her right now and she has some information," Edie said. "You know, the granddaughter who is working at the insurance office a couple of doors down from the Feldmans? Apparently, she knows something, and we should know it too." Edie stood. "So let's go." Then she paused. "Where's Dorothy?"

"She's hiding in the bedroom," I said.

Edie laughed. "Well, it's better this way. Then we don't need to worry about her shooting anybody." Then Edie turned to me and furrowed her eyebrows. "Unless you're going to shoot someone."

"I'm going to skip that today."

"Good."

Edie and I got into the golf cart and sped away. It took me a while to get the hang of driving that thing in flip-flops. After it had taken me a while to just wear flip-flops. And I still didn't make my peace with it. Whoever had the idea that feet should be out in the air like that, was probably stoned.

Marilyn Strobe lived in a pastel-green house on the northeast side of the retirement complex. Just like all the other houses around here, there were gnomes in her front yard. I didn't get the gnomes either. They just gave me the creeps. It was funny that Gran's house was the one that stood out. As far as I could tell, it was the only house in gray paint with an equally gray-colored roof. All the other bungalow-like houses gave off that cheerful vibe. At least that was the intent. I didn't care much for the pastel colors.

I parked the golf cart at the curb of Marilyn's house and Edie and I headed for the front door. We were about to knock when the door opened. A sturdy woman with brown curls and wearing a pink house robe stood in front of us. She looked to be in her eighties. She smiled wide when she saw Edie. Then she nodded at me. We were welcomed into a living room full of antique furniture. This seemed to also be the usual décor around here. As was the layout of the house: bedroom and bathroom in the back, living room and dining nook in the front, kitchenette to the side.

"Edie, I'm so glad you came," Marilyn said. "Come, sit, sit." She pointed to the couch.

A younger woman emerged from the bathroom. "Oh, I thought I heard someone come in." She introduced herself as Victoria Strobe, Marilyn's granddaughter.

I would have guessed she was in her forties. She had long, curly auburn hair and sharp cheekbones with a strong jawline. She wore a tailored blouse with a fitted skirt that she accessorized with fine jewelry.

She took a seat on the chair opposite the couch. She nervously fumbled with her fingers in her lap, signaling a high level of anxiety.

Edie started with a bit of small talk and formally introduced me. Marilyn offered us refreshments, but we declined. Then Edie dove right in.

"Victoria, I hear you wanted to tell us something," Edie said.

Victoria looked over at her grandmother. Marilyn nodded. "That's okay, dear, you can tell them."

Okay, this got my interest.

Victoria cleared her throat. "I think I've seen something that may be important to find out what happened over at the Feldmans' office." She paused. "But first, I need you to keep this between us. I haven't gone to the police with this and I'm not planning to."

Okay, this *really* got my interest.

Edie and I exchanged glances.

Marilyn leaned in and said, "Edie, this is important, and I need you to promise me you will respect Victoria's wishes. I felt you needed to know because you're kind of in charge of this whole thing and I know you're fighting for us to get our money back. I kind of feel guilty because I recommended the Feldmans to you, so that's why I felt strongly you needed to know this." Marilyn turned to me. "And since I know our new resident . . . well, our *temporary* new resident is helping you out, then I figured it was okay for her to know as well."

Good god, this is what it came to. I was Edie's sidekick. It didn't get lower than this.

Edie leaned forward and her eyes almost popped out. If Victoria didn't start talking right now, Edie would combust with excitement and anticipation. "Of course this is remaining between us," Edie said. "You have my word. Go on, tell us what you know."

Victoria hesitated for a bit. "I'm sorry, I need to ask this. I know your grandson is Ryker Donovan, and he is a private investigator and . . ."

Edie waved her hand in dismissal. "I get it, but you have nothing to worry about. Ryker means well and he wants to keep us safe, but often I don't agree with his way of working."

I had to hold in my laughter. What Edie meant by that was she didn't agree with Ryker's *legal* way of working.

"So Ryker won't find out anything from me," Edie continued.

Victoria took a deep breath. "Okay, here's the thing. I've seen some suspicious-looking people going in and out of the Feldmans' office. They look like . . . hit men." She said the last word in a hushed tone.

For a moment, my heart rate went up. Hit men? Like the ones the Falcons probably had on Gran's and my tail? But surely, they weren't looking for us there in the Feldmans' office. I shook my head. This is the way my life would be from now on. Every time I heard something that could be somehow related to us, my antenna went up. Although, I was kind of hoping the subject of hired killers wouldn't come up here in Bitter End. Granted, I had no idea about the criminal landscape here in town; I hadn't researched that field and I wasn't sure I would research it.

It was a fact, though, that Gran and I were scarred by everything that happened. Every time Ryker drove his bike to Edie's house and I heard the once-beautiful roaring sound outside on the street, I'd tense up, thinking the Falcons had found us. I wondered if I'd ever live my life free of those thoughts. How could you *not* live looking over your shoulder when you knew gunmen were after you?

"How do you figure those people are hit men?" I asked Victoria and decided the Falcons were not here in Bitter End.

She cleared her throat again. "Obviously, I'm not exactly sure they are," she said. "It's just that they have that vibe, you know, like in the movies? It's like they were coming straight out of an Italian mafia movie. And they had that look on their faces. Like they never smile. Like they're not nice people."

"Oh yeah," Edie said. "I hate it when people look like that."

I gave Edie a sideways glance. She really had no idea what was going on in this world.

"And what did those people do?" I asked Victoria.

"I don't know what they did in the office," she said. "I've seen them sometimes go in or go out while I went out to have lunch or just take a break. One of them is tall and sturdy, and the other one is way shorter but seems sturdy as well. One of them has a scar on his face, you know, like a diagonal one over his eye and they both always wear a black T-shirt and a leather vest and jeans, and black boots."

"So kind of what Dorothy wears," Edie said smiling at me.

"With the exception that Gran isn't a hired assassin," I said. Edie was close to the truth, but not that close.

"No, of course not," Edie said then paused and mumbled under her breath, "just likes to shoot at whomever."

"Um, who are you talking about?" Victoria asked wide-eyed.

"Never mind," I said and gave Edie a stare. "This is about you and your information. So those guys, do they have any other distinguishing features?"

Victoria seemed to think about it. "No, I don't think so. The short one is bald and the taller one has short dark hair. Other than how they are dressed and how their vibe is, I don't think there's anything else."

"So you don't know what their business was with the Feldmans?" Edie asked.

Victoria and Marilyn exchanged glances.

"That's okay, dear," Marilyn patted her arm. "You can tell them."

Victoria fumbled with her fingers again. "Well, last week I just came from lunch, and I was walking past the Feldmans' office, and you know how they have that glass window and you can see through it?"

Edie and I both nodded.

"As I was walking by, I turned my head and wanted to just wave at them, but then I saw these two guys again," Victoria said. "The short bald one was sitting in the chair in front of the desk and the tall one was perched on the corner of the desk, and he was almost in Lloyd's face. Lloyd looked like a puddle of sweat. And Tammy was next to him also looking terrified. The whole image looked like they were being threatened or something. I can't really explain it. I know; I don't have exact proof, but I swear, something was not right with that image."

"We believe you, Victoria," Edie said, nodding.

I thought about it. It all did sound a bit out there, and I didn't know this Victoria person. She could very well just be a scaredy-cat and see danger in everything and be afraid of everyone. And the cliché about how those guys were dressed and their demeanor . . . wasn't that just a movie cliché? Then I thought about Gran and about the Falcons and the way I used to dress. Yeah, okay, maybe it was not just a cliché.

"Okay, let me guess," I said. "Those two guys have seen you and that's why you don't want to go to the cops with this information, right?"

Edie winked at Marilyn. "See? She's sharp."

Victoria nodded. "Exactly. As I stopped in front of their office, those guys turned and saw me standing there on the sidewalk. They looked at me and I swear they were shooting daggers with their eyes. They didn't even need to verbally threaten me, I already felt that way. They know where I work, because obviously they've seen me go into the office. I'm very sorry for what happened to Tammy, although as I've heard, she was a fraud and so was Lloyd, so maybe I'm not that sorry. I don't know what their business was with those two guys, but I don't want to be part of it, and yes I admit I'm afraid of going to the police with this info because I worry about my safety and the safety of my grandmother."

There was silence for a few beats.

"Fair enough," I said.

"Edie, I'm not sure what you can do with this information," Marilyn said. "But I thought it was important for you to know."

"Yes, yes, but of course, Marilyn," Edie said. "We appreciate you thinking of us. This is really helpful, and Piper and I will come up with a plan."

I raised an eyebrow at Edie. We will?

"I still have some questions," I said. "When did you start seeing these two guys hanging out at the Feldmans'?"

Victoria seemed to think about it. "I'm not sure. I think maybe about a month or so ago? Or maybe two months? Something like that. At first I didn't quite think they were dangerous or anything, but then I started to notice them more and more and they just . . . they're just giving me the creeps."

"Did you see from what direction they came and went when they visited the Feldmans?" I asked.

"They came from down the street in the direction of the laundromat. At least I think."

"Do you know the Feldmans?" I asked Victoria. "Did you have any interactions with them since your offices are close to each other and you work in related fields?"

"Just regular pleasantries," Victoria said. "They seemed like such nice folks. I'm so shocked to hear that they were frauds. Especially since I work in the insurance business, you can imagine how devastated I was to hear these two scammers were doing business right there in the open. And not only that, but my grandmother is involved too, and her money is gone." Victoria looked at Marilyn with a sad look in her eyes. "I really do hope you find Lloyd and get my grandmother's money back. And if he killed Tammy, then I really hope he's going to rot in jail for that."

"Amen to that." "You said it, sister," Edie and Marilyn said at the same time.

I leaned back into the couch cushion. I still wasn't sure if this was helpful information, or if this Victoria chick was just overreacting. But it was still some interesting piece of info.

"Are you working alone in the insurance office?" I asked. "Are there other property owners or staff members from other offices and shops around the area who may have seen the same suspicious guys?"

"I work with Ryan at the insurance office," Victoria said. "I'm not sure he's seen them, and if he did see them then he didn't tell me anything about it. I didn't tell him anything about it either, because it didn't feel necessary for me to share this information with him." Victoria lowered her voice like she was letting us in on a secret about someone. "And also, Ryan is kind of stuck-up and we haven't really discussed anything personal ever."

"Yes, I hate stuck-up people too," Edie said, nodding vigorously.

"Regarding other store owners, I really have no idea if others have noticed something similar about those two guys."

There was silence for a few seconds. It seemed as if everyone was deep in thought about the Feldmans. And the supposed hit men and stuck-up Ryan and the fraud money, and especially where Lloyd was and if he shot Tammy.

"Anyway," Victoria said, "I've taken a leave of absence of one week and figure the police will clear everything up by then. I'm really not so fond of going into the office, knowing those guys know where I work. And yes, I'm aware I want the police to figure this out, but at the same time, I'm not sharing the information that I know with them. I feel guilty about it, but I value my life more." She shuddered.

"That's understandable," Edie said.

"Had you actually seen those two guys at the Feldmans' office yesterday, when the murder happened?" I asked. "Did you hear any gunshots?"

Victoria shook her head. "Unfortunately, no. But as I understand it, the murder happened way earlier in the morning, and I went in to work at about nine a.m."

We all thought about it some more.

"Is there anything else we should know?" I asked.

"No, I don't think so," Victoria said.

"But she'll come straight to you if she remembers anything else, right?" Marilyn said, turning to her granddaughter.

"Yes, of course, you can count on that," Victoria said. "Even if you're not law enforcement, I kind of feel better knowing someone is looking into it and someone knows about those two guys."

"Thank you for sharing that with us," I said and stood.

Edie stood as well and gave Marilyn a hug. "And don't you feel guilty, Marilyn, about recommending the Feldmans to me. They would have gotten to us one way or another."

Edie and I left and drove back to our houses.

"Wow, what a rush," Edie said.

I turned to her. "You're kidding, right?"

"Why would I be kidding?" Edie said. "Hit men, mafiosos, money, murder. It's like a movie!"

"Only you're the one that got scammed. In real life, not a movie."

"Oh." Edie said in a low voice. "I'm trying not to focus on that part too much. I can't undo me giving them my money. I can only look forward, and do what I can to get it back." She paused. "So, what's our next move?"

"Our next move?" I asked. "I thought you were the brainiac here."

"Ha ha, very funny," Edie said. "But seriously, what's our plan now? I really don't know where to go from here."

"Well, same with me," I said. "It would be nice to know what those two guys were up to, but we have zero leads. I don't know where to find them. And I'm not going to interview every person working or living on that street. That would take an eternity and I'm not law enforcement either."

I didn't tell Edie that I kind of figured what was probably going on. If Victoria was correct and those two guys really looked and acted the part, then I would have bet some other criminal organization was behind all this. It didn't even have to be a huge organization, just one person or a couple of people doing illegal stuff and hiring the two scary dudes. From my point of view, even the Feldmans were a criminal organization. And they either worked for another organization and pissed them off, or there was a rival one and they had a beef with the Feldmans.

I decided to keep this to myself; it was no use creeping Edie out, especially since I couldn't prove it. It was just my gut.

Edie pouted. "This is just great," she said. "Well, then we need to sleep on it and maybe we'll get some good ideas tomorrow, after a good game of paintball."

I almost stepped on the break. "A good game of paintball? Now you're really kidding. I assumed that was off. How can you go off and play at a time like this?"

Edie looked at me like *I* was talking crazy. "You mean, *especially* at a time like this. We all need to blow off some steam. We're going crazy sitting around all day, just thinking about stuff. Besides, it's already been paid for. We're losing that money if we don't go."

"It's already been paid for?" I asked. "Gran and I didn't pay for anything."

Edie grinned. "That's because Theodore already paid for you two."

A warmth flooded my chest. Theodore was the epitome of old-fashioned gallantry. Younger guys could really take lessons from him.

"Don't worry," Edie said. "You're gonna love it."

That was what I was afraid of.

Chapter Eight

The next morning at 7:15 a.m., Gran and I sat in Theodore's car on our way to the Bitter End paintball field. He'd brought a thermos with coffee and two cups for us. My heart almost melted. Gran didn't say anything and reluctantly poured herself a cup.

Theodore's car was a sleek, silver Range Rover. It kind of fit his personality. Gran sat in the passenger seat, and I sat in the back. Gran took a bit of convincing. She wanted to be as far away as possible from Theodore.

The one thing I was happy about was that I could finally wear some normal clothes. I dressed in my jeans and black T-shirt, pulled a black sweatshirt over it, and finally, my biker boots. Edie had told us to wear long sleeves and long pants for when we got paint-shot so our skin wouldn't hurt. Gran was in her usual outfit, and she added a dark-gray sweatshirt. Theodore, on the other hand, was wearing a complete tracksuit in light blue. He said most of his wardrobe contained outfits for the Florida type of weather, or slacks and dress shirts.

The day before, I had reported to Gran what we found out from Victoria. Her guess was as good as mine. She figured this may very well not be a personal thing but a crime for money.

"I hope you two ladies are ready for today," Theodore said. He snuck a glance at Gran. "Although, I think you should be the one we need to be worried about."

"You definitely should," Gran said.

"Theodore, I hope you know what you got yourself into," I said. "I mean with Gran here."

Theodore laughed and Gran turned and gave me a death stare.

"That's good, I need a proper challenge," Theodore said.

"Do you know what the challenge was?" Gran said. "Getting up at six thirty in the morning. I really don't know how you let me get roped into this."

"When you live in Florida, you learn how to navigate the heat," Theodore said. "The best time to do anything is early in the morning."

"And what do you do the rest of the day?" Gran asked. "Sit around and do nothing?"

"Have you been doing anything?" Theodore asked. "I'm open to suggestions."

Gran didn't say anything.

"That's what I thought," Theodore said. "Anyway, I'm up since six a.m. That's late for me. I used to start my day at 4:30 every morning."

"That seems extreme," Gran said but didn't inquire further.

I was slightly worried about Gran today. I had to wrestle her gun from her this morning. Chances were just too great that she'd start shooting with her real one. It said something about your relationship with your grandmother when you had to frisk her at 6:50 in the morning.

We drove around Bitter End downtown, then through an industrial area, and after about thirty minutes, we arrived at the paintball place and it was already packed. Theodore took the last parking spot and we all got out.

There was a small mob of people in front of the entrance. I spotted Edie, Beatrice, Belly Man and Raspy, some other known faces, and Sourpuss was also there huddled with her own group.

"What the . . .?" Gran asked. "Looks like a senior convention here."

It was funny that she didn't consider herself one of the seniors.

I took a better look and saw that everyone was wearing some kind of combat outfit, mostly camouflage print. A lot of them also had that camouflage face paint: two lines across the cheeks. They were really taking this seriously. Nobody in the world would ever feel threatened by this image, but hey, let them have their fun.

We approached the group and, after the obligatory hugs and handshakes, a young guy wearing a T-shirt with the words Paintball Crew on it came to us. He had thick blond hair that was bouncing back and forth as he swaggered over. He was twenty-two, tops. He stopped short and frowned.

"Dude," he said and took the image in. "This is like a reunion from Cocoon."

Uh-oh. He should be more careful, or they'll run him over with their walkers. But I had to give him props for his cinema expertise.

Edie put her hands on her hips. "Watch your mouth there, young man," she said. "We're the best in the game. Ronnie can attest to that fact. Where's Ronnie? And who are you?"

"Dude, Ronnie got tired working here," the guy said. "I'm Kevin. Ronnie said he wants to work for himself. Wants to be a business owner and all that."

FOOL ME ONCE

"So what does he do?" Beatrice asked, pushing her glasses further up her nose, smudging the face paint. At least it matched the smudged lipstick.

Kevin scanned the crowd, probably trying to decide where the question came from. Then his head looked down and he spotted Beatrice. "He's opening a weed shop," he said.

There was silence for a beat, and I wasn't sure if this Kevin dude was joking or not.

"You mean like medical marijuana?" Edie asked. "Because there's some people here who would be interested."

Chatter erupted throughout the crowd. Okay, it wasn't a joke. I looked over at Gran and she was grinning wickedly.

"Don't even think about it," I whispered to her.

"What?" she said. "I didn't say anything."

"That's not necessary," I said. "I can see it on your face."

Gran shrugged. "I don't know what you're talking about. It's just good to know there may be a place around here where you can buy pot."

"It's not pot," I said. "It's medical."

"Yeah, whatever," Gran said.

"Hey, dudes," Kevin said, putting his hands up, "I don't know anything more than that. I think

Ronnie told me exactly where he opened his shop, but I don't remember. We had a jam session when we talked about it, you know, dude? Then we had, like, a real heart-to-heart talk and everything, but the darndest thing is, I couldn't remember anything the next day."

I would assume his brain was probably already fried from all the pot he took, and obviously him not being the brightest candle on the cake didn't help matters either.

"Fine, whatever, can we just get on with this?" Sourpuss yelled from the back.

Edie rolled her eyes and said, "Unfortunately, she is right. We want to get started."

Gran and I got the gist of the rules from Kevin dude. The others were not kidding. This was not their first time at the paintball field.

We went inside into a small wooden cabin where each of us got our paintball guns. Gran strapped the gun around her upper body and worked it like the pro that she was, ignoring the glances directed at her. I started to worry that it was a mistake bringing Gran to this.

"Where is everybody else?" I asked Edie and looked around. "You said mostly everybody would play. There's three hundred residents at the complex and we're only thirty people here."

"Oh, the place can't accommodate hundreds of people at the same time," Edie said. "There's about two hundred and fifty people who will play today, because you know the rest are prone to breaking a hip, but we're doing it in shifts."

Edie said this as if it were the most normal thing in the world. Again, I wasn't sure if this was a joke or not.

"I see you look confused," Edie said with a straight face.

"Never mind," I said. Only in Bitter End did retired people play paintball in shifts. I thought about asking if that meant the others were playing later in the day when it got way hotter outside, since that was the reason we had to get up at the crack of dawn, but I let it go. Most likely no answer would make sense for me.

We formed two groups. Obviously, I had the cool people on my team. Sourpuss was not on it. But that meant I had to be extra careful so that Gran wouldn't let out all her aggressions on Sourpuss.

We got some general instructions, like only shooting at each other in the designated areas, or when being hit by a paintball and thus eliminated from the game, we should raise our gun and our arm over our head and exit the playing field as fast as possible. We should put a barrel sleeve on our gun after exiting the playing field, to avoid shooting someone accidentally. Also, no foul language and no knives or other weapons were allowed. Gran and I exchanged glances, and she rolled her eyes.

Edie pulled out red headbands for our team, and the other team had blue headbands. I was amazed at how prepared they were for this.

"Why the headbands?" I asked Edie.

"Because as soon as we put our masks on, we won't recognize each other, so it's easier to identify the enemy by the color of their headband."

Right, how did I dare ask such an obvious question.

Kevin dude came over with a bunch of goggles and started handing each of us a pair. They covered our whole face, and Edie was right; it was harder to recognize someone wearing one of those. I saw a few of my teammates whipping out their inhalers and sucking in a few deep breaths before putting on the goggles. The mask had small openings that allowed for breathing. I shook my head. I guess I shouldn't have been surprised if they came to play paintball with their oxygen tanks.

FOOL ME ONCE

Theodore snuck in beside Gran. "I'm glad we're on the same team," he said to her. "Or else I would be in serious trouble."

Gran made the motion of cocking her gun and said, "You bet you would."

"We could do a bit of reverse gender roleplay, then," Theodore said. "You could defend me from the other team."

Gran stared at him. "What makes you think I'm a team player?"

Theodore shrugged. "I think you're more of a team player than you think."

"My life experience tells another story," Gran said.

"That's all in your past now," Theodore said. "This is your present. You can make a deliberate choice about how you live your life in the present."

Now that was a conclusive victory for Theodore. Gran was speechless. And so was I. What Theodore said hit the right note for Gran's and my life right now. Gran probably wouldn't admit it. And I'd become a master of compartmentalizing my feelings.

Kevin dude showed us the shooting area that was a huge field of dirt and natural terrain. It had a few hills, a few trenches and part of a wood. Wooden bunkers were placed strategically, interspersed with barricades and fortresses. Up a steeper hill there was a wooden fortress, but Edie told me nobody went up there because, well, they were too old to climb. The game was over when every member of one team got eliminated.

The field area seemed huge, and I was curious if the seniors would survive this training or if we'd be calling the paramedics in ten minutes.

The teams were brought onto opposite ends of the field as the starting point, so that they were not in view of each other.

Kevin dude then went back to the main cabin, and we heard a loud sound, like a huge air horn, vibrating through the field.

"Game on," Edie said, and ducked behind the barricade in a combat move.

I watched everyone take positions and get their guns ready to shoot. It felt more like in a sitcom movie.

"Piper, what are you doing?" Edie hissed. "Get down."

I mockingly shook my hands in front of me in a *Oh, I'm so scared* kind of move, that is until a paintball flew past my head and splashed behind me on a wall.

I instantly ducked. "What the . . .?"

"I told you to get down," Edie said.

Come on, was this for real? Who was that good a shooter from the other team anyway?

Another paintball whizzed past us.

Oh, it's on now.

I glanced over at Gran who was a few feet next to me behind a barrel, looking alert. So she's taken this really seriously. As should I, apparently.

Our team was scattered but we could all still see each other. Edie gave out silent hand signals like she was in the military. I didn't understand a single one. She tapped her shoulders, then she put her index and middle finger in front of her eyes like a victory sign, then with the palm of her hand she showed a forward movement, and then she tapped her shoulder twice again.

Were we in a battle or at a baseball game? But the others seemed to understand, so they nodded, and one by one they moved forward. I was next to Edie behind a barricade, and I asked her what her plan was. She told me to follow her. I rolled my eyes. At least we could hear each other through the masks.

Still ducking, Edie told me to cover her while she half ran to the next barricade. The other team opened fire on her as soon as she was exposed, and I fired back until she jumped behind the next barricade. I followed her and was glad I didn't get hit. Man, I really had to up my game.

Gran ran behind one of the wooden walls and dropped to the ground. She lost Theodore somewhere on the way, which didn't surprise me at all. She took aim and shot five times and I heard two people from the other team scream bloody murder and something along the lines of, "Oh gosh-darn it, I was hit." But Gran looked disappointed.

"She just eliminated two people," Edie said to me. "She should be happy."

"Nope," I said. "She shot off five shots and only got two people out."

"Oh," Edie said. "You know, if I didn't know you better, I would say you're joking."

Gran sprang up and ran for the nearest fortress. I looked over at Edie and told her she should let Gran do whatever she does best. She would probably eliminate all the other team players in ten minutes max.

"But I don't want the game to be over in ten minutes," Edie said.

Of course she didn't. I hoped Gran wasn't that selfish and would let Edie eliminate a couple of people as well. Or else we would never hear the end of it.

FOOL ME ONCE

Thirty minutes later we had lost ten players and the other team lost eleven players. I wasn't sure if Gran wasn't on her game or if she held back on purpose. We were dispersed around the whole field, and it got harder and harder to breathe through that stupid mask. Hearing got difficult as well, so we ended up yelling at each other.

I was behind a wooden wall and I peeked out. I was kind of hoping to see Sourpuss somewhere, or better yet, her tight hair bun sticking above her goggles straight into the sky, and bring her down and get it over with. Then we'd have a lesser chance that she and Gran got into a paintball war. But I hadn't seen Sourpuss yet, which kind of made me wonder how good she was at this game?

But I did see Pineapples right across from me behind a barrel. I had forgotten the woman's name a couple of weeks ago, but it didn't matter to me. You really couldn't miss her since everything she wore had a pineapple pattern. Even her combat clothes had pineapple ornaments. She was on the other team, so I aimed my gun at her and took a shot and hit one of the bigger pineapples on her thigh.

She screamed in pain and fell to the ground.
Oh crap. Was she hurt?

I knew it wasn't a good idea for seniors to be playing this game. She was lying there on the ground, aching, and I felt really bad. I got up and, just as I was about to jog over to her and see if she was all right, Sourpuss appeared behind Pineapples and shot in my direction. I instantly ducked down and dragged myself back behind the wooden wall.

I cursed beneath my breath. That sneaky Sourpuss. That was a trap! Pineapples played the card of the little old lady who got hurt to lure me out.

I smiled. I could respect that.

"Nice try," I yelled over the wall. "But your aim is totally crappy."

"Don't get comfortable so soon," Sourpuss yelled back. "I will get you and your annoying grandmother. I will win this game."

"Then bring it on," I said and started shooting her way while she was shooting my way. The wooden wall was now probably full of color.

After a couple of rounds of shooting, I took a break, leaning on the wall and breathing hard. That damn mask, I could hardly breathe with that thing on.

"I hope you have good stamina, because I can do this all day," I yelled.

No answer came.

"Do you hear me?" I yelled louder.

Nothing.

I peeked out and saw no movement. I didn't know if Sourpuss really decided to leave her post or if she only pretended to, getting me to draw near to her hiding place. After five minutes of zero movement, I decided Sourpuss had left and was plotting her next move. Which I should have been doing as well.

I decided the highest fortress on that steep hill would be the perfect spot to see everybody.

I ran from cover to cover and escaped a few shots. I decided to go with it and have some fun but at the same time, definitely take this game seriously. I also decided to not think about the other players. I couldn't really control Gran so she wouldn't hurt anyone, I couldn't control what happened between her and Sourpuss, I couldn't control what Edie did, and I was not their mother. They were all responsible for themselves in the end.

I shot three people from the other team while going to the top of the hill. I was feeling kind of proud of myself. They would all walk around with bruises the next day, but hey, this game wasn't my choice, was it?

DEANY RAY

I finally made it to the fortress at the top of the hill, and I went inside and sat down and took off my mask and breathed heavily. I was hot, I was sweaty, and I was thirsty.

The floor of the fortress was creaky and had loose wooden tiles, but all in all, it looked like a small cabin. At least this fortress had a roof that seemed to be pretty solid, so no sun came through. I put my mask back on and peeked through an opening. From my vantage point I could see most of the playing field. On one side of the hill was the even terrain, and on the other side was the woods.

I needed a break, so I sat on the floor, opposite the entrance, and leaned on the wall. I took the mask off again. It was only then that I realized what was on the floor scattered around. Empty coffee cups, empty and half-full chip bags, some power bars, and small bottles of water. A blanket was in a corner and a fluffy paint container from one of the paintball guns, that was probably used as an impromptu pillow.

I frowned. This looked like a shelter for a homeless person. Was someone really living here? If this fortress wasn't so popular with the paintball players, then I guessed someone desperate could have turned it into a place to live. But who was that desperate?

Just as the idea started to dawn on me, I heard movement coming from the entrance. I didn't have time to jump up, so I instantly aimed my paintball gun at the door.

Lloyd Feldman came crawling in, looking down at his phone, and yelped when he looked up and saw me.

Chapter Nine

"WHAT THE HELL?" Lloyd said, then turned around and bolted right out again, dropping his phone on the floor in the process.

I got you now, you jerk!

I recognized Lloyd Feldman, although I hadn't really seen his face at his office yesterday, what with him leaping up from behind the boxes in the room that barely had any light coming in. However, it didn't matter that I hadn't seen his face properly. His slim body shape, his short sandy-blond hair, his rumpled gray suit—that was enough to know this was Lloyd Feldman.

I jumped up but stumbled over one of the loose wooden tiles. I cursed under my breath, while I shook it off and took off behind him. He had a head start and man, he was fast—just like back in the alley. He ran down the hill like there was no tomorrow. I expected him to pull out his gun, the gun he presumably used to kill Tammy, but just like yesterday in the office, there was no gun. He just kept on running.

I noticed Lloyd's appearance looked even more rumply and disheveled than the day before. Which made me wonder what the heck was going on? Obviously, he was living like a bum. Since he was caught by us at his office, he didn't return there. Neither to his apartment above the office. But shouldn't he have a lot of money, money that he had stolen, to get a fake passport and a plane ticket and just disappear? Why was he still here? Didn't he have access to his money? Then it dawned on me. Why of course. The cops probably froze the Feldmans' accounts. Hmm. No. It wasn't the cops. They'd barely filed the fraud charges from the residents. And I doubted they'd had previous similar charges on them. So it could have been some other law enforcement authority who restricted Lloyd's access to his accounts. That was the only explanation. Lloyd Feldman had literally no money.

But I decided to ponder that later. I needed to catch him now and end this.

Lloyd ran down the hill like a pro and I ran behind him like a bigger pro. I was hoping he wouldn't get to the tree part of the woods, because then I would probably lose him. He still had a good head start, though, so I needed to turn on the turbo. Thankfully, I was wearing my boots and not those damn flip-flops.

DEANY RAY

I figured Lloyd snuck into the paintball area through the woods. It was perfect, actually. It gave him enough cover, and probably Kevin dude didn't check the paintball perimeter every day.

As Lloyd was running for his life and I breathed hard running after him, paintball shots started coming from everywhere.

Were they even kidding? Really?

Now was *not* the time! We had a situation here. Then I thought about it. Actually, they could shoot all they wanted, but preferably at him! It didn't make sense for me to stop, aim, and shoot at Lloyd with that toy gun. I needed to close the distance between us and catch him.

Did these people, whoever were shooting at us now, realize this man didn't belong in the game? Did they not see he was wearing a suit, for crying out loud? Did they not see it was Lloyd Feldman, the guy who stole their money?

Paintballs were hitting me hard all over. And Lloyd as well. He howled every time he got hit. We were absolutely exposed running down that hill. Again, didn't these people see we had an urgent matter at hand? Didn't they see me running after the person that had scammed them out of their money?

Why the hell were they shooting at me, then? I still had my mask above my head, so my face was visible.

In a more normal circumstance, my pride would have been hurt losing at this game, but I had something bigger at stake and had to focus on Lloyd, not my pride.

Now I understood why we were supposed to wear long pants and long sleeves. Those paintball suckers burned like hell! I was glad there was a layer of fabric between the paintball and my skin.

"Why the hell are you shooting at me?" I shouted at no one in particular. "Can't you see what's going on here?"

The paintballs didn't slow Lloyd down one bit. He yowled every time he got hit but kept on running. I guess desperation does that to you. Now, he had on a multi-colored suit. And unfortunately, he disappeared into the woods before I could reach him.

Crap.

I followed him, swerving around the trees, then stopped and tried to listen for footsteps. Sunlight barely streamed throughout the lush greenery. I wiped away sweat from my face and held the paintball gun in a ready position. I wasn't sure why; it was not like you could really harm someone with it, so I guessed it was just a reflex.

I was focused on detecting movement, when I heard a voice echoing. "You're out of the game, doofus," the voice shouted. "Get off the field."

I straightened up. Did someone just call me a doofus? Was this for real? I was after their scammer! Who was the doofus here?

I ignored the voice and kept on searching. But I realized soon it was a lost cause and Lloyd was gone. If he lived in that fortress up the hill for the last two days then he already knew his way around here way better than me, and he knew the best routes to escape. Searching for him now would tally zero results.

I looked down at myself. I was pelted with paintballs. My jeans were a wreck, and my black sweatshirt bore the colors of the rainbow. And now it started to sink in that I'd lost in this game. I lost to eighty-year-olds at a shooting game. My new life just kept on getting better and better. Not.

I turned around and bumped into someone. It took a few seconds for me to recognize Edie, since she had her goggles on.

She was breathing hard as she took her mask off. "What the hell happened to you?" she asked and looked me up and down. "Wow, they got you really good."

"Wait until they find out who they let slip away," I said.

Edie frowned. "What do you mean who they—" Just then, paintballs whizzed past us.

Edie dropped to the ground and didn't even bother with me.

"Gee, good to know you don't care about me anymore," I said.

Edie looked up from the ground. "Well, you already got hit. You're out."

"So I don't matter anymore?" I asked half-jokingly.

"I'm sorry to burst your bubble, but not in this game, no," Edie said. "We're here to win, not to comfort the injured ones."

I rolled my eyes and lifted the gun over my shoulder, then started to march out of the woods. Then I turned back around. "Say, how many people are still in the game?" I asked Edie.

"Me, Dorothy, and Theodore on our team, and Lucretia, Otto, and Maude on the other team," Edie said, while scanning the perimeter around her.

"Huh," I said.

"What?" Edie asked.

"This game started over an hour ago and I thought we would be done in five minutes," I said.

"Yeah, you really don't have any faith in us, do you?" Edie said.

"I'm having more now," I said.

I left Edie doing her thing and hopefully winning this game, and decided to let them have their fun. I pondered calling the cops and telling them about Lloyd. It was just that I couldn't get rid of that nagging feeling every time I had contact with law enforcement. I knew this wasn't only about me anymore, it was about Edie and the other residents, but still, I wasn't comfortable even being near cops. Besides, they worked by the book, meaning they were often a bunch of slowpokes. And I figured Edie and the others, and also myself, had a more vested interest in catching Lloyd. I wished nothing more than to hurt him. For me, it wasn't so much about him potentially killing Tammy Feldman. I didn't really care that much about that. I cared about the fraud part against the residents.

I exited the forest area and looked up at the fortress up on the hill. I made sure no one was near me and started walking back up. I knew what I had to do. No, strike that. Not what I *had* to do, what I *wanted* to do and what I *would* do: get Lloyd's phone immediately. I got really lucky with that.

Moreover, if Lloyd was living in the fortress for the last two days, then maybe there were some clues there that could be helpful. And yes, I wouldn't mind finding those clues before the cops did. Just like I didn't mind snatching that phone before they got to it. Regular people would probably feel a sense of guilt, but I was not regular people. The cops could have the phone after I was done with it. If I felt like it. I could send it in anonymously or plant it somewhere for them to find it.

We already had information the cops didn't have. Like Lloyd being in his office and those two thugs that Victoria had seen, so hopefully, with Lloyd's phone, maybe we could put the whole puzzle together. One thing I didn't need to worry about were my fingerprints in the fortress. I was playing paintball so had every right to be there.

If someone dared call me "doofus" again for not exiting the playing field, I would take them down. But this was way more important. At least the fortress wasn't a highly frequented spot in this game, so I could search it in peace.

On my way up there, I wondered if Lloyd bought a burner phone. After Tammy was shot, the cops couldn't get ahold of him, as Edie had said. They said Lloyd's phone was turned off. He would have to be really dumb to turn on his phone again. So my guess was he bought a new one with a prepaid card.

Two minutes later I was in the fortress again. I wiped some more sweat off my forehead. I was going to need three showers after this. I picked up the phone and pressed the button on the side to unlock it. On the screen appeared a small window requesting a PIN number. Damn it. I was afraid of this.

Okay, what now? In my former life I knew people who would have been able to help me out with this issue. I was not a pro at this kind of skill. It never bothered me, because I always knew people who were pros. But now, I had a problem. I needed to get past the PIN and see what was inside this cell phone. I needed to see Lloyd's calls and messages and files. I needed a hacker.

Okay, baby steps. First, I was going to slip the cell phone into the back pocket of my jeans. And then I'd figure out some way to get past the PIN security number. I was sure there were people here in Florida who would be right for the job. It was only a matter of how to find those people, especially being in the witness protection program and having to obey legal rules. Yuck.

FOOL ME ONCE

I scanned the inside of the cabin, looking for any other clues. The blanket, the chip bags, the cups of coffee, that was all pretty normal. I walked around the cabin and looked into every corner and on every surface. I even looked up on the walls and on the ceiling just in case I found something. With a thick twig that was lying around, I lifted the blanket and looked underneath. There was nothing there. There was also nothing underneath that paint container. Again using the twig, I moved around the bags of chips and the coffee cups. Nothing.

I threw the twig away and exited the cabin.

This time, I put my mask back on just in case there was more shooting. Although, with only a few people remaining in the game, chances were slim. With the paintball gun over my shoulder, I walked down the hill. I was about to pass around the edge of the wood and go back to the event field when a voice shouted out loud, "We eliminated you! Get out of the game! Just admit that you lost."

I stopped in my tracks and turned around, trying to detect where the voice came from. "Don't get your panties in a bunch, I'm walking out right now," I shot back.

"You're a sore loser, that's what you are," the voice yelled.

Wait a minute, I knew that voice. It was Sourpuss.

"Like I said, Lucretia, I'm walking out now, so just chill," I said.

A paintball hit me in the back. I stopped in my tracks. "Okay, that's very mature," I said. "What part of I'm getting out now didn't you understand?"

Sourpuss appeared from behind a tree with her paintball gun aimed at me. And her bun sticking up high. She slid her mask over her head and grinned wickedly at me.

"You do know that's not a real gun, don't you?" I asked. "Because if we were in a real gunfight, you would be the sore loser."

"That's a nice little threat," Sourpuss said. "But as it is, you even lost in a make-believe gunfight. So turn around and walk off the playing field right now."

"You're going to leave her alone!" another voice yelled.

From out of nowhere, Gran appeared, hanging from a branch, and for a second, I thought maybe I'd inhaled too many paint vapors and was hallucinating. Huh. Who knew I would have to call the paramedics for *Gran*. Surely she would break something any second now.

Sourpuss ducked as Gran let go of the branch and jumped to the ground. She straightened herself and pointed the paintball gun at Sourpuss like a pro. Sourpuss was too slow to lift her gun and Gran pulled the trigger. The only problem was, her paint container was empty. Nothing came out. Gran stiffened and Sourpuss had the wicked grin on her face again.

"Well, well, well," Sourpuss said. "How the tables have turned. Get ready to lose, grandmama."

Sourpuss lifted her gun and, just as she was about to shoot, another voice shouted, "Not so fast, Lucretia."

Mental forehead smack.

What was up with these people? Where the hell did they hide and why the hell were they so good at it?

I saw Theodore, with his mask up over his head, coming forward from behind a tree about forty yards behind Sourpuss. Hmm. Did paintball guns even shoot that far? The shooter had to be good as well. No way would Theodore make the shot.

He got in position. He aimed. And like a pro, he shot only one paintball and hit Lucretia's . . . butt.

I couldn't decide if I should cringe, laugh, or pat Theodore on the back. I guessed I was about to do all of them. I was very surprised at the clean shot Theodore took even from that distance. And his body language as he took the shot was nothing close to an amateur.

Sourpuss' face went dark red and steam came out of her ears.

Gran smiled as Theodore came forward. Everybody was speechless for a couple of seconds. That is until Edie came running up from behind me and stopped short. She frantically looked around us.

"What happened?" She asked. "What's going on here? What did I miss?"

Theodore just got Lucretia," I said to Edie, smiling. "What about those other two on her team?"

"I just eliminated Otto and Maude," Edie said and put on a wide smile.

"So that means we won?" I asked.

Edie flipped Sourpuss off. "We won."

Chapter Ten

"I KNOW IT'S HARD to admit that I saved you," Theodore said smiling.

We were in his car driving back to the retirement complex.

"But you know that's what happened." He snuck a glance at Gran who was sitting next to him in the passenger seat. He had a twinkle in his eye.

Oh my, he was poking a hornets' nest.

Gran looked at him with her death stare and I knew she was sorry I made her leave her gun at home.

"You saved me?" Gran asked. "You didn't save me. There wouldn't have been any point in saving me. The point of the game was to eliminate the other team. So great job for doing what you were supposed to do. And may I remind you, I was out of paint, meaning I was the one who did the most shooting and I wiped out eight people in total."

I was curious how this conversation was going to turn out. And if Theodore would still be alive when we got back to the house.

"Still, it would have really stunk if Lucretia had gotten you," Theodore said. "And I made sure she didn't get you."

"If she had gotten me," Gran said, "then you would have shot her just as well, thus completing the goal of this game. I know you want to go all macho here because you're a guy and that's what guys do, and if you want to live your life thinking how great you are because you saved me, then go right ahead."

I smiled and looked outside the window. Gran was taking this way better than I would have expected. But again, the reason for that is probably just that she didn't have her gun with her, so she had to use other ways to defend herself.

"I'm not macho," Theodore said, still with that twinkle in his eye. "I just like to tease you."

"Well, gee, do I feel like the lucky one," Gran said.

Theodore stopped for a light and turned to Gran. "You *should* feel lucky."

Gran stared back at him but didn't say anything.

Ten seconds went by, and they were still staring at each other. I rolled my eyes. They were good at this staring contest, but I really wanted to get back to the house and take that shower.

The cars behind us started to honk, and that's when Theodore broke contact and started driving again.

"Say, Theodore," I decided to change the subject, "I'm curious about something. How did you manage that shot at Lucretia? You were pretty far away. Do you have some kind of hidden talent that we don't know about?"

"I probably could have made that shot with my eyes closed," Theodore said.

Gran instantly whipped her head toward him with a raised eyebrow. I knew that got her interest. I assumed Gran hadn't seen Theodore in his shooting position. She was too busy being miffed about not having any paint left.

"Well?" Gran asked Theodore when he didn't say anything.

He smiled again. "So you'd like to know?"

"See?" Gran said. "I told you, you were macho. You're turning this around so that I will beg you. But I'm not going to do that."

Theodore laughed. "Oh, Dorothy, I'm just having fun. The reason why my shot was so clean is because I was a Navy Seal."

A what?

Crap.

Gran and I were both speechless. This was so not what we needed in our new lives right now. Or ever. I thought Ryker could be a problem, him being a PI and all, but now a former Navy Seal? Could the universe hate us that much?

I needed to wrap my mind around this for a minute. It totally blindsided me. A Navy Seal? Theodore? Okay, that would explain some things: his build, the way you could tell he was an athlete, the way he took that shot back there in the woods. The fact he woke up that early in the morning. It was all the discipline he'd learned. I just didn't expect this. Now that I thought about it, Theodore hadn't mentioned what it was that he did before retiring. And we never asked.

I knew Gran must have connected the same dots: us having a criminal record in our former lives and now being in WITSEC . . . we didn't need a trained professional who could sniff us out and blow our cover. But from the back seat I spotted the way Gran was looking at Theodore. It was totally different than before. It was like Theodore earned some brownie points in Gran's book. Being a good shooter, chasing targets, the physical fitness and mental toughness—that was hot! If only he'd been operating according to *our* interpretation of the law.

I also knew Gran would have liked nothing more than to grill Theodore about it, but she most likely didn't want to seem too eager.

So it was me who finally said, "You were a Navy Seal? Wow, I did not expect this. What was your rank?"

"I was captain," Theodore said.

Whoa. Now we were getting into deep water.

"Are you serious?" I asked. "Theodore, that's . . . amazing." And I really meant it, despite me feeling uneasy about Gran's and my real identities.

"Piper, let me tell you; it was one hell of a job," Theodore said.

"I believe you," I said. "I can't even imagine what it must have been like and what training and stress you have gone through. So you were in Vietnam?"

"I was," Theodore said in a more gloomy voice and didn't expand on it.

"How long did you serve?" I asked.

"I served for thirty years," Theodore said. "Then I retired."

For a couple of seconds, nobody said anything. Gran was stoically keeping her mouth shut.

"You lived near Chicago, right?" I asked Theodore. I couldn't help it; it was all so fascinating.

Theodore nodded. "Yes, I lived there with my wife, and after all the time I was away from her, I just wanted to enjoy time with her. You know, it's not easy keeping relationships intact when you're away from home fifty percent of the time, so most marriages end up in divorce. Thankfully, mine only kept on getting stronger."

I saw Gran sneak a glance at Theodore. More brownie points for him.

Theodore continued. "We didn't have any children, although we really wanted to. But that just wasn't in the cards for us. I loved my wife very much and I cherished the time I spent with her. After I retired, we started a business; we had a shop selling fishing equipment right by Lake Michigan. You know, living the slow life. Not that being a business owner means you're stress-free—by all means, that's not the case—but it was certainly a slower pace than what I was used to. I enjoyed that time very much after my time serving this country." He paused. "Then my wife died of breast cancer three years ago and I decided to leave everything behind and move here to Florida. So there you go, that's my resume in a nutshell."

Gran and I were silent again. We were both mulling over what Theodore just told us. I'd only met him three weeks ago, but I was now even more certain that any woman should be calling herself lucky to be with Theodore. It was not what he was telling us about himself, it was more his actions. Most people got blinded by words. Got blinded by lies. Got bedazzled by flattery. Women, especially, got blinded by flattery from men. But it was the actions of that person that mattered. With Theodore, I was liking what I'd seen so far, despite just finding out he could put Gran's and my new identity in danger.

"I'm sorry about your wife," Gran said, and by the tone of her voice, she really meant it.

Theodore smiled faintly. "Thank you, Dorothy," he said. "She was something else. You would have liked her."

Gran didn't say anything.

"What about you?" Theodore asked Gran. "Was there a Mr. Dorothy?"

Gran's attitude did a one-eighty. "That's really none of your business now, is it?"

Theodore laughed and I just shook my head.

"I shared with you facts of *my* life," Theodore said.

"That was voluntarily," Gran said. "I didn't ask you to."

"You're right," Theodore said and looked in the rearview mirror. "*She* did."

I put my hands up. "Whoa, whoa, whoa, don't get me involved in your little repartee, okay?"

"As you wish," Theodore said with a wink. "Anyway, it's interesting how well you knew about the shooting distance at the paintball field," Theodore said while giving me another glance in the rearview.

Damn it. I've done it again. I didn't keep my mouth shut.

"Well, you know, I'm a big fan of forensic TV shows," I said. "I know it sounds silly, but I think you learn a couple of things if you regularly watch those shows."

I could feel Gran tensing up in the passenger seat. This was my go-to lie every time I slipped up and made it look suspicious about how on earth I knew stuff like this. And I always hoped the other person would buy it. "I've also been to the shooting range a couple of times," I added.

Theodore gave me a long glance in the mirror, then he turned his attention back to the street. "I guess that makes sense," was all he said.

I couldn't get a read on him. I had no idea if he believed me or not. Man, I was getting rusty. On the other hand, if he was a Seal, that was like ten levels superior to mine.

Theodore dropped us off back at Gran's house. It was already noon, and it was hot outside. I was thankful for the few clouds up in the sky. This way, I didn't feel the burning sun, at least.

"Thank you for everything, Theodore," I said as I got out of the car. "Especially for being on our team and for treating."

"It was my pleasure," Theodore said smiling. Then he looked at Gran. She just nodded, turned on her heel and got into the house.

"This is what you would have to deal with, Theodore," I said, laughing. "Just saying."

"I'm looking forward to it," Theodore said, laughing with me.

I said goodbye and headed for the house.

"What did he treat?" Gran asked as soon as I stepped into the house.

"Why didn't you ask him that?" I asked.

Gran shrugged.

"I know why; it's because you didn't want to seem interested in him," I said.

"Yes, fine," Gran said. "I didn't want to ask him because I didn't want him to rub it in my face, okay?"

"Are you ever going to let your guard down?" I asked.

Gran put her hands on her hips and narrowed her eyes at me. "You're the one to ask."

I felt a blush creeping up my cheeks. "What do you mean?"

"You know very damn well what I mean."

Okay. Fine. Gran was right.

"Fine, I give up," I said. "He paid for us to play today at the paintball field. It wasn't for free, you know."

"Oh," Gran said. "Guess that was nice of him. But I didn't ask for it; it was totally his choice. If you remember correctly, I didn't even want to go there."

"But you did have fun, didn't you?" I asked. "It's not like you stood at the side of the field and watched. You were totally into the game."

Gran scoffed. "It may have looked like I was into the game, but actually I just used it as an outlet to get some shooting done around here. Even if it was just with stupid paint."

"That's exactly my point," I said. "You liked it."

Gran's eyes bore into me.

I continued. "And I know you won't admit it, but you didn't dislike Theodore . . . rescuing you." I emphasized the last two words. I could barely hold in my laughter. This was way too much fun. I knew that Gran would probably combust if told that a man rescued her, especially if guns were involved.

"Are you *trying* to provoke me?" Gran asked.

"No, it's just so easy," I said.

"Well, stop it," Gran said. "Besides, you know we need to keep our distance from him from now on, don't you?"

I knew what she meant. And I knew she was right, but I didn't like it. I mean, couldn't Theodore just have been like a plain old factory worker or something?

"You know," I said, "it doesn't have to be that way. Theodore is retired now, and he is—"

"I'm going to stop you right there," Gran said and put her hands up. "We are not doing this. We are not going there. You know very well, even retired, he is a Seal at heart. He is trained to spot, let's just say, abnormalities. Exhibit number one, you almost giving yourself away today with that whole shooting distance thing. You think I didn't see that? Even with that old broad in front of me, even with me focusing on her, I saw him way back there behind that tree and I knew something was up. His whole posture, his whole vibe screamed professional. But did I ask him that? No, I didn't."

"Oh," I said. "I wasn't aware that you—"

"Exactly," Gran said. "I know you weren't aware. Because I kept my mouth shut."

Damn it. Sometimes I wondered if I would ever advance to Gran's level.

"Okay, but still," I said. "With the risk of you shooting me now, I still have to point out that he is a *retired* Navy Seal and that he is living at the same retirement complex you are, and that he seems to be a very cool person, he seems to be courteous and gallant, and he has the hots for you. I don't think you avoiding him is going to be successful, especially since he keeps orbiting around you."

"Well, then I guess I'll just have to do my best to avoid him."

"I really don't think that's possible," I said.

"Okay, then here's only two words for you," Gran said. "Edie's grandson."

Oh. I stood there dumbfounded.

"See?" Gran said. She had her I-won-face on.

"Fine, I don't want to talk about it anymore," I said. "I'm going to hit the shower."

I headed for the bathroom and, as I started to shed my sweaty clothes, I sensed the cell phone in my back pocket. Crap. Lloyd's cell phone. What with

Theodore, and him revealing his life to us, that cell phone slipped my mind.

Screw it, I was still going to hit the shower first.

As the cold water washed over me, I let the events of the day run through my mind. Gran was Gran and there was nothing I could do about her attitude toward life, toward people, toward the world. We just found out Theodore was a former Seal, and who knew the things he'd done and the things he'd seen during his time of service. Gran's and my past were probably nothing compared to that. I wondered how Theodore adjusted to civilian life after he retired. I bet his wife provided essential guidance for his life after the Navy. He seemed to act normal . . . well, whatever normal meant around here, or in general for that matter. All these past few weeks, we'd had no idea about Theodore's past. I kind of wished it had stayed that way. Now it got even more complicated. And who was to blame for finding out? Me of course. Stupid me had to ask about his shooting. On the other hand, we would have found out about his former job sooner or later. I guessed only time would show how big of a role Theodore would play in our lives.

Then my mind drifted to Lloyd and the cell phone. That was a more urgent matter. So urgent, I'd decided to shower first. I already gave up on the idea of calling the cops, because frankly, I really didn't care about them. I didn't care about them my whole life; moreover, I actually had negative feelings toward them. I was raised to avoid them. I was raised not to deal with them. That wouldn't change now with this situation. Besides, I was absolutely sure I could do a better job in finding out who murdered that woman and in finding out where Lloyd was hiding.

I wasn't hindered by red tape, I didn't work with bosses telling me what to do, and I didn't work with stupid technicalities, like needing a warrant to search a place.

All this was to say that I officially got involved in investigating a murder. Again. And a fraud case. That sneaky Edie. She did it again. I was hooked.

I let water wash over my face. Who was I kidding? It was my responsibility. It was not like she held a gun to my head. I was responsible for my own choices in life.

So far, nobody knew about my encounter with Lloyd up on that hill and about me finding his cell phone. I wasn't sure the residents were aware that they were shooting paintballs at Lloyd, of all people! Either way, I needed to figure out what to do next.

I took a longer time with the shower; it felt liberating and cathartic. That is until Gran banged on the door telling me that she would like to shower too, please.

I got out of the bathroom with a towel wrapped around me and with my hair wrapped in another towel, and felt like a new person. "The stage is yours," I said to Gran.

About one second after Gran closed the bathroom door, someone knocked on the front door and just came in. Like, literally, the door opened and somebody just came inside.

I sprang to the kitchen counter, grabbed a knife, and taking a combat stance, I almost threw the knife in Edie's direction, just as she was chirping, "It's meee!"

Her eyes landed on me, and she instantly ducked. "Oh, Jesus Almighty!"

I relaxed my shoulders. "Are you kidding me, Edie? What the hell are you doing?"

"What am I doing?" Edie screeched, still in a squatting position. "What are you doing?"

"I'm defending myself from an intruder," I said. "You don't just come in!"

"Then don't leave your door open!" Edie said.

That was a thing I chose to worry about later. Was it Gran or me who'd left the door unlocked? Either way, it was a sign we were getting sloppy. Maybe Gran and me had started to feel way too comfortable around the retirement complex. I had to remind myself that the Falcons were after us, WITSEC or no WITSEC. We had to be careful.

"Why did you try and see if the door was open?" I asked, placing the knife back on the counter.

"I don't know," Edie said. "It was just a reflex, I guess."

She took a seat on the couch this time instead of her chair at the kitchen table. She probably wanted to put as much distance between the knife and her as possible.

I know why she tried the door without even thinking. She was so often here at Gran's; it had become like a second home to her. In only three weeks' time. That was scary.

Edie exhaled a long breath then said, "Were you really going to throw that knife at me?" Then she looked me up and down. "In that outfit?"

"In my defense, again, I thought you were an intruder," I said.

"It's interesting what reflexes you have when you think an intruder comes in," Edie said. "Usually, people try to run away or something, not go full battle mode."

"Well, I'm different than most people," I said.

"That you are," Edie said.

I grabbed a couple of clothing items and went to the bedroom and changed. I had already given up on blow-drying my hair since that would just make me all sweaty again, even with AC. So I just let my hair get the natural Florida frizz this way.

Gran was still in the shower when I joined Edie back in the living room.

"So did you enjoy the paintball game?" I asked Edie.

"I loved it!" she said then pouted a bit. "Although I do wish I hadn't missed the fun."

I smiled. "You mean eliminating Sourpuss?"

"Who?" Edie asked. "Oh, you mean Lucretia. Yes, exactly. I wanted to take her down."

"I know you did," I said.

"But we did win nevertheless," Edie said. "And the baskets should get here tomorrow."

"The baskets?" I asked. "What baskets?"

Edie looked at me like I was the one who didn't know what she was talking about.

"The baskets, Piper," Edie said. "The spa gift baskets. The ones we won?"

"We won gift baskets?" I asked. "You never told me that."

"I didn't?" Edie asked. "Huh. I must have forgotten. You didn't think we just played like that without a prize to win, did you?"

"The nerve! How could I have thought we were playing just to play?"

Edie narrowed her eyes at me. "Don't think I don't get your sarcasm. You still have a low opinion of us older folks. You think we can't be competitive at our age?"

I put my hands up in surrender. "You're right, I'm sorry. So, spa baskets?"

Edie nodded. "The losing teams order the baskets for the winning teams. Expect yours and Dorothy's to be delivered tomorrow. We demanded express delivery. We love their foot powder. And Lucretia loves it too." Edie put on a wicked grin. "But she ain't getting a gift basket. She's buying one for us."

Wow, it amazed me every time, all the different ways these seniors here were sticking it to each other. Apparently, getting foot powder as a prize for winning a paintball game was one of those ways.

Gran came out of the bathroom in the same outfit I had before: wraparound towels. "I don't have to wonder why you're here again, do I?" Gran said to Edie.

"Not unless you want to throw knives at me too," Edie said.

Gran raised an eyebrow and looked from Edie to me.

I shook my head and Gran didn't ask any further questions. She turned around and stomped into the bedroom, mumbling something about Edie practically living here, and shutting the door closed behind her.

"She's something else, isn't she?" Edie asked.

"That, she is," I replied.

Edie looked in the direction of the bedroom and smiled. "I like that."

"Despite the fact she's insulting you?" I asked.

Edie brushed it off. "Like I'm gonna break down and cry because of that. I'm a tough cookie, you know?"

I laughed. "I do know." I went to the fridge and got out a beer. "You want one too?"

"Yes, please," Edie said. "I came over to let you know Ryker called and told me some news about the Feldmans. Their accounts have been frozen. There's no money going in and no money going out."

I smiled. *Just as I thought.*

"Why are you smiling?" Edie asked. "You don't seem surprised. Why don't you seem surprised?"

I handed Edie her beer and opened mine and took a long swig. "Because I had an encounter with Lloyd today."

"You had a what?" Edie asked, frowning.

I told Edie about Lloyd's hiding place at the paintball field and about me taking his phone and about the phone being locked. Like Edie would have put it, I needed to confer with someone. And Edie was the perfect person, since she was personally involved and had something at stake. Gran would find out soon enough, but she would most probably go straight into the darknet to find a good hacker. I couldn't deal with that right now. Maybe later when I would realize that was the only way. I just hoped Edie wouldn't run to the cops with this information. My gut told me she wouldn't. She was a good person, but she had a bit of a bad bone as well.

Edie chugged half her beer in excitement. "This is great news!"

"I'm glad you see it that way," I said. "So you're not going to the cops with this info?"

"Heck no," Edie said. "I mean, not right now. Maybe later. I like having the upper hand."

I laughed. "I know you do."

"And somehow, I feel safer with you," Edie said.

Again she managed to get me all soft inside. "Thanks, Edie," I said and smiled at her.

"Now we know Lloyd is really desperate if he had to sleep in that cabin at the paintball place," Edie continued. "And now that you found his hiding place and his cell phone . . . he's screwed."

"I hope you're right," I said. "But what if he somehow finds a way to get money and to disappear?"

"Then we have to find him before he does that," Edie said. "That phone is the key. We need to know what's on it."

"I agree, but that's easier said than done," I said. "Do you happen to know a phone hacker?"

Edie thought about it for a second, then she grinned wide. "Actually, I do."

Chapter Eleven

"This is such a dumb plan," I said.

"Nonsense," Edie said. "This will work."

It was about 5:00 p.m. and I was sitting at Edie's table in her dining corner and eating peach pie. Edie poured some more coffee.

"Whoa, whoa, that's enough," I said. "The paintball game this morning already got me hopped up."

Edie took her seat next to me and dug into her own piece of pie, while she was staring at Lloyd's phone on the table.

"When did she say she'll be here?" I asked.

"In the afternoon," Edie said.

"No exact time?"

Edie shook her head. "No. I didn't want to seem too official, so I didn't push for an exact time."

I had to admit, she did good with that.

"And why am I here exactly?" I asked. "Is that also part of the master plan?"

"You're here in case we need a diversion," Edie said, like that was the most normal thing.

Oh, goody.

"So I'm supposed to wing it if we need a diversion?" I asked.

"Yeah, I think you're good like that," Edie said.

About twenty minutes later we heard a roaring car outside. And about one minute later the doorbell rang. That got me thinking for the first time since I'd arrived at the retirement complex in Bitter End— why was everyone here knocking on the door instead of using the doorbell? Was this a generational thing too?

Edie opened the door and Samantha Braveheart stepped inside. She was working at Ryker's PI firm, and according to Edie, she just made associate.

I'd only seen her once from afar shortly after moving here. Her dress code was grunge-anime movie. She was two inches shorter than me, so about five foot five. She had short dark-pink hair, and wore black-rimmed glasses. She wore a white T-shirt and plaid cargo pants, combined with black Chucks and a camouflage backpack. Geeky nerd was the best way to describe her. So if she really could hack a phone, then she definitely dressed the part.

Edie seemed to like her a lot, but I was curious about my own opinion of her. I knew I had to keep my guard up and even higher than usual, since she was about my age and worked in the investigative field, making her sharper than the senior community residents.

How could this be our luck, Gran's and mine? Of all the locations in the country, we had to land in a place where we had to deal with a private investigator, a former Navy Seal, and now a technology buff. We were so close to so many people who could sniff out our real identities. This had just become so ridiculous.

Edie was sure Samantha could help us out with Lloyd's phone. I pointed out the obvious: why would she help us if she was working alongside Ryker? She would probably not be doing anything felonious either. Edie replied we didn't have to tell her it was Lloyd's phone, and she had a plan for that. I told Edie that if we got caught, I would deny everything and blame it on her. She shook my hand on that.

"Sam! So glad you're here," Edie said as Samantha walked inside.

She took one step and I swear she flinched for just a second. Why wouldn't she? The wallpaper with the busy floral pattern could give any person an instant headache. Never mind the stuffy antique décor of Edie's house. It was those dolls on the couch that gave you shivers down the spine. I tried hard to ignore the dolls every time I came over to Edie's.

"So good to see you, Edie," Samantha said and gave her a hug. "It's been a while."

"I know," Edie said. "That's why I'm so glad you managed today."

"Well, when you said you needed my help, I carved out some time for you," Samantha said and smiled at Edie. She looked up and her gaze landed on me.

"Sam, I want you to meet Piper," Edie said and led her to the table. "She lives next door with her grandmother. Well, actually, she only lives there temporarily."

I stood and reached out my hand. "Nice to meet you."

"Oh, same here," Samantha said and shook my hand with a strong grip.

We maintained eye contact a bit longer and I kind of got a vibe from her that she already didn't like me. Which wouldn't surprise me. Ryker probably had told her stuff about me. Well, so be it. He can tell people whatever he wants. Not that I was so self-centered thinking Ryker told people about me. But surely he would have mentioned his grandmother's new neighbors to his colleagues, especially since we'd butted heads in our own investigations.

"Sit, sit," Edie said and brought a plate with a fork for Sam. "Let me pour you some coffee as well."

"Thank you, Edie," Sam said and glanced in my direction again.

Edie had told me Sam was thirty years old, but there was something about her demeanor that made her come off more mature.

"So, Piper was it?" Sam asked me, placing her backpack on the floor next to her. It was interesting to see she was all smiles when she talked to Edie, but the smile disappeared as soon as she talked to me.

"Piper Harris," I said. In the last few weeks, I'd gotten the hang of pronouncing my whole name without stuttering. I had troubles at the beginning remembering what my last name was, since Gran and I had to change it. Our first names we got to keep. "And you are Samantha . . . Braveheart?"

Sam nodded. "That's right. And I've heard all the jokes there are about my last name, just so you know."

"Gotcha," I said. "Then I will refrain from the three references I just thought of now."

Sam cracked a subtle smile my way. I had no idea if she meant it as a sign of respect, enjoyment, or just annoyance.

Edie brought over a cup and poured some coffee for Sam. "So how is your mom? Is she still . . ."

"In jail?" Sam said. "Yep."

Um. Okay.

"Still?" Edie asked. "I thought she was already out."

Sam shrugged. "She landed back in. I'm tired of always bailing her out, so I'm letting her stay there the night."

I swear I think my mouth was hanging. This was way better than the supposed crime shows I was watching.

I couldn't hold it in anymore; I had to ask. "Excuse me, Samantha—"

"You can call me Sam," she said.

"Sam, why is your mother in jail? Again?"

Sam leaned back in the chair and said, "She gets involved with a lot of environment stuff, like in an extreme way, and she pushes boundaries that get her in trouble."

Sam said this like it was no big deal.

"I've dealt with this all my life, so it's not a big deal to me anymore," she said, as if she could read my mind.

"She's one of those environmental lawyers, you know?" Edie said to me, as a way of explanation. "The ones that prostrate themselves before buildings that are supposed to get torn down." Edie turned back to Sam. "You know I always liked Donna. And she is doing good, in her own way. Send her all my best."

"Will do," Sam said. "She's coming home tomorrow. Which reminds me, I need to buy some new soap. That ink they use at the station is a million years old and barely comes off."

I frowned. "You live with your mother?" I asked.

"Yeah," Sam deadpanned. "So?"

I put my hands up. "Nothing. I was just curious."

Wow, she really didn't like me. Then again, I asked some pointed questions, so it was only fair.

"So Ryker tells me you moved here with your grandmother from . . . where was it from?" Sam inquired, which I expected.

"From Boise," I said. "Idaho."

"Uh-hum," Sam said and eyed me suspiciously. "May I ask why you moved here?"

"Gran got a place here at the complex and I just kind of came with her," I replied. This was my go-to answer anytime someone asked about the reason. What I didn't tell them was why Gran decided to move to Florida in the first place, if she obviously wasn't a fan of the climate here.

Sam didn't take her eyes off me as she took a bite of the pie. But apparently, she didn't have any more questions now, so she turned her attention back to Edie.

"This peach pie is divine, Edie," Sam said.

Edie blushed a bit and thanked her for the compliment.

"So you said you needed my help?" Sam asked, and I was glad we were finally getting down to business.

"Oh yes," Edie said. "I'm kind of embarrassed to ask this, but I forgot the PIN for my new cell phone, and I know you're so good with technology and stuff and I wondered if you could just access my phone without that PIN number." Edie slid the phone toward Sam.

Sam frowned and took the phone in her hand and analyzed it for a bit. "Don't you have the PUK code in the documents from your provider?" Sam asked. "If you tried entering the PIN number three times and it didn't work, then you need the other code, your Personal Unlocking Key, hence, PUK. And then you can access your phone."

"Oh dear, I have no idea where those documents are," Edie said. "I don't even know what the other code means. You know, when you get to my age, you kind of lose this skill for technology. That's why I hoped you could help me?"

I had to hold a smile in. Edie was very good at playing the helpless little old lady. It was hard for anyone to say no to her. I knew that firsthand.

Sam seemed to think about it but then said to Edie, "Sure, I can try and help you out. But why didn't you ask Ryker?"

Edie waved her hand in dismissal. "I'm asking Ryker so often for so many things, I was kind of embarrassed asking this of him too. So maybe we could keep this between us?"

I cringed just a bit because now this seemed way suspicious. I was curious if Sam bought it.

But then Edie gave the final punch. "You know how it is. Sometimes you're embarrassed to ask a family member for a favor. Again and again."

Holy moly! Edie was so good. She was referring to Sam's mother. She definitely hit that nerve in Sam.

Sam looked down at the phone and nodded. "Yes, I do understand that very well." After a pause she said, "It's okay, we can keep this between us. Good thing I always have my laptop with me. We need that to crack the phone."

Sam pulled out a small laptop out of her backpack and placed it on the table. She took another bite of pie and another sip of coffee and started up the small computer. She then took a cable out and connected the phone to the laptop. This seemed kind of fun. So far, at least.

Edie sat mesmerized next to Sam. "I know you're a genius with this stuff," Edie said. "But I never asked, where did you learn it?"

Sam shrugged. "I just kind of always had an interest in technology and computers. So I started early on and I kind of learned it by doing it myself. I wanted to go to college and to MIT, but I couldn't afford that. I always had to work and bring money home, because you know my mom with her shenanigans; instead of working for a big company as a lawyer, she works against them."

Edie nodded. "Yes, that's a shame."

"Exactly," Sam said. "So money was always tight in our house, and with dad leaving us when I was a kid, academics was not an option."

Edie patted her shoulder. "Yes, you had a hard situation growing up. That's why I'm so glad you've turned into such a pleasant young lady."

I think I saw Sam blushing just a bit. No wonder, Edie had that effect on people. Now I knew the reason Sam seemed to be more mature than her age. Not having a regular childhood and having to always work and worry about money instead of getting a decent education, especially if you wanted one, forced you to mature quickly. She had my respect for it.

"Thank you, Edie," Sam said. "If I had a grandmother just like you, my life would have been way richer."

I swear Edie almost melted.

"You can tell that to Ryker," Edie said. "Sometimes he treats me like I'm not capable of doing anything."

Sam laughed. "That's just because he loves you. Trust me, he knows you're capable of anything."

It was the first time Sam really lit up laughing. She had a nice smile and she actually looked really pretty. It was just hard to see it under all that grunge look.

"But instead of me talking to Ryker, maybe you could talk to my mom sometime and tell her to . . .

you know, grow up," Sam said to Edie while she was hard at work on her computer. "I think sometimes she doesn't get that I'm the daughter and she's the mother. And especially now that I would like to get my own place."

"I would be careful asking Edie a favor like that," I said, smiling at Sam. "You know she'll do it right away."

Sam glanced at me then she smiled back. "Yeah, you're right. Edie would talk to her, and who knows what she would say." Sam winked at Edie.

Edie feigned offense. "I wouldn't hold back, that's for sure."

We all laughed but I kind of had the feeling that Sam appreciated having someone like Edie in her life.

"I hear prices are down in real estate right now here in Bitter End," Edie said to Sam. "If you'd like to buy your own place."

"Yeah, I know about the prices," Sam said. "I also know about the money."

"Surely that shouldn't be a problem now that you're an associate with the PI firm," Edie said.

Oh, Edie, if it were that simple.

"I gather Sam's mother is swallowing up most of the money," I said. "That's why you're driving that car, which by the sound of it could break into pieces at any time now."

Sam looked somberly at me.

"I'm sorry, I didn't mean to pry," I said. "It's just that you all seem to talk so freely about everything and I just thought . . ."

"Oh yes, I apologize as well," Edie said. "Family and money dynamics are probably too sensitive of subjects to talk about with everybody."

"Thank you," Sam said, and she looked at me. "But you're sharp. I like that."

I gave her a weak smile.

"You know, Piper here is looking for a place too," Edie said. "She's looking to rent. And it's a money issue with her too."

I gave Edie a look and so did Sam.

"What?" Edie said. "Now you're even."

Sam turned her attention to the laptop.

"Oh, there's one more thing, Sam," Edie said. "I would rather you not look into the phone after you access it."

I saw Sam raising an eyebrow at Edie. Edie continued, "You see, I have a male, let's say, friend, and we get along really good, and we met a couple of times, and we realize we get along so good that I didn't mind to kind of send him something that was only meant to be seen by him . . . some nude pictures."

Coffee almost came out of Sam's nose, and I dropped the piece of pie from my fork.

Oh, okay, now I got it. Edie had really thought it through. She used the little-old-lady routine, and now the seniors-with-nude-pictures one that made you want to cut off your ears.

Sam cleared her throat. "Um, okay . . . nude pictures? Wow. I can understand that. I'm just going to access your phone and I won't look into your personal files and messages."

"Thank you so much, Sam," Edie said. "This is also one of the reasons I didn't want to ask Ryker."

I had to admit. Edie was a genius.

Sam focused on her laptop and Edie and I just watched as she furiously tapped the keyboard . . . then, five minutes later, the phone screen woke up.

"Okay, there you go," Sam said. "It's done."

Edie took the phone and swiped the screen—and got in just like that, without a PIN number. I was really impressed. Now I was anxious to see what was on that phone. I hoped Sam really got what Edie said and she didn't access the phone herself.

"Oh wow, Sam, thank you so much," Edie said. "Now I can finally talk to my honey again. And send him some more pictures."

Sam put her hands over her ears, and I rubbed my forehead. There were so many images in my head fighting for top billing.

Sam took the last bite of pie and gulped down her coffee. "Edie, I'm sorry I can't visit longer but I really need to go and see about my mom."

"Oh, that's fine," Edie said. "That's totally understandable."

"It was nice meeting you," Sam said to me.

I nodded. "Same here."

"And Edie, I'm sorry to hear about the Feldmans," Sam said, shoving her laptop in her backpack. "I hope the cops get this resolved fast. If not, then Ryker will."

"Thank you, my dear," Edie said. "Do you happen to know anything about the investigation?"

Sam shook her head. "Unfortunately, no. I'm out of this one. I'm working other projects right now. Ryker won't tell you anything, right?"

"No," Edie said. "And that totally annoys me."

Sam laughed. "I bet it does. But don't worry, he only has your best interests at heart."

Edie rolled her eyes. "Yeah, yeah, yeah."

FOOL ME ONCE

Sam packed up the rest of her stuff, gave a hug to Edie, then Edie walked her to the door where she thanked her again for her help. Then she left.

As soon as I heard Sam's roaring car drive away, I gave Edie a high five.

"Nice work," I said to her.

She looked cocky. "I know. Now let's see about that phone."

We both went back to the table and huddled around Lloyd's cell phone.

I swiped the screen and, just like that, we were in.

First, I checked the previous calls. The first one was outgoing and the last two were incoming, from a number Lloyd hadn't saved into his phone. The first went out on Monday afternoon, so the day Tammy was killed. The other two calls came in yesterday. There were no other calls made or received since Monday. There weren't even any other calls registered before Monday. It became pretty clear Lloyd bought this phone after the murder of Tammy. There was barely any data on it.

Which confirmed my suspicions: Lloyd had bought a burner phone. That was Criminal Minds Thinking 101. You always ditch your phone when you're the prime suspect in a murder. That's why the cops couldn't get ahold of him.

"Lloyd got this phone after everything went down the drain on Monday," I told Edie and explained about the precious few records.

"Oh, okay," Edie said. "I kind of expected to see my name there too with the other calls."

"You talked on the phone?" I asked.

"Of course we did," Edie said. "They called and we made the monthly appointments when I was to go to their office for making my deposit."

"Well, that would be on Lloyd's former phone, which could be in the Atlantic Ocean by now."

"So we need to focus on this phone right here," Edie said. "That unsaved number is suspicious, right?"

I nodded. "Let's see if he has messages too."

Lloyd was using one of the popular apps for text messaging and I clicked on the icon. There was only one chat there. With the same unsaved, unknown number. I clicked on the chat and all I saw was an audio file that Lloyd sent to that number on Monday afternoon. The audio file was only eighteen seconds long. I clicked on the play button while Edie was breathing down my neck.

"Edic, for the love of god, I need some space to breathe," I said.

"Well, excuse me for getting too excited," Edie said. "My blood pressure is so high right now, I'm going to have to take a second pill today."

So there we were huddled together with Edie's blood pressure through the roof and my own excitement rising high, when I pressed the play button. But what we heard made our hair stand up. Well, more Edie's hair than mine.

We heard voices in the background and some static in between. I got the impression the voices came from another room.

Edie and I huddled closer together to hear better.

I said we need the money today, a man with a deep voice said. The tone of his voice sounded like he wasn't the sharpest tool in the shed.

Please, I already told you, we don't have it today, I swear, a female voice said in total panic.

Edie mouthed to me, "That's Tammy."

Mr. Moose is not happy with you. If we don't get the money now, there'll be consequences, a second voice belonging to another man said, and I could hear the cocking of a gun.

No, please, I'm begging you, we really don't have it, the woman said, more panic rising in her voice.

Then we'll get the money from your husband, especially after sending this signal, the second man said.

Then we heard a gunshot, and then there was silence.

Good thing Edie was so close to me because she almost fainted.

What we just heard, was Tammy getting shot.

As I was about to ask Edie if she needed her blood-pressure pill now instead of later, a voice behind us asked, "What on earth are you doing?"

It was Ryker and he was standing in Edie's doorway.

Chapter Twelve

NOW EDIE ALMOST fainted for real.

I caught her just in time and I reacted fast. "Ryker, why the hell are you scaring us?" I asked. "We were just watching some movie clip. Of some crime movie. Someone just got shot. But I don't think we're liking this one, so we're probably going to look for some good old rom-com."

I watched him and hoped he would buy it. I was betting on the fact that he only half heard the shooting, and me planting the lie of crime movie in his mind would make it all believable.

I elbowed Edie.

She seemed to come out of the shock and nodded her head, making her white curls bob along. "Ryker, are you trying to give me a heart attack? Why the heck are you coming in without knocking? Just as we were watching this movie scene with the shooting. You really picked a good time."

I almost burst out laughing. Edie was so good when she put her mind to it. And also, she was preaching to Ryker about letting himself in? After she did that at Gran's house? Now that was hilarious.

Ryker almost blushed. He cleared his throat. "Grams, I'm sorry, I just . . . I did knock but there was no answer, so I just tried the door. I'm sorry I scared you."

Edie stood from the table, pushing Lloyd's phone toward me, and she gave Ryker a hug. I took that as a sign for me to slip the phone into my pocket. Edie was such a good weasel when she had to be.

"Do you want some pie?" Edie asked Ryker. "It's peach."

"I could never say no to your peach pie," Ryker said.

I took that as my cue to leave, although I had a burning desire to talk to Edie about what we'd just heard. But as usual, Ryker had the knack for ruining such beautiful moments.

Just as I stood from the table, Edie nudged me to sit back down. "Piper, I'm sure you want a second piece of pie, right?"

Ryker was staring at me, and he didn't exactly have a welcoming facial expression. He turned to Edie and said, "Actually, I need to talk to you." He paused. "Alone."

"Talk to me alone?" Edie asked. "About Tammy and Lloyd?"

Ryker nodded.

"Then Piper can stay," Edie said. "She knows about everything, so you can talk freely."

I saw Ryker hesitating.

"Look, Edie, you don't need to put Ryker in this position," I said. "I can respect that he doesn't—"

Edie put her hand up. "Let's not play coy. Ryker, you know I'm going to tell Piper everything you tell me, and Piper, you know I'm going to come over and tell you everything Ryker told me. So let's just be efficient and cut to the chase. Now both of you sit down and eat your pie."

I smiled and did as requested. Ryker smiled too although I could tell he tried to hide it.

"Does anybody need coffee?" Edie asked.

Ryker and I both shook our heads. But we did dig into the peach pie. It was official. I had to join a gym. I snuck a glance at Ryker and admired his ripped arms and chiseled chest. This guy really stayed in shape. I felt some tingly feelings in my stomach, so I ignored them immediately. Must be the climate here.

"So what did you find out?" Edie asked Ryker after she took her seat at the table.

"There were some calls about Lloyd Feldman," Ryker said. "He was seen at the paintball place here in Bitter End." He looked from Edie to me then back to Edie. "Do you happen to know something about it?"

"Oh," Edie tried to feign innocence. "He was seen at the paintball field? Really? Hmm . . ." Edie tapped with her index finger on her chin, and she gazed at the ceiling like she was mulling over this question.

"Weren't you and everybody else from the Bitter End retirement complex at the paintball field today?" Ryker asked as he bit into his pie.

"Yes, we were," Edie said.

"And?" Ryker asked. "Didn't you see him there?"

Edie put on her most innocent face and said, "No, I don't believe I did." Then she turned to me. "Piper, did you happen to see Lloyd at the paintball field today?"

"I obviously didn't see Lloyd there," I said. "Or else I would have told you."

Ryker eyed us suspiciously. But I knew he had nothing to pin on us.

"So who reported it in?" I asked.

"Some of the residents," Ryker said. "But they said that Lloyd was running down a hill and he was followed by someone. Someone who ran fast and who was part of the game as well."

Ryker stared at me.

"So a resident was on his tail?" I asked and pretended not to get where he was going with this. "Too bad they didn't catch him."

"Yeah, too bad," Ryker said. "It's also too bad the residents here don't have the best eyesight. They couldn't identify who the person was that ran after Lloyd." He paused. "If it was Lloyd they saw to begin with."

"I totally get that," I said. "And the person who supposedly ran after him didn't come forward and admit it?"

Ryker shook his head.

"That's interesting," Edie said. "Maybe they didn't know it was Lloyd they were running after. But either way, now we know Lloyd is still in Bitter End, right?"

"Right," Ryker said. "Then a couple of other people reported seeing Lloyd running into the woods at the paintball field and he was supposedly splashed with paintballs. They say he looked like a run-down, rumpled clown."

Edie and I both burst out laughing.

"Why is this so funny?" Ryker asked.

"I'm just picturing him now," I said. "He got shot at with paintballs while running for his life. Now that is funny."

Ryker stared at us as we finished laughing.

"What was he wearing beside paint?" Edie asked, and that was a good question to try to keep the guilt away from us. Because we knew what he was wearing.

"We think it was a gray suit," Ryker said. "Which is now a gray suit with lots of color in it."

"Do you think it's possible he still has some unfinished business here?" I asked. "I mean, it's two days since the murder and he's wearing a suit, meaning he probably got up that morning, put on a suit for work and didn't have the chance to change since then, right?"

"You're correct," Ryker said. "We've yet to find out why he's still here. My guess is he needs money. I gather Edie has told you his accounts were frozen."

I nodded. "I agree with you. I think it's about money too. I'm also curious how he's going to get his hands on his money with the restricted access. And now that he is suspect number one for killing his partner . . . I wouldn't want to be in Lloyd's shoes."

I actually didn't even want to be in *my* shoes, in the witness protection program in freaking Florida instead of my home in Oregon, but Lloyd's shoes seemed even worse right now.

I was pretty sure Lloyd didn't kill Tammy, but I couldn't share that with Ryker without disclosing the cell phone story. What Edie and I had heard was Tammy getting shot and Lloyd recording it. I was rolling the dice that Lloyd wasn't that perverted as to hire someone to kill his partner and then record it. For what? That wouldn't make any sense. No, what I suspected was that Lloyd probably went into that storage room while those two hit men came in and threatened Tammy. Lloyd didn't make a sound when he heard them come in and Tammy didn't give him away. When things got heated and the thugs pulled the gun on Tammy, Lloyd had the sense to think fast and pull out his phone and record the whole thing. That would make him non-guilty for Tammy's murder. But I still had to play along for Ryker.

"I would be really shocked if Lloyd didn't kill his wife," Ryker said. "I'm assuming it has something to do with money as well. Maybe there was a fight between them, it got heated, Lloyd pulled out the gun and shot her."

Edie gave me a subtle sideways glance and I knew she was thinking the same thing as me. Lloyd couldn't have killed Tammy. "Yes, you're most probably right," I said to Ryker.

"Okay, something's up," Ryker said. "Why do you agree with me so much?"

Crap.

I kept underestimating this guy. He took me by surprise again. And I wasn't prepared for that. Again. I needed to buckle up.

"Now you're skeptical of me because I'm agreeing with you?" I asked. "There's no way to win with you, is there?"

Ryker examined me for a couple of seconds. "Yeah, I guess you're right. Sorry."

Ha, gotcha.

"See?" Edie said. "You two work so well together when you let go of your egos. Why can't you do that more often?"

Ryker and I both turned our attention to the pie on our plates.

"There's just one small thing that's bothering me," Ryker said.

Uh-oh. Here it came. The ace up his sleeve. The rabbit out of the hat. The surprise attack. What was it? Someone saw me taking Lloyd's phone? Someone saw Gran shooting at Lloyd? Sam realized what was going on and told on us? Ryker found out my identity was phony? What? What?

"It's the short range," Ryker said.

"The what?" I asked.

"The short range Tammy was shot at," he said.

Oh. I let out a long breath.

"What about it?" Edie asked.

I relaxed my shoulders and bit into my pie. "It was too close. It looked more cold-blooded, more like an execution. Too clean. An angry husband would have been more . . . careless. If he—"

I looked up and stopped with my fork in midair. Edie and Ryker stared at me.

Ryker blinked twice. "Wow, that was exactly what I was thinking."

"What did I just tell you?" Edie said while taking a sip of coffee. "You two think alike."

"You really do know about these things, don't you?" Ryker said.

"Yes, but like I already had told you, I'm not a spy and I'm not CIA or FBI, nor do I work as an undercover agent for the Russians, okay?"

Edie nearly snorted her coffee out. "Oh geez," she said and grabbed a napkin, sounding nasal.

"Grams, are you okay?" Ryker asked and patted her arm.

"I'm fine, I'm fine," Edie said then turned to me. "You're not *what* now? Why are you going there?"

I nodded my chin toward Ryker. "That's what he said."

Three weeks ago, when Edie and I solved the mystery of her neighbor, Edgar, Ryker actually asked me if I was CIA or FBI, or a spy or an agent. He knew my knowledge and physical abilities were not the regular kinds for a hairdresser. Funnily enough, he assumed I worked for the government. For the "good guys," as one would put it. If he only knew.

Ryker put his hands up. "Something is definitely up. She knows too much for just a regular civilian."

"But she watches all those crime—" Edie started.

"Shows," Ryker finished for her. "Yes, I know, so I've been told." He paused. "Numerous times. I just don't buy it."

I folded my hands on the table, leaned over my plate until I was only inches from his face, and looked him straight in the eye. "You know what?" I said in my softest, lowest, most sensual voice, "I don't care if you buy it or not."

Edie whistled and leaned back in her chair.

FOOL ME ONCE

Nobody said anything for a good fifteen seconds while Ryker and I had our own staring contest.

"Okay, you want me to arrange a duel between you?" Edie finally asked. "We could do it on my lawn. We could invite everyone to watch. We'll have a blast. I can tell people to bring sodas and corn dogs and popcorn too. Twelve p.m. sharp sound good for you?"

Edie was really laying on the sarcasm, but I honestly didn't mind. What I did mind was Ryker. He came by at the worst time and now he was wasting our time with things we already knew. Boy, if he knew what we knew. Then he'd probably deliver us personally to the police station for interfering with an official investigation and not disclosing crucial information.

Ryker broke the eye contact, smiled, and got back to his pie.

"So did you find out what Lloyd was doing there at the paintball field?" Edie asked.

"We searched the place and found a cabin up on a hill, and by the looks of it, Lloyd has been spending the last couple of nights there. We found coffee cups and a blanket and bags of chips."

Edie seemed impressed. "Oh, wow. Do you think he'll go back there?"

"Doubtful," Ryker said. "Since we now found his sleeping spot."

"And what do you think the chances are of us getting our money back if his accounts are frozen?" Edie asked.

"I don't know what to tell you," Ryker said and put his hand on Edie's arm. "It's definitely a good sign the accounts are frozen, because that means an investigation is underway. I'm not informed how that's going, but I hope they sort it out fast enough and hopefully there's enough money left for you all."

We all munched on our pie and thought about that. I could see a sadness crossing Edie's face. In my opinion, she was handling the situation admirably. She knew she had to do something because it was her money and she cared about the other residents as well. At the same time, I bet she tried not to think about the scam all the time; that would be counterproductive and wouldn't help one iota right now. What was done was done. She could only look forward. But now and then when the subject of money and Lloyd and accounts came up, I could tell she realized once again she'd invested a lot of money in a fraud, and she wasn't sure if she was going to get a cent of it back.

I finished my pie and was craving another piece, but I resisted the urge. I hadn't done a lot of exercise since I'd arrived here in Florida. Okay, I'd barely done any exercise. Just regular walking. But that was nothing. Back home in Oregon, I didn't go to the gym or anything, but me and the Falcons were so often on the move, investigating our competitors, doing surveillance . . . and then there was me working at Choppers. So I always was involved in that kind of exercise and there wasn't that much time to stuff many calories in myself.

I was never the kind of girl to finish her shift at the bar at four a.m. and then grab fatty fast food on her way home. Moreover, Gran and I cooked a lot at home. That was also something we let slide here in Florida. Granted, we had a dining hall here at the complex, so the incentive to cook for ourselves really diminished.

"I'm curious about something," I said to Ryker. "How come you're working so close with the cops?"

"What do you mean?" Ryker asked.

"I mean usually cops kind of hate PIs because they're always in the way," I said. "But you're always telling us that *we went to investigate* and *we found this out* or *that out* and *we think* whatever you all think. How come?"

Ryker grinned. "See? I told you something's off if you know stuff like this. But to answer your question, it's because I'm a serious investigator. I don't do any of those cheating spouses cases. Not that they're not important—I can see the point to that—but that just wouldn't satisfy me professionally. I have a criminal degree, but I've always wanted to be my own boss and have my own hours. And I've known Greg, my associate and my friend since high school, and he kind of thinks the same way I do. So we both got our PI licenses and opened up the firm. Samantha Braveheart is our third associate as of last month. We also have security projects that we handle, for midrange to high-profile companies here in Bitter End."

"So you and Greg both went to school in Georgia and decided to move here to Bitter End in Florida to open your firm?" I asked.

Ugh. My plan was actually not continuing this conversation, so that Ryker would leave as soon as possible, and Edie and I could continue with the sensational news we just found out. But the questions just came out of my mouth. I had to admit, I was curious. Damn it. On the other hand, as long as

I kept Ryker talking about himself, that would take the heat off me.

Ryker grinned some more. "Somebody is curious."

I shrugged. "Just as you are with me."

Edie let out a snort. "Ha. Touché."

Edie had mentioned her daughter was Ryker's mother, and together with her husband, she lived in Georgia, where Edie came from.

"I went to school near Augusta in Georgia, yes," Ryker said. "And so did Greg. I was often here in Florida on vacation with my parents and with my grandparents, before my grandpa died." He squeezed Edie's arm and she looked sad again.

"Ryker's parents found other vacation spots for them, but I kept on coming here and Ryker often came with me," Edie added. "I finally moved here five years ago, and one year later, Ryker decided to move here as well. Greg was between jobs and decided to come with Ryker."

Ryker nodded. "We also used the fact that the private security market was pretty sparse around here."

"Oh, and there was also Ryker's ex—" Edie started, but Ryker gave her such a stern look, she immediately closed her mouth tight.

I raised an eyebrow but didn't probe further.

Ryker leaned in his seat. "So, now you know about me." And with that, he signaled that this conversation was over.

That was fine by me since we were done eating the peach pie. Ryker looked at his watch and I enjoyed the view of his skull tattoo on his arm again. I wondered if Ryker had a girlfriend or a dating partner or an affair going or anything like that. Edie hadn't mentioned anything, but that didn't mean there wasn't somebody. And Ryker shutting Edie up with that "ex" thing . . . that only piqued my interest. Then I shook it off. Why was I interested? I shouldn't care about Ryker's personal life.

Ryker stood and said he needed to leave. He said if we knew something we should come forward, and whatever we did, we should definitely not get in the way of the investigation, like he already knew we were doing just that.

Edie walked him to the door, then Ryker gave her a warm hug. He peered in my direction for the last time and left.

I walked to Edie's window and watched Ryker get on his bike. Now that was a beauty! The bike, not Ryker. Well, maybe Ryker too, but I couldn't feel that way about him. It ached that I couldn't get my own bike around here. My eyes squinted, peering across the street at the golf cart in Gran's driveway. Ugh. Such a slap in the face.

Edie clapped her hands together. "Oh my god, I thought I was going to faint when Ryker came in before."

"Yeah, you almost fainted on my shoulder," I said. "Your grandson really has a knack for showing up at the worst possible time."

"Thank you so much for thinking on your feet," Edie said and planted herself at the table again. "Do you think he bought it?"

I shrugged. "I couldn't tell you. I'd say he bought it. Or else he would have grilled us about it. But I mean, he's your family, and you know him best. What does your gut tell you?"

Edie seemed to think about it. "I think he bought it too or else he would have been all over us." Edie looked thoughtful. "I really hate lying to him, but it's just . . ."

"What is it?" I asked.

"Well, he always wants to do things his way, the right way, and I'm a bit more . . ."

"Alternative?" I asked.

Edie laughed. "Yeah, you could say that. Just like you are."

I pulled Lloyd's cell phone out of my back pocket and took a seat next to Edie at the table again. "That's why we go so good together."

Edie gave my arm a squeeze and I felt that warmth again. It was totally unnerving.

"I know it's totally disturbing what we heard, but play it again," Edie said.

I pressed play again and we heard the audio file again. Twenty minutes later we had heard it about one hundred times.

"I really don't know what to say," Edie said, letting out a long breath. "I know it's weird, but it's like being there. It's like Tammy's death is so close to us. I'm probably going to have nightmares because of this." Edie paused. "What do you think?"

I wasn't as shook up as Edie was, although I never expected to find something like this on Lloyd's phone. I told Edie about my take on this. That I thought Lloyd wasn't a killer and that he just happened to be in the storage room and had the inspiration to press record as soon as he heard what was going on in the room next door.

I also told Edie my gut was telling me that Lloyd was now blackmailing the killer or the killers. We heard two voices on that audio file. Only one pulled the trigger, but there were still two people there.

Then Lloyd sent the audio file to that unknown number after Tammy was killed. That was the start of the blackmail, sort of. And then that unknown number called Lloyd twice after the audio file was sent, according to his callers list. I would say Lloyd and those thugs tried to make a deal. Or were still trying. Who knew?

"But if Lloyd didn't do it, then why didn't he just send the audio file to the cops?" Edie asked.

"Because first of all, his fraud scheme has now been uncovered, so he's still guilty of that, and secondly, even if he can send the audio file to the cops without turning himself in, why would he do that? He could blackmail the killers, especially now that his accounts are frozen. Don't forget this is still a criminal we're talking about. He's looking for a way out now. He needs money and he can get that money through this audio file. And then a fake passport and leaving the country."

Edie's eyes went wide. "Whoa, this is like one of those spy movies."

"Could be, only this is real life unfortunately," I said.

I told Edie this could be an explanation why Lloyd was still sticking around; he was probably in negotiation with the killers to get the money. And now that we had Lloyd's cell phone, he was in big trouble. Those two voices we heard on the audio file had to be those two hit men Victoria had mentioned to us. And she was right. They sounded exactly like that. They even mentioned a Mr. Moose. That was most likely their employer. An employer who gave them the order to kill Tammy Feldman. Or maybe they would have killed Lloyd if he was in the office and Tammy was gone.

They said they needed the money. So whatever was going on, the Feldmans were involved with this Mr. Moose and they were giving him money. When Mr. Moose didn't get his share, he did what any criminal entity would do. Murder someone to get the message across to the others. In this case, to Lloyd Feldman. Only Lloyd got lucky-clever and recorded the murder. He turned the tables on Mr. Moose and was now blackmailing him for money. The irony.

God, how I missed this life.

I wondered if Lloyd really went to the cops with this audio file, if the cops would know who they were hearing was the two men. Would that have been evidence enough to make an arrest?

"So what now?" Edie asked. "Shouldn't we go to the cops with this? I mean, we heard it first and all but I really don't know what to do with this."

I thought about it. And I thought about all the possible consequences. We could go to the cops with this audio file or just plant it in a way so that we wouldn't get blamed for withholding evidence.

One of the consequences would be that we were putting Lloyd's life on the line. If he didn't have any bargaining power against the killers, he was fish bait. But the thing was, I really didn't care about Lloyd or his life. I would finish him off myself for what he did to Edie and the other residents. Yet we might still need Lloyd to get to the money, even if his accounts were frozen. I knew people like this. They usually also had some offshore accounts. Lloyd probably needed to get out of the country to access those accounts. We wanted to catch his butt before he did just that.

The reality right now was that Lloyd was still around and he didn't have any way of contacting Mr. Moose and his posse. Unless he had money somehow to buy another cell phone. And also assuming he knew the unknown number by heart.

"So what exactly can we do with Lloyd's cell phone to track him down or track down those two guys?" Edie asked. "And what about that Mr. Moose? How do we get him?"

"Well, those thugs and Mr. Moose don't know that we have Lloyd's cell phone," I said. "Assuming negotiations between them are not closed yet, then shortly they would call—"

At that second, Lloyd's cell phone started vibrating on Edie's table.

Edie jumped back and almost fell off her chair.

I looked at the screen.

The unknown number was calling.

Chapter Thirteen

Edie and I looked at each other wide-eyed.

"Go ahead, answer it, or we'll lose them," Edie said.

"But they're expecting Lloyd," I said. "And I'm not Lloyd. And I can't fake a male voice."

"Then use yours," Edie said.

"And then what?" I asked.

Edie threw her hands in the air. "Wing it!"

Without having any plan how to proceed, I hit the answer button and waited.

My heartbeat slightly accelerated and I had a flashback of my former life. The excitement, the high of doing something wrong . . . ah, nostalgia was hitting hard.

"Hello?" a male voice said and I recognized it as thug #1 from the audio file. Even the hello sounded dumb and uninspired.

"Hi, who's this?" I asked confidently.

There was a pause on the other end, and I knew Thug #1 was thrown.

Edie was on the edge of her seat, biting her nails and her eyes were almost bulging out.

Then Thug #1 said, "Who is *this*? I want to speak with the Feldman guy."

"The Feldman guy isn't available anymore," I said. "But I am. Do you want the audio file?"

There was another pause and I heard Thug #1 holding the phone away from his ear and saying something to another person. "There's a chick on the other line. I think she offed the Feldman guy."

"What?" the other person in the background said and I recognized the voice as Thug #2. "What do you mean? What chick?"

Still with the phone held away, Thug #1 said, "I don't know. It's like I said. A chick answered the phone."

I rolled my eyes. I was dealing with idiots here. And I'd dealt with idiots before. The funny thing was, they somehow didn't get caught as fast as one would expect. They always got lucky through their own dumbness. I wondered who Thug #1 and Thug #2's employer was. Who on earth would even hire these two? Even put together, they probably didn't own enough brain cells to pull off something of this magnitude.

Thug #2 continued in an annoyed voice. "Well, then ask her what she wants."

Thug #1 returned to the phone call. "What do you want?"

"Whatever deal you had with Feldman, that's off," I said. "You're dealing with me now. I want a million dollars for the audio file."

Edie leaned forward so far she slipped off the chair and fell on the floor.

Thug #1 said, "You're crazy."

I heard Thug #2 in the background. "What the hell is going on there? Why is she crazy?"

Thug #1 held the phone away again. "She says she wants a million dollars for the audio file."

"What?" Thug #2 said in a louder voice. "She's crazy!"

"That's what I said," Thug #1 replied.

"Tell her we don't have that kind of money," Thug #2 said.

Thug #1 returned. "We don't have that kind of—"

Okay, this could go on forever and I didn't have that much time or patience for these fools.

"Put the other one on the phone," I demanded.

"Put the—" Thug #1 was obviously confused.

I heard some rumblings, then Thug #2 said, "What?"

"She wants to talk to you," Thug #1 said.

I heard an annoyed sigh, then Thug #2 took the phone. "What? Who are you? And what do you want?"

"I want one million dollars for the audio file or you can kiss your freedom goodbye," I said. "Tomorrow night, eight p.m., Liberty Square."

"But we don't have—"

I disconnected.

Edie got back on her chair and stared at me with her mouth hanging open.

"I don't know if I should applaud you or be terrified," she finally said.

"You can do both."

Edie grinned. "I told you you're good with the winging it."

Especially when I had to deal with idiots. Then it was easy. They didn't even inquire further who I was.

"So tell me, tell me, what did they say?" Edie asked.

I told her about our conversation.

Edie blinked twice. "What idiots!"

"I know!"

Edie thought about it. "I can't believe you just talked on the phone with Tammy's killers. I wonder what was up between the Feldmans and these guys."

FOOL ME ONCE

"I would sure like to know that," I said. "Possibly Mr. Moose found out what the Feldmans were doing, scamming you out of your money, and wanted a piece of the pie."

"Yeah, those two could never be the brains behind it, anyway," Edie said.

"Exactly. The fact that they're still out there and not in jail is actually a miracle. It just says something about our current legal system and the law enforcement competence." Then I thought about it. "On the other hand, they may have come here from another state. Tracking them down gets harder then. Hit men usually don't stick around in one place too long; they're like freelancers looking for jobs."

"Oh, okay," Edie said. "And we don't know anything about a Mr. Moose, right?"

I shook my head.

"So let's say Mr. Moose gave the order to shoot Tammy or one of the Feldmans," Edie continued. "How can the police catch him as well, if he wasn't the one who really shot the gun?"

"That's the brilliance behind it," I said. "The hit man gets caught and is convicted because he pulled the trigger, and the cops have to prove that there was somebody else who gave the order. That's obviously way harder. But hit men don't usually have any emotional connection to their employer, so they are presented a deal for spilling the beans on their boss."

Edie shook her head. "By the way, I still think it's surreal what kind of conversations we're having. One day everything is fine, the next day, we're talking killers, hit men, convicting, gun-shooting . . . What is this world coming to?"

I resisted the urge to tell Edie the world was always like this.

"You know," I said, "we're not really sure if this Mr. Moose is working alone or if he's part of a whole criminal organization."

Edie rubbed her forehead. "This is getting way complicated." She took another piece of pie. "So why did you tell them you want one million dollars anyway? And the meeting tomorrow night? I mean, where were you going with that?"

The heck with it. I took another piece of pie. "I wanted to put the heat on them. This way they'll scramble to somehow get the money, leaving them less time to think about how to turn the tables on us. Right now, we have the upper hand with the audio file. They have to play by our rules. As long as we keep this status quo, we can bust them tomorrow."

"We can bust them?" Edie asked. "And how do you think we can bust them?"

"Well, we have a little over twenty-four hours to make a plan," I said.

Ah, the anticipation of making a plan for busting the opposing group. This surely wasn't my first rodeo. The only difference was that in my former life I had the Oregon Falcons to back me up. I was not alone. In my current life, I had Gran, who was like a ticking bomb ready to shoot whomever and whenever, and Edie, a seventy-five-year-old regular civilian in a polka-dot dress, whose only weapon could be her peach pie, if she threw that in your face.

"By the way, you were awesome on the phone," Edie said to me. "I wish I could do stuff like that."

"That's probably the weirdest compliment I ever got," I said. Then I smiled at Edie, and she smiled back.

"You really think we can get them?" Edie asked, munching on her piece of pie. "I mean, I don't know how to picture this. Those two guys are going to be at Liberty Square, and that's assuming it's just them and not their boss too, and then you and me hiding behind a bench and jumping on them? And since

Dorothy likes shooting so much, we'll have her hide behind a bush as our sniper?"

Yeah, okay, the way Edie put it did sound stupid. It sounded more stupid because Edie would be involved. Even without the Falcons, I was pretty sure Gran and I could take them down. But I still wasn't sure how best to approach this. We may need the cops as well, but I didn't know how to do that without putting ourselves in their line of sight. But then, if we did this without the cops, how would we explain it to them?

I sighed. Stuff like this was so much easier in my former life. If we had a beef with other groups, we didn't have any reason to involve law enforcement. We dealt with it among ourselves. But now with Edie and the other residents, I felt that the game rules had changed, and I had to take that into account. Sheesh, I really did hate the law.

It was evening by the time Edie and I polished off almost the entire pie. I told her we needed to let this sink in and we should talk in the morning about how to best go about it. I let Edie know I would discuss this with Gran too.

"Please remind her to reflect on the situation first before shooting anyone," Edie answered.

I laughed. "I will."

Back at Gran's house, I found her lying on the couch and watching TV with a beer in her hand.

"What? No poker today?" I asked.

"Nah," Gran said. "Not after today's outing. I've already seen too many of these people this morning at the shooting place."

"It's not a shooting place," I corrected Gran. "It's a paintball place."

"Whatever," Gran said. "Were you at Edie's this long?" Gran asked without taking her eyes off the TV screen.

"Yeah, but I brought you some peach pie," I said and placed a slice on a plate for Gran. Then took a seat at the table.

Gran joined me. "Thanks. I can't say no to pie." She dug in. "So what were you doing? Plotting your next move?" She let out a honk of a laugh.

"We kind of did," I said.

Gran stopped eating and raised an eyebrow.

I told her about Lloyd at the paintball field and his cell phone and the call I had.

Gran chewed on a bite of pie and seemed to think about it. "Good thinking, I would have done the same. So I'm thinking my position could be behind one of those palm trees at Liberty Square. It's too bad I don't have a rifle, but I can manage with my gun just as well and then we'll—"

I put my hand up. "I'm going to stop you right there. This is not how we're going to do it."

Gran looked at me like I was talking gibberish. "What are you talking about? Of course that's the way we'll do it. That's the way we've always done it."

"I know that," I said. "But things are different now. We have Edie. And we have the other residents here. It's not just us anymore."

Gran huffed.

"Not to mention the fact we're already in big trouble if this comes out," I said. "Dillon would pull us out of here immediately and we'd be royally screwed."

Brett Dillon was the US marshal who'd gotten appointed to us. He probably regretted that, starting with his first day through to his last day. He was the one who acted as our bodyguard, our babysitter, our protector, our consultant—everything it took for him to keep us alive while we waited for the trial against the Falcons to begin. Then throughout the trial, then relocating us here to Florida. He took care of everything, of every bit of red tape; he moved with us from motel to motel until we got the house here in Bitter End.

He was also the one we took all our frustrations out on. Some days I pitied him that he got stuck with us. But most days, all I wanted to do was take his gun and shoot ourselves free.

He always wore a dark gray suit, and he was always put together. In a parallel life, I would have contemplated him as a potential partner.

"So what do you want to do, then?" Gran asked.

I sighed. "I don't know. Yet."

"What do you think that Feldman guy will do?" Gran asked.

Now that was a most interesting question. What with the call to those idiots, I almost forgot about Lloyd. I asked myself what his plan was now. Did he still have the same clothes on? The gray suit splashed with paintballs? He would actually be a walking target that way. Anybody could spot him from anywhere. So he literally needed to change his appearance and his clothes. I was thinking he probably had some money on him when this whole thing started. That's why he could afford to buy chips and coffee and the blanket and another cell phone. I figured he had a couple of hundred dollars on him. So he needed to keep an eye on his remaining cash and spend it wisely. He was on a budget. And now his cell phone was gone as well. He probably freaked out that he couldn't reach the idiots to make his deal happen.

But what if Lloyd spent the rest of his money on another cheap phone and called the thugs himself? Assuming he knew their number by heart. Then what would happen? What would he tell them? Lloyd didn't have the audio file anymore. We had it. So he didn't have any leverage over the idiots. He could call and convince them he still had the audio file or he even made a copy of it. Then my deal with the idiots would be off.

There were so many possibilities to consider. Even if I did make a good plan for tomorrow evening and we busted those two idiots, where would that leave Edie's money and the rest of the residents' money? We still needed to find Lloyd and deliver him to the cops. That way the investigation would move further along, and Edie and the rest would get their money sooner, assuming there was enough money left.

"See?" Gran said. "I told you not to get involved. And then you do get involved and you get me involved, and then you forbid me to be who I am."

"I feel a headache coming on," I said. "I'm getting a beer."

"Awesome," Gran said. "Get another one for me too."

I came back to the table with two brews.

"So was the phone unlocked?" Gran asked.

Oh. I hadn't told her that part.

"It was locked," I said. "We had some . . . help with that."

I told Gran about Samantha Braveheart and Edie being sneaky.

Gran shook her head. "You're hot and cold with me. It's okay when you do stuff like this, but it's not okay if I do stuff like this."

I threw my hands up. "Your stuff is shooting people!"

Gran waved her hand in dismissal. "Potato, potahto."

After a pause, Gran said, "By the way, that one million dollars you requested . . . is there any chance that we could, you know, keep the money? Go through with the deal for real?"

I stared at Gran. Up until a couple of months ago, I wouldn't have even blinked at that question. Moreover, Gran wouldn't even have to ask. It would have been a "duh" situation. Of course we would have gone through with the deal. For us. But now, after going into the witness protection program, after those excruciating thirteen months and seeing what happened to the Falcons, and knowing what would happen to us if we got off the "right path," my answer to that changed. It didn't change for Gran. She was still Gran. How would anyone expect her to change in her seventies? She lived the outlaw lifestyle through and through. Heck, she could hire the two idiots and show them a thing or two about that kind of life.

Gran got my drift, and she rolled her eyes. "Fine, we don't go through with the deal. I don't understand how you can say no to a million dollars, but whatever."

It was dark outside when I finished my beer. Although I'd had a long day and I felt super tired, my brain kept running scenarios through my mind. Thoughts of money, fraud, blackmail, and Lloyd and Tammy Feldman swirled in my head. What was going on there between the Feldmans and Mr. Moose? I was sure Mr. Moose had to have found out somehow what the Feldmans were doing and wanted a piece of the pie. But how experienced could this Mr. Moose have been if he hired Idiot #1 and Idiot #2? And where would Lloyd go to now? And would he get in touch with the idiots and ruin the plan for tomorrow night? Whatever the plan was, because I still hadn't thought of anything else besides showing up at 8:00 p.m. at Liberty Square, then wait for the thugs to arrive, then bust them. Yeah, brilliant plan. Could it be just as simple as that?

Finally, I decided not to think about it anymore, so I crashed on the couch and watched some mind-numbing TV shows with Gran sitting beside me.

Chapter Fourteen

THE NEXT DAY AT 8:00 A.M., I was driving the golf cart to the dining hall. Gran was in the passenger seat and Edie was in the back.

Gran and I were wearing dark sunglasses and Edie was squinting in the sun. We looked like a girl band where each of us had our individual outfits. I had on khaki shorts, a T-shirt and flip-flops. Gran had her usual biker outfit on, and Edie wore a red-and-green polka-dot dress and maroon chunky sandals. We could have gone to a girl-band casting right now and gotten the part.

We talked about the Lloyd situation on our way to breakfast. I left Lloyd's cell phone back at the house, and even if I was a bit paranoid, I stuck the cell phone in the sugar jar. The jar was inside the cupboard. There was barely any sugar in the jar, but I didn't want that phone just lying around.

I knew I was probably way overreacting, but life had taught me that the craziest things can happen. See our current life for example. I didn't want to take the chance of someone breaking into the house and finding that cell phone on the table right there in the open. Granted, with a thorough search, an experienced person could find the phone anywhere; however, this way I reduced the likelihood of someone finding it. And it was not like Gran had nooks and crannies in the house where you could hide stuff.

We had a hidden safe in our old house in Oregon where we stashed a lot of cash and jewels, gold, and diamonds, but the marshals made us give that away. We had to sell everything. Gran needed to pay her back taxes to the IRS and she needed money to live off after entering the witness protection program. The monthly subsistence checks from WITSEC would end eventually. So she had to sell the house we lived in and the cabin near Mount Hood in Oregon, our second home.

I could say we formerly lived a fairly good life, money-wise, and we'd never been poorer than we were now. Which should make me go out and get a job right away, but that only got me deeper into my depression tunnel. I was glad we had the Lloyd situation on our hands, because that gave me something to do.

"Piper, we only have about twelve hours until we're meeting those guys," Edie said. "What are we going to do?"

"I don't know," I said. "I mean, I do know. We're waiting for them to show up and then we bust them."

"And how the hell are we going to do that?" Edie asked.

Gran was about to say something when Edie turned and stopped her. "No, you won't just start shooting at them. That will get us all thrown in jail."

"You two always ruin the fun," Gran said.

"I say we go to the cops," Edie said.

"And tell them what?" I asked. "How would we explain withholding evidence like this? Then they sure would throw us in jail."

Edie pouted. "But we did them a favor. They should be thanking us."

"Ha," Gran said. "I want to be there when you tell them that."

"You know very well they're not going to thank you for this," I said. "But I'm starting to agree with you that we need the cops, as much as I hate saying it. But we have to go about it in a clever way so that we come out clean at the end of it."

We drove the rest of the way in silence, and I parked the golf cart in the only spot that was still available.

FOOL ME ONCE

"Why is it packed here?" I asked, as we all stepped out of the golf cart.

Edie grinned. "Because they're delivering the baskets today and everybody who won wants to pick them up."

Gran looked questioningly from Edie to me. Oh yeah, she didn't know about the spa baskets that we won.

"There was a prize for winning the paintball game," I said. "We won spa baskets."

Gran blinked twice.

"Apparently, the foot powder is to die for," I said by way of explanation.

Gran still stared, absolutely unimpressed. Then she shrugged and mumbled something about the odd way people had fun around here.

We walked past the swimming pool and the rec hall and entered the dining hall and stopped short. It was so packed and so loud I almost went spontaneously deaf.

"You know what?" Gran said loudly. "Let's just have breakfast at my house."

She started to turn around, but Edie grabbed her arm. "Nonsense, Dorothy. We won that game and we're not going to hide in our houses."

Did Edie really grab Gran by her arm? Did she know what she was doing? I saw Gran reaching for the small of her back where I was sure her gun was tucked, but then apparently she changed her mind and just gave Edie her usual death stare.

Beatrice waved at us from a table in the back. She almost had to get on top of the chair so we could see her. She was that small. Theodore was sitting next to her and waved at us as well.

We made our way to Beatrice's table while Edie was greeting everybody and giving them a high five. She definitely was downplaying being in the spotlight and being on the winning team at the paintball game.

Beautiful gift baskets lined the sidewalls of the dining hall. The baskets were wrapped in cellophane and had the winners' names on them on a blue ribbon. Wow, these people really took this seriously.

"We thought you'd never get here," Beatrice said. "This is the second time I'm saving these seats for you while almost getting tackled by the mob here." I saw Beatrice and Theodore blocking other people's way to those chairs.

We took our seats and Jim came over with a fresh pot of coffee and some coffee cups. Jim was a staffer at the retirement complex and seemed like a pretty decent guy. He looked to be in his forties, and he had the most piercing blue eyes I'd ever seen in my life.

He always seemed to smile when he saw me. I smiled back and thanked him for the coffee. Then I turned, and three pairs of eyes were staring at me and grinning. Edie, Beatrice, and Theodore. Gran was trying to pretend she was somewhere else.

I frowned. "What?"

"I wish I were your age again," Beatrice said, taking a sip of coffee.

"What are you talking about?" I asked.

"Do you even know that guys have the hots for you?" Edie asked. "First Ryker, now Jim."

"Are you crazy?" I asked. And took a big gulp of coffee. That's so not true."

"Of course it's true," Beatrice said. "You just don't realize it. When you get to our age there's a lot of stuff that's just so transparent you could see it from space. That's why I'm saying I wish I could be your age again."

"But with the wisdom we have now," Edie said.

"Amen sister," Beatrice said, and they both clinked their coffee cups.

"Okay, did you go for the Irish coffee today" I asked.

Yes, I knew Jim smiled a lot more when I was around. I was not stupid. But I just didn't want to think about it. Having a potential romantic involvement was the last thing I needed right now. Besides, how could I ever have a partner again? I would have to lie to him all the time about my previous life and about being in the witness protection program. How was that ever a good foundation for a relationship? With this logic, I wouldn't be able to ever enter a relationship. Wow, that was scary. Better not to think about it.

"We went for the harder stuff today and skipped the coffee and went straight for the Irish part," Theodore said smiling.

He glanced over at Gran who was totally ignoring him. Did Gran have the same wisdom as well? Clearly, she knew Theodore liked her, but she just gave zero damns about it.

Edie, Gran, and I somehow made our way to the buffet to get some food on our plates. We had to stop every two seconds so that Edie could greet and talk to everybody.

Back at the table, the conversation quickly diverted to the paintball game from the day before. People were psyched. Actually, the winners were psyched; the losers were rather neutral. Except for

Sourpuss. I saw her a couple of tables over with her gang, shooting daggers at us with her look.

"So how did Lucretia take it?" I asked. "Is she planning her revenge for losing the game?"

Everybody rolled their eyes. "I'd be surprised if she didn't plot the revenge already," Beatrice said and pushed her glasses further up her nose. "I'd sleep with my eyes open if I were you."

"Yeah, Piper, make sure you put that knife right beside your bed," Edie said, laughing.

Everybody turned to Edie, then to me. I waved it away. "Long story."

"Oh, did you hear about Lloyd being at the paintball place?" Beatrice asked. "I can't believe he was there. I swear if I'd seen him, I would have taken him down." She patted her crisp, freshly ironed shirt.

I had to smile. I could just see it now. Tiny Beatrice with her glasses thick as Coke bottles running after Lloyd in the woods.

"The problem is that we are too old and he's too young, so he can run fast," a person from the table next to us said.

"You're right about that, Burt," Theodore said.

"But let me tell you, my anger would be enough to catch up with him," Burt said.

I took a closer look and Burt was wearing his favorite color again: green. He had a walker next to him.

"I think Lloyd should be more afraid of us than the police," Beatrice said. "If we get our hands on him, he'll be toast."

"Damn skippy," Burt said, and my eyes landed on his walker again.

Gran looked at me like, *Oh, yeah, this is a dangerous mob right here.* I had to stifle a laugh.

"I hear people are setting up a neighborhood watch," Burt said. "If he's still around here, he's going to show up sooner or later, and when he does, then *pow!*" He put his fists in the air.

I had to take a bite out of my granola cereal or else I would have really started laughing. Then I thought about what Edie kept saying to me, that I kept underestimating the people here. So who knows, maybe a neighborhood watch would help catch Lloyd. Now that was a sad way to go; being run down by an angry elderly mob.

A couple of other residents had joined the conversation, and the anger toward Lloyd got even more intense. Wow, Lloyd should really skip town as soon as possible, before these people got their hands on him. Then again, if someone scammed me out of that much money, I'd probably do things to him that were beyond anyone's wildest imagination.

By the end of breakfast, there was a small crowd of people gathered around our table, all talking about their experiences with the Feldmans. Some were sad about Tammy; others said she got what she deserved. Some were planning to go down to the station again and put more pressure on the police to solve the fraud case. For the first time in my life, I felt pity for the cops.

After about two hours, my stomach was full and I kind of got tired of hearing the residents telling what they'd do if they got their hands on Lloyd. Mostly because *I* was the one who *really* needed to plan how to get her hands on Lloyd tonight.

Gran decided to head over to the rec hall with her poker-playing posse, so I took her gift basket with me. Underneath the cellophane, I could see there were soaps, lotions, shampoos and the infamous foot powder. Edie and I loaded the three baskets in the back seat of the golf cart and drove back to the house.

"Ooh, I can't wait to use that stuff," Edie said rubbing her hands in anticipation.

"If you like the foot powder so much, I'm sure you can have Gran's and mine as well," I said.

"Nonsense," Edie said. "Trust me, you'll love it. And Dorothy could use the powder since she's wearing those boots all the time."

I laughed. "Yeah, I think you're right about that."

Gran was one stubborn broad. I wondered if she would ever give up her boots here in Florida. I still had a hard time myself wearing those damn flip-flops, and I sure missed my own biker boots. That's why I liked my white sneakers so much. It was like a compromise between the flip-flops and the boots. It was a shame my feet got hot in those things as well.

I parked the golf cart at the curb and Edie headed to her house holding her beloved basket. I took the other two baskets in my arms and headed for the door. But then I stopped short. The door was slightly open. I felt my blood freezing. Somebody picked the lock!

My mind and body instantly went into battle mode. I slowly put the two baskets on the ground and made the move of pulling out the knife from my boots. *Crap*. Again, there were no boots and there was no knife. I really hated this.

If the intruder was still inside, then there was only one thing left to do. I took in a breath and barged through the door into the living room—just in time to see two legs jumping out of the right-hand window of the living room. With a quick glance, I saw the sugar jar on the counter. And the lid open. *Double crap.* I turned back around and took off.

Chapter Fifteen

I ROUNDED THE CORNER just as the intruder disappeared into the hedges behind Gran's house. But I recognized him. It was Lloyd with his sandy-blond hair. He'd ditched his colorful suit, and he was wearing blue sweatpants with a matching blue sweatshirt. So he *did* have enough money to buy himself a new outfit. Or, who knew, maybe he shoplifted.

It didn't matter right now; all that mattered was that I busted him. If he took his cell phone back, then we were really screwed. Honestly, I really thought I was being paranoid hiding the phone in the sugar jar. It turned out, I wasn't. How the hell did Lloyd even know to go there? How did he even find Gran's house?

These were all thoughts for later. Right now, I needed to focus on catching him. He was running fast and, unfortunately, I had on those damned flip-flops. I could barely run in them! Lloyd ran in a zigzag pattern through bushes and hedges, through backyards and front yards, but I kept close behind him. As close as I could in that footwear. It was just my luck that we were talking about a neighborhood watch, and all the neighbors were still gathered in the dining hall. There was nobody around here. *Thanks for nothing.*

Lloyd jumped through a hedge and ran across the street. I followed him but when I jumped through the same hedge, I lost one of my flip-flops. I got up fast and tried to ignore the fact that I was running half-barefoot now. Sadly, I couldn't ignore it too long because I stepped on a freaking huge twig. I yelped and stopped in my tracks. All I could do was watch Lloyd disappear behind a house.

I cursed so bad a sailor would have blushed. I was sweaty, I was angry, and I had a twig coming out of my foot.

I trudged back to the hedge and found my other flip-flop. Then I limped back to the house in the burning sun. Where I found Edie standing on the porch, trying to peek in. She jumped when she saw me coming from behind her.

"What's going on here?" Edie asked. "I saw your baskets on the ground through my window and thought something was up." Edie looked at me from head to toe. "What the hell happened to you?"

"Ugh, only the worst," I said and trudged into the house. Edie was right behind me. She brought the two baskets inside and set them on the floor next to the couch. I went straight to the sugar jar and looked inside. The cell phone was gone. I cursed again.

"Okay, now you're starting to scare me," Edie said. "What happened here? And is your foot bleeding?"

I had taken the twig out of my foot, but now it was indeed bleeding. I washed it off, then I realized Gran and I didn't have any adhesive bandages.

I told Edie what just happened, that Lloyd broke into Gran's house and took his cell phone back. I told her where I'd hidden the phone and that I didn't have any explanation why the sugar jar was on the counter and not in the cupboard, where it was supposed to be. That made it way easier for Lloyd to find it. Because it looked so out of place somehow.

Then I opened the cupboard and saw two bottles of rum where the jar used to be. *Mental forehead smack*. Gran probably exchanged them and didn't have time or didn't want to think about what to do with the sugar jar since we barely used it. Awesome. Gran would be thrilled. If she even cared.

"So you're telling me his cell phone is gone?" Edie asked. "Like, with the audio file and everything?"

I nodded and wiped the sweat from my forehead.

"But why didn't you send the audio file to your own cell phone?" Edie asked.

"Are you kidding me?" I said. "If somebody knew we had the phone in the first place, we'd be in so much trouble. But then to actually have that evidence on my own phone would just be plain stupid."

Edie threw her hands up in the air. "Well then you should have sent it to my phone because I don't care."

"Well, good to know now," I said.

What I thought was a scrape that the stupid twig had made, was in reality a fairly deep cut. I didn't even feel any pain because I was so pumped up with adrenaline. It was more of an anger adrenaline on account of Lloyd being here in Gran's house. And I didn't bust him. Now there were Lloyd cooties everywhere. It gave me goosebumps just thinking that a stranger was here in the house.

It was kind of funny actually. It was not like I hadn't been into anybody's house in my former life. I just never thought how it would feel to know someone was in mine.

"Oh man, he really searched the place, didn't he?" Edie said.

I looked around and it was only then that I saw things were out of place. It was not that obvious because Gran and I didn't have that much stuff. I went into Gran's bedroom and into the bathroom and everything seemed to be in place there. The clothes were hanging neatly in the closet and the bed was still made and nothing seemed out of place in the bathroom. So Lloyd only had time to search the living room and he'd hit that jackpot really fast.

I plumped down on the chair next to Edie. I pressed a tissue against my foot.

"I have some bandages for you at my house," Edie said.

"Thanks, you can bring them by later," I said.

Then we both sat there in silence, and I had a feeling Edie had to process this as well.

"I can't believe Lloyd was here and he took the cell phone," Edie said. "Just the thought that a stranger was in your house . . ." Edie shuddered. "How do you think he found you?"

"That's what I've been trying to rack my brain about just now. How did he find me?"

This was extremely worrisome. I felt totally blindsided. How did Lloyd know to search this house, and most importantly, what did he know about me and Gran? What was the connection between him and us? Then it dawned on me.

"Edie, have you told Lloyd anything about Gran and me?" I asked and narrowed my eyes at her.

Edie looked surprised. "Who me? I didn't mention your names to Lloyd, it was just . . ." She paused. "Oh, crap."

"What did you tell him?"

"We talked on the phone last week to make the appointment for this week, and you know I told you how we just got to talking about stuff and I happened to mention something about my new neighbor and her granddaughter and how cool they are and that I like them very much and they're just so different and refreshing than the other people around here. That's about it."

I stared at Edie.

"But how did he go from me just mentioning my new neighbors, to you having his cell phone here in this house?"

"Because he had seen me running after him down that hill at the paintball place," I said and let out a sigh. "I didn't have my goggles on. If he was smart, then he kind of got that only seniors were playing that morning. Since I was the only non-senior person there, he put two and two together. If you mentioned a granddaughter and if Lloyd is not completely dumb, then he took a chance that your neighbor's granddaughter was the one running after him on that hill. And he also knew that I saw him dropping his phone, so he probably assumed I took it with me. He had your address because you're his client; hence, he knew where your neighbor and her granddaughter are. And he came looking."

Edie let out a groan and leaned in her seat. Then she got up, took a few steps to the cupboard, and took out a bottle of rum. She took two shot glasses and poured us some. Then she came back to the table and handed me one of the glasses, taking a seat again.

We said cheers, I didn't know what for, and gulped down the rum.

"Piper, I really am so sorry," Edie said, and I could tell that she really felt guilty.

But how could I have been mad at her? I leaned over the table and squeezed her arm. She put her hand over my hand and smiled weakly.

"Round two?" I asked her.

She smiled wide and nodded her head.

I poured us more rum, and we continued to sit there at the table and stare in vain.

"So what now?" Edie finally asked.

I shrugged.

"The meeting tonight is off, right?" Edie asked.

I nodded.

Edie took another gulp of rum and looked around.

"How the heck did Lloyd find the cell phone?"

I told her about me hiding the phone in the sugar jar and Gran switching the jar with the rum bottles. Edie looked down at her glass. "Well, at least it's good-quality rum."

"Yeah, silver lining," I said, and we clinked glasses again.

After another twenty minutes Edie said, "Okay, I don't know where to go from here. That cell phone was all we had. We know about those two bad guys, we know they shot Tammy, we know Lloyd is on the run, we know there was some blackmail and money exchange going on between them, but we don't know where any of them are right now."

"Unfortunately, no," I said. "And Lloyd probably already called them, and they made a new deal. There's probably going to be a money-for-audio-file exchange somewhere. Lloyd needs cash and anything else is too trackable. We have no idea where that exchange will take place."

I was only slightly sorry for not making a copy of the audio file, but any copy I would have made, I had to store somewhere, making me liable in this investigation. And also, who on earth would have thought that Lloyd was going to find Gran's house and search it? I beat myself up that I didn't hide the phone better. Or that I didn't take it with me to breakfast. Funny how I figured the phone was better hidden in Gran's house, as opposed to my back pocket.

Now with the phone gone, my feeling of disappointment really sank in. I felt disappointed that the excitement about the meeting tonight had vanished. I had gotten a whiff of my old life and it smelled good. I felt alive again. And now . . . I had no idea where to go from here.

I drank some more rum. That always helped when I felt bummed out.

"Didn't you memorize that number we called?" Edie asked. "We could call them from our phones."

I gave Edie a look. "From *our* phones?"

She looked at me sheepishly. "Yeah, okay, from *my* phone."

"That's funny, because every time we need to make a call, you conveniently don't have your phone with you and it's always easier to use my phone," I said.

"Yes, but this time, we could really use my phone," Edie said. "I could go get it right now. But how does that help us if we don't know that number?"

I thought about it. I had looked intently and carefully when I analyzed Lloyd's phone. A couple of digits most probably got imprinted in my brain.

I hated this. In my old life, I would have noted the number down at least. But then again, in my old life, I wasn't worried that much about leaving a trace of evidence. Now, with the cops here in Bitter End that were definitely *not* like the cops we had in our pockets back in Oregon, and with being in WITSEC, things were different and I knew I was losing my touch. Or better yet, I had to adapt to this new situation.

"Maybe I know half the number," I said.

Edie immediately stood, searched the living room, looked around and seemed to be at a loss. "You don't have any paper here." It wasn't a question; it was more a reality.

"You mean like a piece of paper?" I asked.

"Yes," Edie replied. "And a pen or something." She looked around more intently. "You really should get some more stuff than you have right now. I remember when you moved in here, you barely had stuff with you. Where are all your belongings from back in Boise? You should have a U-Haul with stuff, at the very least. Even the piece of paper where you had written down potential apartments was from me."

Yes, I did know that, and way to rub salt into the wound. But what Edie didn't know was how Gran and I were yanked out of our home and had to sell almost everything we owned. We had only a few boxes when we arrived in Bitter End.

"We didn't need much stuff with us," I said. "People have too much stuff. Let's go to your house." I hoped that was enough explanation for now and I hoped she didn't inquire further.

"Fine by me," Edie said and headed to the door. "I have lots of stuff. Everything you need, I have."

I thought of the gnomes in her front yard that looked like real little people when it was dark outside and the creepy-looking dolls on her couch, that fit so good with the stuffy, antique vibe of her house. I preferred having no stuff to that stuff.

"Um, Edie," I said, and she stopped and whirled around. I looked down at her glass she was still holding. "Should we take the rum with us?"

"Oh. Not necessary." She gulped the last of the rum and set the glass on the table. "I'm ready. Let's go."

I smiled and followed her to her house.

Chapter Sixteen

We took our seats at Edie's kitchen table. She gave me a bandage for my scrape then she brought a notebook to the table and wrote down the first digits I remembered.

"Now all we need are the rest of the digits," Edie said, looking thoughtful.

"Cool, easy peasy," I replied.

Edie rolled her eyes. "There's no need for sarcasm here. If you could have just memorized the number, we would have it now."

"If I had just... why didn't *you* memorize it?"

"I'm seventy-five years old," Edie threw her hands up in the air. "You're thirty!"

"Thirty-*one*," I said.

"Fine, thirty-one," Edie said. "Much older, indeed."

"Okay, okay, let's not get into a fight," I said, pressing on the bandage. "I need to think. We need the last three digits."

"Exactly," Edie said. "We'll think about all the possible ones and all the possible combinations and I'll write them down."

"Are you kidding me? Do you know how many permutations we'll have?"

"Permutations?" Edie asked. "What are you, good in math or something?

"No, it's basic knowledge," I said.

"Maybe in your neck of the woods in Idaho," Edie snickered.

I shook my head. "Never mind, we're getting sidetracked here. Even if we do write down all the possible . . . combinations, then what? Do we phone each of them and ask for Mr. Moose's henchmen?"

"That's an idea," Edie said in a small voice.

"That's a terrible idea," I said.

"Do you have a better one?"

Damn it. She got me there.

"Besides, do you have somewhere to be and something else to do?" Edie prodded further.

I narrowed my eyes at her. This seemed to be her go-to reason to involve me in her shenanigans. I had nowhere to go so I could take part in whatever Edie's crazy plan was. The worst part was, she was right. I didn't have anywhere to go. Edie knew that and used it against me.

"You do know I *will* get a job one of these days, don't you?" I asked her. "Then you'll have no buddy to take advantage of."

"One of these days?" Edie asked and gave out a snort. "You're heading straight into semipermanent unemployment at this rate."

Wow. That kind of stung.

"I just got here three weeks ago," I said. "Give me a break, will ya?"

"I am," Edie said. "That's why I'm keeping you busy with this."

I gave her a look but couldn't help smiling. "Really? That's why?"

Edie blushed and smiled back. "And because we kind of make a good team."

"That we do," I said and couldn't believe what I just said. Now me and *Gran*, yes. We always were a good team. But because Gran was Gran. She was always packing and wasn't afraid to use it. Edie, on the other hand, made sure her white curls were bouncing every day and that her peach pie came out with the perfect crust. I never would have thought I would ever fight crime with such a person. Better yet, I never would have thought I would fight crime, period. That was like fighting against myself.

"Okay, so let's see," Edie said and turned her attention to the notebook. She wrote down a couple of digit combinations then stopped. "We already have, like, two million possibilities, and we're not done yet. Could you at least try to remember some of the last digits?"

I closed my eyes and thought about it. I imagined me seeing the number on Lloyd's phone. I imagined how I found the audio file that Lloyd sent to that number. I tried to visualize that number. Then I opened my eyes. "The last number is five," I said.

"Are you sure?" Edie asked.

"I'm sure," I said.

Edie wrote down number five. "Okay, now we have only one million other possibilities."

"Do you have somewhere to be and something else to do?" I asked Edie with a grin.

She rolled her eyes. "Very funny, Piper."

"You know what?" I said. "We're never going to actually call all the possible numbers. Let me call a few, maybe we'll get lucky. If not, we have to figure out something else."

"Fine," Edie said and went to her bedroom.

She came back with her brick of a cell phone. I raised an eyebrow.

"What?" Edie said. "It's not one of those fancy phones, but it gets the job done."

I took the phone and pushed some buttons so that Edie's number would be displayed as anonymous. Then I called one of the possible numbers.

"Hello?" a woman's voice croaked out.

I contemplated hanging up but decided to leave no stone unturned. Who knew? Maybe there was a woman involved as well. For all I knew, Mr. Moose could have been a woman.

"I need to speak to Mr. Moose," I said while Edie was sitting next to me, her body all tensed up.

"Who?" The woman said. "I can't hear you."

I rolled my eyes.

"Mr. Moose" I said louder. "I'm looking for Mr. Moose."

"I don't have any booze. What kind of call is this?"

"Never mind," I said and hung up.

This could take a while. And I didn't have that much patience.

"What happened?" Edie asked.

I told her what happened.

"Booze?" Edie cringed. "See? This is what happens when old fools are not wearing their hearing devices."

"At least she had her phone on her," I said. "Unlike some people."

Edie narrowed her eyes at me but didn't say anything.

I tried another number. A man picked up after the first ring.

"Whadda ya want? I told you I don't wanna talk to you. I never wanna talk to you again. You slept with my brother! I don't wanna talk to you ever again and I don't wanna see you ever again. And don't even think 'bout coming over, 'cause I'm changing the locks first thing tomorrow. No, you know what? I'm changing the locks today. I'm gonna change them right now. I'm getting up right now and then I'm gonna—"

"Mr. Moose?" I interrupted the rant.

There was a pause. "Wait. Who the hell is this?"

Then I heard some rustling in the background. "You're not Jennifer." The man stated.

No, thankfully I was not.

"No, I'm looking for—"

He disconnected.

I banged my head against the table. We were getting nowhere this way and I started to develop a craving for Gran's gun.

"They can't all be that bad," Edie said.

"Really? Then you try one."

Edie dialed another number. After a few seconds, she said into the phone, "Hello, my name is . . . um . . . Martha, and . . . um, may I speak with Mr. Moose regarding a matter of—"

Then Edie frowned.

"No . . . I'm not . . ." She paused and listened. "Now wait a minute . . ." She frowned some more. "I most certainly won't!" Then she blushed a bit. "Now listen, young man, you should be ashamed of what you're asking me—"

She took the phone away from her ear. "He hung up."

I grinned. "So what did he want?"

Edie blushed some more. "I can't even repeat what he said to me."

"You still think they all can't be that bad?" I asked and leaned forward in my seat.

Edie let out a breath of air. "People are mean. And stupid."

"I agree," I said.

"Come on, one more," Edie said and handed me the phone.

"Fine, but last one." I dialed another number.

After the third ring, a man's voice answered and said hello. The voice sounded familiar. It was Thug #1.

"I said hello?" he repeated in his dumb-sounding tone.

Okay, I had to admit, I did not expect this. And again, I felt just a bit unprepared about what to say.

I cleared my throat. "It's me again. We need to change the time for tonight. Nine p.m. instead of eight p.m."

There was a pause, and I could almost hear the wheels beginning to spin in his brain. "But the guy said ten p.m. You working with him now?"

I smiled. At least the doofus gave us one bit of information. "Yes, um, we're working together. So just to confirm, it's ten p.m. tonight and where exactly—"

At that moment, I heard rumblings on the phone. "Who is this?" Uh-oh. That was thug #2 and, as I recalled, he seemed a bit brighter than his companion.

"This is Lloyd's partner," I said. "The deal we made is—"

"I don't know who you are, but you're not Lloyd's partner and our deal is off," he said and hung up.

Crap.

"Oh my god, it was them, wasn't it?" Edie said, wide-eyed.

I nodded and reported back our short conversation.

"I don't know what I'm more shocked about," Edie said. "The fact that the guy told you the meeting time, or the fact that we actually got the right number."

"I would say both," I said then paused. "Wow."

"I know," Edie said. "It's good we know the time now, right?"

"We have two problems regarding the meeting time. First, we don't know the location. And second, if they're smart, they'll change the time knowing that I know about it too."

"But I thought you said those guys are pretty dumb," Edie said.

"They are," I replied. "Well, one of them is. The other one seems to have a better grasp of reality. Then again, I'm not sure the second one even got the fact that the first one told me about the meeting time."

"Let's hope that he didn't," Edie said.

"And then what?" I asked. "If we don't know the location, then it doesn't help we know the time. It's not like we can search every corner of the whole town at exactly ten p.m."

"You're right about that," Edie said. "So what do we do now?"

"I have no idea," I replied.

We sat there at Edie's table, staring at the floor, and not coming up with any good ideas.

"So let's assume Lloyd is going to meet with those guys tonight at ten p.m.," Edie said. "Lloyd is going to hand them over the audio file in exchange for blackmail money, then Lloyd is probably going to skip town and, like you always say, get a fake passport and leave the country."

I nodded. "That's what I would do."

Edie stared at me. "Theoretically, if you were a criminal, right?"

"Right."

"Then we can't let Lloyd and those guys get away with it," Edie said.

"You know, exchanges like that almost always don't end the way they're expected," I said. "Usually, one party or both want to have their cake and eat it too. In this case, how can those thugs trust that Lloyd hasn't made a copy of the audio file and won't blackmail them again in the future? Or how can Lloyd rely on the fact that those guys managed to get whatever amount of money in this short amount of time? Maybe those guys are rolling up hundred-dollar bills over five-spots."

Edie stared some more. "Whoa, you're good. And then if Lloyd catches on, then he won't hand them over the file."

"Or he already hands them the file, and realizes only after that he's been duped," I said. "It can get pretty heated pretty fast, and one group or the other could very well have an ace up their sleeve. Or some guns ready for action."

Edie shuddered. "Yeah, okay, I get it. Boy, I wouldn't want to watch those crime shows you do. I would get nightmares."

If only Edie knew those crime shows I kept mentioning had actually been my real life.

There was a loud knock at Edie's door and we both started.

"I swear, if that's Ryker again, I'm going to jump out this window and bail," I said to Edie as she headed for the door.

"Well, at least he didn't just come in," Edie said.

She opened the door and there stood Gran, hands on hips. She looked at Edie, then looked over Edie's shoulder at me.

"What's going on here?" Gran asked.

Edie frowned. "You mean, more than usual?"

"My place looks like it was searched," Gran said.

Uh-oh. I forgot about Gran. I assumed she would spend the whole day at the rec hall playing poker. I didn't expect her back at the house this soon.

Edie sighed. "Come on in, Dorothy. There's been some developments."

Gran took a seat on Edie's couch, pushing away one of the freakish-looking dolls.

"What did you do now?" Gran asked.

***

Two hours later, we were mentally exhausted. Gran and I were still at Edie's, having dissected and talked about the Lloyd situation until there was no more to say.

"I can't believe you let that slimeball enter my house," Gran said.

"Well, it's not that I let him," I said. "I'm just as pissed as you are that he did."

"Well, if you hadn't been involved in this, then that wouldn't have happened," Gran said.

"And if we wouldn't have been involved in this, then where would our money be?" Edie asked.

Gran opened her mouth, then closed it. I knew what she wanted to say. She wanted to say it was

Edie's fault in the first place. She let herself get defrauded out of the money. The old Gran would have just come out and said it, but apparently the new Gran had learned a couple of things since she got here.

"By the way, if you wouldn't have switched the sugar jar with the rum, we wouldn't be having this problem," I said to Gran.

"You could have told me you hid that phone in the jar," Gran said. "Besides, rum is way more important than sugar."

I huffed and Gran blew out a raspberry.

"Okay, this is real mature," Edie said. "Listen up, we're getting nowhere this way. We have six hours until the meeting takes place, and that is only if they haven't changed the time. I say we go to the cops."

"No way." "Not in a million years," Gran and I said in unison.

"Why not?" Edie threw her hands up in the air. "You would rather let Lloyd and those bad guys get away?"

Gran and I exchanged glances. Neither of us was able to say no.

This whole going-to-the-cops-or-else-the-bad-guys-got-away thing was totally new to me. I didn't even have a strict separation between good guys and bad guys. That didn't exist in my world. At least, in my former world. There was *us* and *the others*, whoever those others were: cops, feds, other gangs, ex-cons . . . we didn't care. The line was very blurry between good and bad.

Now, Gran and I were forced to think like regular civilians. Like, what was that? How did that even go? I saw how Edie thought and I tried to emulate that. But I didn't feel it from my heart. Back home, we didn't take care of things by going to the cops. We took care of them ourselves. If we didn't succeed, we tried again the next day. Going to law enforcement agencies of any kind was simply not an option. It was laughable at best.

I was just about to tell Edie we were going to figure out something, when there was a loud knock on the door. Again.

All three of us jumped.

Gran said, "If that's your grandson, I'm diving out the window."

I laughed. "I'll be right behind you."

"Jesus, what's up with people today?" Edie said, half-annoyed as she headed to the door.

"Well, they could just come right in after they knock, like you did," Gran deadpanned, and Edie stuck her tongue out at her.

Edie opened the door to Sam. Which made me wonder how come we didn't hear her falling-to-pieces-any-moment-now car outside. I really must be losing my touch.

Sam came in, gave Edie a hug, and scanned the room. Her eyes landed on Gran. She looked Gran up and down, took in her biker outfit, and frowned. Then she turned back to Edie.

"I need to talk to you," Sam said to Edie. Then Sam looked at me. "And to you too."

I had a bad feeling about this.

"We can talk here," I said. "This is my grandmother, and she's always in the loop, so . . ."

Sam hesitated for a bit then said, "Whose cell phone did I crack?"

Uh-oh.

Edie cleared her throat. "What . . . what do you mean? What cell phone? The one with the PIN number? Well, that's mine, like I said."

"It's not yours," Sam said. "I installed a tracking program on the phone and the phone is far away from here right now."

Chapter Seventeen

We all stared.

I scoured my brain for a lie, but I came up empty. At the same time, I fought the urge to do a happy dance right there on Edie's table, because now we could track down Lloyd if Sam shared that info with us. I wasn't sure if she already knew who the phone belonged to and if she'd just tested us to see if we were telling the truth.

Unfortunately, it was time to come clean with Sam. I knew we couldn't get out of this one. If she called the cops, though, I would bail and deny everything.

Like reading my mind, Edie said, "Sam, why don't you sit down?"

As Sam took the few steps to the armchair across from the couch, Gran scanned her outfit. Sam was wearing a plaid skirt today and a black T-shirt, combined with her black Chucks and red socks that were rolled up to her knees.

"Interesting style," Gran said to Sam. "I like it."

Sam took in Gran's outfit as well. "I like yours too. It's definitely different than those other . . . the people around . . . I mean, than what you would usually see at a retirement complex."

I could tell Sam had a hard time articulating what she really meant. It's not like she was going to say, "You look really hip for someone your age."

Gran's mouth twitched at the corners, and Sam smiled at her. Was that some sort of code for "I respect you because I like your outfit?"

Edie made the introductions between Gran and Sam. I had to give Gran props for not even flinching about Sam's last name.

"So, care to tell me what's going on?" Sam asked.

Edie and I told her about the phone belonging to Lloyd, and the thugs with the unknown number, and the meeting that was supposed to happen tonight at ten, if that was still on.

"Okay," Sam said, letting out a long breath. "I did not expect this. I thought the phone maybe belonged to another resident and you're playing pranks on them or something. I thought about just letting it go and letting you deal with it among yourselves."

I was dumbstruck. But of course. A prank on another resident. That would have been the most perfect lie. Damn it.

"So why did you come here, then?" I asked her.

She shrugged. "My gut told me I had to know what was going on."

"So you tracked down the phone?" I asked and tried not to be too excited about it. I so wanted to know where Lloyd was hiding.

Sam nodded. "Yes, as long as the phone is turned on, I know where it is."

"And would you care to tell us where it is?" I asked.

Sam waited for a couple of beats. "What is this? Vigilante justice? You're going to venture out for yourselves and apprehend Lloyd and those other guys? Why didn't you go to the cops?" Sam turned to Edie. "Why didn't you tell Ryker?"

"Well, how could I do that without getting myself into trouble?" Edie asked. "And without getting Piper and Dorothy into trouble?"

"Me?" Gran said. "I'll have you know I refused to be involved in anything. I was forced to get involved."

"Forced?" Sam asked.

Edie waved it away. "Never mind her, she's just overreacting. She loves being involved."

Gran gave Edie her death stare. Ha—Edie got Gran good. Again.

"Sam, you know I have a personal interest in this. It's my money and the residents' money that Lloyd and Tammy stole from us. I couldn't just stand around and wait for other people to handle this stuff. So we went out to search for clues, to search for Lloyd, and we got deeper and deeper until the point where, if I went to the police, I would have to tell them everything we did, and that would get us into trouble. Especially with Ryker. He would probably lock me in my own house."

Sam smiled. "I'm sure he would do just that."

"Yes, exactly," Edie said. "Now we still have a few hours until the meeting tonight and we need to come up with something good."

Nobody said anything for a long moment.

"Look, I don't know what you got yourself into here," Sam said, "but this is totally out of your league. I will talk to Ryker, and I will talk to the cops, and I will make sure to leave you out of it, if that's even possible. They will ask where I've gotten this information from, but I can probably get away with saying it's a confidential source."

My heart sank. It was like I had a toy and now somebody took that plaything away from me. I kind of wanted to take part in whatever would go down tonight. That rush of anticipation about a meeting including a money exchange—where guns were involved, and strategies were being laid out to double-cross the other party—that was always one of the highlights of my former life. And now it had been taken away from me. Again.

"You almost seem disappointed," Sam said to me. "Who are you anyway?"

"Who am I?" I said. "I'm Edie's neighbor. We've already been through this."

Sam eyed me suspiciously. "There's something off. Why didn't you go to the cops like normal people do?"

"Like normal people?" Edie said and I could see she felt offended.

"I mean, like normal people of her age," Sam said and closed her eyes tight. "I mean, not *her* age, I mean . . ."

I grinned wide. She couldn't get out of this one. Best just to say nothing else, or she would only make it worse.

Gran cackled. "This is fun."

Edie crossed her arms and stared at Sam. "Thanks for the compliments."

"You know what I mean, Edie," Sam said. "Either way, you shouldn't have withheld evidence. What did you plan on doing anyway? One civilian and two retirees were going to bust some criminals all by themselves?"

I would have told her I was not a regular civilian, and at least one of the retirees was also not a regular retiree. I couldn't say that to her, though.

"Like we have said, we tried to come up with a plan for tonight," I said.

"Ryker told me you're a hairdresser," Sam said. "What on earth would make you think you can handle this?"

I felt my jaw clench. The urge to let her know who I was became overwhelming. Gran could sense my edginess. "It's okay, hairdressers are capable of doing a lot, right?" Gran fixed me with a look that said, *Don't go berserk now, it's not worth it.* That was the thing with Gran. She knew when to stay calm and she had a way of calming me down too.

"Yes, I'm a hairdresser," I said to Sam. "But I still have a brain and can put myself into the shoes of other people. Most criminals today are so very stupid. It's not that hard to see right through them."

"And how do you know how criminals are nowadays?" Sam asked.

"Oh, she watches those crime shows all the time," Edie said. "The things she knows sometimes, it's frightening."

Geez, thanks a lot, Edie.

"Edie is right and that's the truth," I said. "Which is why I'm curious: why did you even think in the first place to track down that phone?"

Sam smiled. "Because I knew something was up. It was just my gut telling me so."

"Well, your gut was spot on," I said.

"Can we wrap this up soon, ladies?" Gran asked. "Do you have a plan for tonight or not?"

"I already told you what the plan is," Sam said. "I'll go to the cops with this and try to leave you out of it, for Edie's sake."

Try to leave us out of it? I did not like the sound of that.

"Look, do what you want, but if the cops come knocking, I'll deny everything," I said.

"Me too," Gran said. "I didn't want to get involved in the first place."

"Well, if they're denying it, then so will I," Edie said.

She winked at me.

Sam rubbed her forehead. "Fine, then you'll all deny it," she said.

"Would the cops accept your tracking program as viable evidence?" I asked. "Or better yet, any lawyer Lloyd would get?"

"Yes, they will," Sam said. "I didn't steal his phone to put the tracking in. It was fair game at the point when Edie handed it to me."

Well then, at least she had that.

I stood. "If we're done here, we'll get out of your hair."

"But . . . but . . ." Edie looked frantically from me to Gran and to Sam. "This is it, then?"

Oh yes, I could see Edie was just as disappointed as I was.

"If Sam is going to the cops, there's nothing for us to do. We're done here."

It almost kind of hurt saying it. Deep down inside I didn't want it to be over.

"But . . . surely there's something we could do," Edie said.

"Edie, there's nothing you can do," Sam said. "You have to trust law enforcement and Ryker that they won't let Lloyd get away. You know that."

Edie pouted. "It's just that, I felt so useful, you know? I felt more in control being involved."

Another checkmate statement from Edie. That was exactly how I felt.

"Will you let us know how things turned out?" I asked Sam.

She nodded.

FOOL ME ONCE

Gran and I headed for the door, but just as I was reaching for the knob I turned around. "Sam, just out of curiosity, where is Lloyd now? I understand you're going to the cops and all, and we won't interfere. I'm just curious where that weasel has been hiding."

Sam studied me for a bit then probably decided I was telling the truth. "He's at the Sunrise Peak Motel off the highway."

"Thank you," I said. Then I turned to Edie. "Don't be sad, okay? Surely, the cops will catch Lloyd and the other guys." What else was I supposed to say to her? I tried to be comforting. "And, hey, now you can enjoy that spa gift basket. You haven't even touched it yet." I nodded toward the basket, that sat between two plants against the wall.

"I guess you're right," Edie said. "There's nothing some good foot powder can't make right again."

I smiled. "See? You're already feeling better."

Then I left with Gran close on my heels.

We passed by Sam's car that was parked by the curb. It really did look like it was about to fall into a thousand pieces at any moment now. I was still shocked I hadn't heard the car driving in.

Back at the house, Gran went straight for the fridge and brought us two cold beers.

"Well, that took an unexpected turn," Gran said, crashing on the couch and taking off her boots.

"That it did," I said and sat at the kitchen table.

Gran turned to me. "You look peeved. Why do you look peeved? Are you really sorry you're out of the equation?"

I stared at the floor. "I kinda am."

"Well, get over it," Gran said. "It's their business, not ours. We're dealing with people here who like going to the cops. Did you ever? Like, going to the cops—what is that?"

"I guess it's what normal people do," I said.

Gran snorted. "Yeah, I'll never understand that."

I took a swig of my beer. It was harder letting this go than I thought. But I needed to let this go. Sam was going to Ryker and to the cops with all the information she got from us. They didn't even need the time of the meeting. They could just track Lloyd's phone and follow him to wherever he went. It was a perfect plan. As long as Lloyd's phone was turned on, they could get him at any time. They just needed to make sure they got the other guys as well.

I cared more about the getting Lloyd part, since they probably needed him to get to the money he and Tammy stole, but I would have found it even more satisfying busting Lloyd blackmailing the other guys. That would net him a higher sentence in the pokey. I had really come to dislike Lloyd Feldman with all my being.

I heard a loud rumbling outside and moved to the window. It was Sam leaving. I wondered if she'd go to Ryker or the cops first.

Ugh. I moved away from the window. I tried to force myself to think of something else. And I also tried to force myself not to worry about the cops or if they would come after Gran and me. I meant what I'd said to Sam. If they came to us, we would deny everything.

It was almost 7:00 p.m.; that meant three more hours until showtime. If the time of the show hadn't changed. God, I so wished I could be a part of this. But without the cops and without Ryker. Just me and Gran. Yeah, okay, and Edie. She could have been our lookout.

"Stop thinking about it," Gran said. "There's nothing you can do." She took the cell phone and started typing. Gran and I shared the same phone.

"Are you texting anyone?" I asked. "I've never seen you do it since we got here."

"So what if I'm texting someone?" Gran said.

"That's totally fine, it's just unusual. So who are you texting?"

"Just some people around here," Gran said.

I waited for further explanation but none came. "Are you texting Theodore or are you texting your poker-playing buddies?"

"Obviously I'm not texting Theodore," Gran said, her eyes still on the screen.

"Why obviously?" I asked, already knowing the answer.

Gran gave me a look.

Yup, I knew the answer.

"So you're going out tonight?" I asked.

"What else is there to do?" Gran asked as the cell phone vibrated. She looked down at her screen. "Okay, so Irene is free tonight. What else would she be doing around here anyway?"

While Gran was busy texting her new poker friends, I looked out the window toward Edie's house. I thought about how Ryker would react when he found out what kind of evidence we had been withholding from him. Or maybe Sam made good on her promise and left me out of the narrative. I was so deeply involved, that would be hard to do.

Then I thought about Sam. Samantha Braveheart. She seemed like a clever cookie. Too bad she gave out the vibe she didn't like me, but hey, what was new?

I realized it was dinner time, but I wasn't really hungry. Gran didn't rush out to the dining hall either. So I decided to watch some brain-numbing shows on TV. I had to take my mind off the Lloyd story somehow.

I parked myself on the couch next to Gran and asked her when she was going to meet her group. Gran said it was still undecided, because one of them may or may not have had shooting pains down their left arm.

"How can anyone be unsure of that?" I asked, frowning.

Gran rolled her eyes. "Beats me. Arthur lifted some fifteen-pounders. His arm hurts now. He probably hadn't exercised since the eighties, and his muscles gave out on him."

Gran took the remote and zipped through the channels.

One hour later, Gran and I were still on the couch watching TV and we were on our second beer. We'd also gotten to be slow drinkers around here.

I got up and stretched my limbs. "You know what, Gran?" I eyed the gift baskets. "I think I'm going to try that foot powder Edie's been talking about. You should try it too since you're the one walking around in boots here all the time."

Gran looked at her feet then looked at her biker boots then looked over at the basket. She shrugged. "Fine, I guess there's no harm in trying," she said. "Might as well do that too, if I'm condemned to rot here in this retirement hell."

"You know very well it's not that bad," I said.

Gran mumbled something but I ignored her.

We unwrapped the baskets and pulled out face masks, a lot of soaps, lotions, small shampoo samples, and a plethora of food powder.

"What's up with these people around here and foot powder?" Gran asked.

"I have no idea, but I guess it doesn't hurt if we try it," I said.

I looked at the bandage on the sole of my foot. I'd have to sprinkle the powder around the scrape, if that was possible.

We took some paper towels and spread them on the floor in front of the couch. Gran rolled up her jeans to her knees. Just as we were about to open the container of foot powder, Edie came bursting inside. Gran instantly reached for her gun, but I was faster this time, and blocked her hand. Who the hell keeps leaving the door unlocked?

she gave out the vibe she didn't like me, but hey, what was new?

I realized it was dinner time, but I wasn't really hungry. Gran didn't rush out to the dining hall either. So I decided to watch some brain-numbing shows on TV. I had to take my mind off the Lloyd story somehow.

I parked myself on the couch next to Gran and asked her when she was going to meet her group. Gran said it was still undecided, because one of them may or may not have had shooting pains down their left arm.

"How can anyone be unsure of that?" I asked, frowning.

Gran rolled her eyes. "Beats me. Arthur lifted some fifteen-pounders. His arm hurts now. He probably hadn't exercised since the eighties, and his muscles gave out on him."

Gran took the remote and zipped through the channels.

One hour later, Gran and I were still on the couch watching TV and we were on our second beer. We'd also gotten to be slow drinkers around here.

I got up and stretched my limbs. "You know what, Gran?" I eyed the gift baskets. "I think I'm going to try that foot powder Edie's been talking about. You should try it too since you're the one walking around in boots here all the time."

Gran looked at her feet then looked at her biker boots then looked over at the basket. She shrugged. "Fine, I guess there's no harm in trying," she said. "Might as well do that too, if I'm condemned to rot here in this retirement hell."

"You know very well it's not that bad," I said.

Gran mumbled something but I ignored her.

We unwrapped the baskets and pulled out face masks, a lot of soaps, lotions, small shampoo samples, and a plethora of food powder.

"What's up with these people around here and foot powder?" Gran asked.

"I have no idea, but I guess it doesn't hurt if we try it," I said.

I looked at the bandage on the sole of my foot. I'd have to sprinkle the powder around the scrape, if that was possible.

We took some paper towels and spread them on the floor in front of the couch. Gran rolled up her jeans to her knees. Just as we were about to open the container of foot powder, Edie came bursting inside. Gran instantly reached for her gun, but I was faster this time, and blocked her hand. Who the hell keeps leaving the door unlocked?

Edie looked flushed and she was barefoot. She held her hands high and even her white curls looked totally out of place. She took in the paper towels and the foot powder and yelled, "Don't do it! Don't use the foot powder!"

Chapter Eighteen

EDIE SNATCHED THE powder containers from our hands.

"What the . . .?" Gran asked. "Are you crazy?"

Then I looked down and saw Edie's feet had bright red spots.

"What happened to your feet?" I asked.

"It's Lucretia!" Edie yelled. "That shrew put something in the powder. My feet are splotchy! And they itch! I swear, I'm going to take that witch down!"

Gran cracked a smile while Edie was pacing around the room.

"Why are you smiling?" Edie stopped and asked.

"She took revenge on you," Gran said. "On all of us. She futzed around with the foot powder containers. I can respect that."

Edie threw her hands in the air. "You can respect that? What the hell are you talking about? How can you respect that? Giving someone a rash in this most evil way is earning respect?"

This was often the situation with Gran and Edie. It was stuff like this that showed me the difference between them. I knew exactly where Gran came from. In our world, even someone trying to screw you over—the more creative, the better—could earn some sort of respect. It was weird, yes, but that's just the way it was. And then we had Edie, a regular retiree, as Gran put it, who obviously didn't see the whole picture. She just saw what was in front of her. Which was now itchy feet.

"How about you thanking me for warning you just in time?" Edie asked, looking down at our non-splotchy tootsies.

I stopped Gran from saying anything else about Sourpuss and respect. "Yes, you're right," I said to Edie. "We are thankful you warned us just in time. But what about your feet? Do you need to go to a doctor?"

Edie limped to the kitchen table. "No, I don't think so." She touched her feet and looked at them from all sides. "I have some lotion for skin rashes at home."

"So you haven't used it yet?" I asked, confused.

"No," Edie said. "I came to you first. Well, actually, I called Beatrice first so she can tell the others. And then I ran over here. A golf cart almost hit me."

"Oh my god, Edie!" I said. "Please pay attention on the street!"

"Well, my feet were burning," Edie said. "Do you know how hot that concrete gets around here? I had to be fast."

A rush of coziness filled my chest. Maybe sometimes it wasn't so bad being just a regular retiree. One who thinks of the others, before she takes care of herself.

"That was very nice of you, Edie," I said and elbowed Gran. "Thank you."

"Oh yes," Gran cleared her throat. "We are definitely thanking you." She said in a rather passive voice.

"You're kind of bummed out now, aren't you?" I asked Edie. "You were really looking forward to this foot powder."

"I was looking forward to it, yes; and I'm not bummed, I'm pissed," Edie said. "Wait till I get my hands on her."

"What did she put into the powder, anyway?" Gran said. "Can you prove that she tinkered with it?"

Edie stared. "I don't need any proof, I know she did it."

Gran rolled her eyes. "Okay, if you say so."

"I do say so," Edie said.

"Are there even any signs that someone fiddled with the powder?" Gran asked. "Was the container sealed?"

We all looked at Gran's and my foot powder containers. We'd opened them just like that. No plastic wrapper. No tamper seals. No nothing.

"Maybe it's the powder itself," Gran said. "Maybe it was the manufacturer who botched it."

Edie shook her head. "No way, Jose. I just know it in my gut that it was Lucretia."

"Fine," Gran said and put the container aside. "Then it was Lucretia."

Edie sighed. "This can't get any worse. First, we're out of the loop with Lloyd and those guys, and now this."

There was a pause. I honestly didn't know what to say to her. I was bummed as well. Or maybe even pissed, just as Edie put it.

"Did Sam say anything else after we left?" I asked.

Edie shook her head. "Not really. She tried to make it clear that I shouldn't have withheld information, especially from Ryker, blah blah blah, heard it before. She didn't say anything else that could be useful. Just what you already know. Lloyd is at that motel." Edie paused. "You don't think maybe we could go—"

I put my hand up. "No way. I know what you're thinking, and no, we're not going to the motel."

"Why not?" Edie said. "We're already so involved in this."

"You can be sure they're going to lock us up for interfering with their investigation if we go to that motel," I said. Not to mention Gran and I would be out of the witness protection program.

"But we're not sure of that," Edie said. "I'm thinking we could just lurk around somewhere and just watch what happens."

"Yeah sure, because that went so good the last couple of times," Gran said.

Edie ignored Gran's comment, then said, "Come on, we have to do something. I can't just sit around here thinking about the meeting and knowing I'm not going to be part of it, knowing I'm not going to contribute in any way. I'm going nuts."

I sighed. I was probably going to go nuts listening to Edie about how she was going nuts. I was just as bummed as she was, knowing we were out of the loop. However, knowing that getting back into the loop would mean dodging cops and PIs, that was more reason for me to go nuts. Gran and I had a lot more at stake.

"Okay, then how about this," Edie said. "Let's assume those guys are really dumb and didn't change the time and they're still meeting at ten p.m. Yes?"

"Yes, so?" I asked.

"Let's just assume that," Edie said. "Okay?"

"Fine, let's assume the meeting is still at ten p.m.," I said.

"Good," Edie said. "Now about the location. Piper, what made you suggest Liberty Square when you talked to those guys? What was your reasoning for it?"

"My reasoning was that Liberty Square is an open, public place with enough people around to avoid a bloody showdown." I said. "If I would have chosen something like a warehouse, well, that's just asking for trouble. In public places, people are usually less inclined to pull out their guns."

Edie glanced at Gran. "You don't say."

Gran rolled her eyes and rolled down her jeans.

"For most people, anyway," I said, smiling.

"Interesting," Edie said and seemed to think about it. "So what if Lloyd had the same reasoning and chose Liberty Square for the meeting as well?"

"Honestly, I don't know how smart this Lloyd is for a deal like that," I said. "I mean, yes, he managed not to get caught until now and he knew to search Gran's house. That suggests maybe an ounce of intelligence, but still, it would be an awfully big coincidence for him to choose Liberty Square for the meeting as well."

"But let's assume that he did," Edie said. "Then we could drive by Liberty Square at ten and see if there's something fishy going on. Liberty Square is an open public space, just like you said. We have every right to be out for a stroll tonight in that area."

"We?" Gran said. "What do you mean by we?"

"What do you think I mean by we?" Edie said, leaning forward in her chair. "We're not going to have this conversation again, are we? You're involved in this too."

Gran looked at me like she was begging for help. I put my hands up. "Sorry, Gran, Edie is quite convincing."

"Well, isn't that just sweet?" Gran mumbled.

"Are you meeting your poker buddies tonight?" I asked her.

Gran paused, then said, "No, they can't make it tonight."

was more reason for me to go nuts. Gran and I had a lot more at stake.

"Okay, then how about this," Edie said. "Let's assume those guys are really dumb and didn't change the time and they're still meeting at ten p.m. Yes?"

"Yes, so?" I asked.

"Let's just assume that," Edie said. "Okay?"

"Fine, let's assume the meeting is still at ten p.m.," I said.

"Good," Edie said. "Now about the location. Piper, what made you suggest Liberty Square when you talked to those guys? What was your reasoning for it?"

"My reasoning was that Liberty Square is an open, public place with enough people around to avoid a bloody showdown." I said. "If I would have chosen something like a warehouse, well, that's just asking for trouble. In public places, people are usually less inclined to pull out their guns."

Edie glanced at Gran. "You don't say."

Gran rolled her eyes and rolled down her jeans.

"For most people, anyway," I said, smiling.

"Interesting," Edie said and seemed to think about it. "So what if Lloyd had the same reasoning and chose Liberty Square for the meeting as well?"

"Honestly, I don't know how smart this Lloyd is for a deal like that," I said. "I mean, yes, he managed not to get caught until now and he knew to search Gran's house. That suggests maybe an ounce of intelligence, but still, it would be an awfully big coincidence for him to choose Liberty Square for the meeting as well."

"But let's assume that he did," Edie said. "Then we could drive by Liberty Square at ten and see if there's something fishy going on. Liberty Square is an open public space, just like you said. We have every right to be out for a stroll tonight in that area."

"We?" Gran said. "What do you mean by we?"

"What do you think I mean by we?" Edie said, leaning forward in her chair. "We're not going to have this conversation again, are we? You're involved in this too."

Gran looked at me like she was begging for help. I put my hands up. "Sorry, Gran, Edie is quite convincing."

"Well, isn't that just sweet?" Gran mumbled.

"Are you meeting your poker buddies tonight?" I asked her.

Gran paused, then said, "No, they can't make it tonight."

"Oh, it was Arthur, wasn't it?" Edie said. "Who may or may not have had shooting pains down his arm."

"How do you know about that?" I asked Edie.

"Beatrice told me," she replied.

Duh. I forgot how gossip worked around here.

"So this means that you're free tonight," Edie said to Gran.

"Great," Gran said. "But if the cops bust us, I'm going to tell them you forced me to come along."

Edie waved her hand in dismissal. "Yeah, sure, whatever."

I weighed my options. When it really came to it, I had to choose between staying in the witness protection program and potentially being kicked out of it. It could only be one way or the other. Ugh. But I couldn't change who I was at my core. So I agreed to Edie's plan. She was right. I couldn't just sit around on the couch watching TV knowing the meeting was going to go down. It would have driven me insane as well. Better to just hop in the car and drive around town and see what was up. At least this way, we would feel like we were doing something. I was sure Ryker would call Edie tonight and tell her they caught Lloyd and the other guys. So we would be staying out of trouble but still have the feeling that we were doing something.

We still had about two hours until showtime, so Edie went to her place to take care of her feet, Gran said she was going to stay in the house, and I decided to go out for a walk and clear my head.

First, I ate a bag of chips since I hadn't had any proper dinner. Not that chips were ever a proper dinner, but I still wasn't hungry.

I exchanged the flip-flops for the sneakers, especially since now I had that stupid scrape on my foot. Then I went outside. It was dark but still warm. The streetlights were on. Now and then I nodded to one of the other residents also out for a walk.

As I walked around aimlessly, I took in the pastel-colored houses with the gnomes in the front yards and thought about my current life versus my former life. Just as I often did. I got a soaring ache in my heart, a pining for my old life. For my day-to-day life. For the people that I knew. For the house I lived in with Gran.

When would it stop hurting? Would it ever stop hurting? Or would my former life just get blurrier and blurrier as time went by, making it someday just a distant memory? Dillon had told us we could never go back home again. That was a hard concept to

"Oh, it was Arthur, wasn't it?" Edie said. "Who may or may not have had shooting pains down his arm."

"How do you know about that?" I asked Edie.

"Beatrice told me," she replied.

Duh. I forgot how gossip worked around here.

"So this means that you're free tonight," Edie said to Gran.

"Great," Gran said. "But if the cops bust us, I'm going to tell them you forced me to come along."

Edie waved her hand in dismissal. "Yeah, sure, whatever."

I weighed my options. When it really came to it, I had to choose between staying in the witness protection program and potentially being kicked out of it. It could only be one way or the other. Ugh. But I couldn't change who I was at my core. So I agreed to Edie's plan. She was right. I couldn't just sit around on the couch watching TV knowing the meeting was going to go down. It would have driven me insane as well. Better to just hop in the car and drive around town and see what was up. At least this way, we would feel like we were doing something. I was sure Ryker would call Edie tonight and tell her they caught Lloyd and the other guys. So we would be staying out of trouble but still have the feeling that we were doing something.

We still had about two hours until showtime, so Edie went to her place to take care of her feet, Gran said she was going to stay in the house, and I decided to go out for a walk and clear my head.

First, I ate a bag of chips since I hadn't had any proper dinner. Not that chips were ever a proper dinner, but I still wasn't hungry.

I exchanged the flip-flops for the sneakers, especially since now I had that stupid scrape on my foot. Then I went outside. It was dark but still warm. The streetlights were on. Now and then I nodded to one of the other residents also out for a walk.

As I walked around aimlessly, I took in the pastel-colored houses with the gnomes in the front yards and thought about my current life versus my former life. Just as I often did. I got a soaring ache in my heart, a pining for my old life. For my day-to-day life. For the people that I knew. For the house I lived in with Gran.

When would it stop hurting? Would it ever stop hurting? Or would my former life just get blurrier and blurrier as time went by, making it someday just a distant memory? Dillon had told us we could never go back home again. That was a hard concept to grasp. You couldn't just take people out of their homes and tell them they were never going back again. That just wasn't . . . done.

Sometimes I missed my old life and old home so much, I even thought about going back to Oregon in disguise. Why wouldn't that work? I could put on a wig and wear non-biker clothes. But then what? Walk up and down the street where I used to live? See strangers going in and out of my home? How could I just be there without talking to any people that I knew? I wouldn't be able to talk to anybody because most of them were part of the Oregon Falcons. Who were now after us. Surely, they'd put up a bounty for finding and killing us.

What about my girlfriends? There were only a few, since I always seemed to get along better with guys, but those few girlfriends and I had been through thick and thin together. Breakups with boyfriends, surveillance going wrong, bailing someone out of a night in jail—when a rookie cop had no idea who he or she was dealing with—the usual stuff for me back then. Fast-forward to now in Florida. I was spending my time with people who were almost triple my age, who collected yard gnomes for fun and played paintball to win a spa basket, including one person giving the others skin rashes as payback. I really missed people my age.

However, this longing was also met with fear and anxiety. How could I build a friendship based on lies? How could I look someone in the eye and lie to them about my background and about why I was living in Florida? What kind of friendship was that?

Then Edie came to mind. I was lying to her all the time.

I tried to shake these thoughts away as I went on with my walk. When we moved here three weeks ago, I never would have thought I would end up involved in murders that didn't even have anything to do with me. So why did I get involved? It was probably a combination of lack of activities, feeling useful—again, lack of activities—and somehow our neighbor Edie growing on me.

Thinking of Edie made me think of Ryker. Six feet two of perfectly engineered features. I shook my head. It didn't make any sense to think about Ryker. I had no idea why my thoughts even went there. Maybe I just missed being attracted to a man, and Ryker was the only one around. I'd had two steady boyfriends in my life. The first one I dated for two years, and the second one, for one year. They were both part of the Falcons. So they knew who I was.

FOOL ME ONCE

There were no lies about our personas. There was a potential third boyfriend, but he was all into marriage and kids right away, and I wasn't ready for that. At thirty-one now, I still wasn't sure if I was ready for that. I guess time would tell. But how could anyone have a family and be in the witness protection program at the same time? Not telling your spouse and your kids who you really are? I could almost laugh. WITSEC had some serious deficits in their handbook rules.

It was shortly after 9:00 p.m. when I got back to the house. I realized it was a good thing to go out, or I would have gone nuts from having these existential thoughts.

Ten minutes later, Edie came by and then we all hopped into the Ford Taurus and sped away.

Edie was wearing socks and her chunky sandals.

"That looks hideous," Gran said. "At least wear some tennis shoes if you're putting on socks."

"I don't have any tennis shoes," Edie said. "We're in Florida here, although I know you try to tell yourself otherwise." Edie glanced at Gran's boots. "I put some antihistamine lotion on my feet, and I need to wear the socks now. But who knows? Maybe I'll spark a trend."

"If that trend is ever coming here, shoot me now," Gran deadpanned.

It was 9:45 when we arrived at Liberty Square. This idea Edie had was either pure genius or the dumbest idea ever. There usually was a thin line between them.

The square itself was pedestrian only, but there were narrow side streets going to and from the area. I parked on one of those streets where we had a clear view of the square but were not too close. We needed to keep a low profile. The square and the streets were lit and there was still a good amount of people walking by. I'd never been in town at this time of day so this was new for me as well. I was surprised to find out Bitter End was more vibrant than I had expected.

"You know, I kind of feel stupid doing this," I said. "It's ten at night and I'm sitting in my car on pretend stakeout, hoping to spy something that may very well not happen."

"But what if you're not just pretending?" Edie said. "What if I'm right?"

That was a good question. What if Edie was right? What would we be doing then?

"On the off chance you're right," I said, "I am not calling the cops. I don't want to have anything to do with them. So I hope you have your cell phone with you to call them if you wish. But then I'm out of here."

Edie looked at me sheepishly.

I rolled my eyes. "You don't have your cell phone with you, do you?"

"Sorry, I didn't think to take it with me," Edie said.

Gran mumbled something from the back seat about old people and slowpokes and landlines.

"Edie, do I really have to tell you explicitly to take your cell phone with you everywhere you go?" I asked. "Especially for a trip like this?"

"Well, it's not a reflex," Edie said. "So yes, you have to tell me that."

"Fine, whatever," I said. "I don't think we're going to need a cell phone either way, so let's just drop it."

"I'm not going to hope we don't need a cell phone because that would mean there's nothing to see here and that would be a bummer, wouldn't it?" Edie said.

I honestly didn't know what to tell her. I kind of wanted the action, but I didn't want the consequences. I didn't have the cushion of the Falcons network here in Bitter End. I was totally exposed to law enforcement. Even worse, I now had to be extra careful being in WITSEC and all. And Gran as well.

We kept our eyes on the square and scanned the shops around it. Gélato, the ice cream place, was getting ready to close up shop. The last customers came out with ice cream cones. An ice cream would be good right now. First chips, then ice cream. *Way to eat healthy.*

Some couples were strolling by, holding hands. Some teenagers were out and about, probably looking for a party. A lot of elderly people were sitting on the benches around the square, watching the mesmerizing spectacle of the fountain's dancing water illuminated by the colorful lights.

At about 9:55 I saw a guy sauntering through the square and taking a seat on one of the empty benches. He stuck out like a square peg in a round hole. Oh my god, this had to be Thug #1. Victoria's description was right on the mark.

He had on jeans, a black T-shirt, and a black vest over it. He was tall, had good muscle tone and short dark hair. Victoria also mentioned the tall one had a scar on his face. I was too far away, and it was too dark for me to see if he had a scar, but I was sure this was him.

FOOL ME ONCE

I exchanged glances with Edie and Gran.

"I can't believe this," Edie said, and her voice was an octave higher. "I think that's one of them. I think I'm going to pee my pants."

"Why?" I asked. "It was your idea to come here. You expected this to happen."

"Yes, but I'm amazed I was right," Edie said.

I was just as amazed. And slightly thrown by this turn of events. We could have used Edie's ideas back in Oregon.

I surveyed the surroundings but didn't see Thug #2 and didn't see Lloyd either. And where were Ryker and Sam and the cops anyway?

"I don't know what's about to happen, but I think I'm going to need my heart medicine," Edie said.

Gran sighed out of boredom in the back seat. "I'm going to take a nap. Wake me up when we're done here."

"Okay, everybody, you know what?" I said. "Let's just wait and see what happens before we get our panties in a bunch."

Edie and I leaned over and held our breath while we watched what would come next. Thug #1 stretched out on the bench and lit up a cigarette. He pulled out his phone and scrolled and casually puffed away. He didn't seem too concerned. He didn't seem alarmed; his body language was very relaxed. I remembered Thug #1 not being exactly the sharpest pencil in the bunch, so I would expect such behavior.

Two minutes later he put out his cigarette on the ground.

"What a litterer," Edie said.

"I'd say that's the least of our problems," I said.

We kept watching him. From out of nowhere, the guy pulled out some weird-looking fruit and vigorously bit into it while he kept scrolling his phone.

"Is he serious?" I asked. "What is this?"

Edie shrugged. "Well, maybe he's just hungry. Even bad guys have to eat, right?"

Thug #1 tore into his fruit with gusto then seemed to frown. He studied it, then spit some out. Then he placed the remaining fruit next to him on the bench and did a shiver of disgust.

"Now that is just sickening," Edie said.

"I agree," I said. Being a criminal does not mean you have to be a complete boor. I was taught to have good manners either way.

We kept our eyes fixed on Thug #1, when all of a sudden a man was standing before him. He was wearing blue sweatpants and a sweatshirt. Thug #1 looked up and smiled. Then he rose. He stood in front of Lloyd.

"Oh my god, that's Lloyd!" Edie said. "It's really him!"

"Edie," I said and turned to her. "Please let me know if you get any chest pains."

I had to admit I felt my heartbeat speed up as well. This felt like the action I missed so much.

The two men stood in front of each other, and Lloyd pulled out something from the pocket of his sweatshirt. It looked to be a small device, but I was too far away to recognize it. I had to assume it was a flash drive. Okay, so they were doing the exchange. But what did Thug #1 have to give him? Lloyd had to have demanded money in exchange for the audio file. It had to be cash too. But I didn't see any suitcase or duffel bags or trunks anywhere near Thug #1.

Thug #1 took whatever device Lloyd had just handed to him and then I saw their mouths moving. Thug #1 was calmly saying something, and in response, Lloyd became agitated. He began flailing around with his hands. I was so focused on their exchange that I didn't see another shorter guy approaching until he was suddenly standing behind Lloyd. The shorter guy was definitely Thug #2. He looked exactly like Thug #1, only he was shorter and was bald. It was like Thug #1's mini-me. There was no doubt these two were the guys Victoria described to us.

The shorter guy was suspiciously close to Lloyd. Lloyd seemed startled by someone behind him, and I saw his back stiffening. Oh wow, I knew what was going on.

"What's happening there?" Edie asked with her eyes almost bulging out the windshield.

"The shorter guy is threatening Lloyd with a gun to his back," I said.

Edie whipped her head toward me. "What? Are you serious? How do you know that?"

"I can read body language," I said.

We kept watching. The three men were still standing there, the shorter guy still behind Lloyd. They were most probably negotiating something. So much for choosing a public place to avoid exactly this.

Then they all started moving, with Lloyd leading the way and the thugs extremely close behind him. I was sure they had the gun still pointed at Lloyd. What rookies. You never let the victim walk first. You sandwich the victim between you. I shook my head. Losers like this were running free. Unbelievable. That only made my life harder.

"What's going on?" Edie asked.

"Looks like their deal is off," I said. "They are taking Lloyd with them at gunpoint."

Edie sucked in some air. "Oh my god, oh my god, what do we do? We need to call the cops!"

Now I was the one who whipped her head around at Edie. "What did I just say ten minutes ago? I will not call the cops."

"Are you kidding me?" Edie said "You mean we're just going to let them escape?"

"Well, Ryker was supposed to take care of it. And Sam was supposed to take care of it. And the cops were supposed to take care of it. Right? So where the hell are they?"

Edie was silent for a bit. "I don't know where they are but we have to call them."

We both turned our attention on the men again. They were on one of the side streets, and three seconds later, they disappeared from view.

"See?" Edie said. "Now they're getting away. Then we need to follow them. So come on, step on it."

I thought about it. Was it really wise to start following them? And that was only if we could catch up with them. What was their plan? Well, for starters, the plan was to double-cross Lloyd. I was guessing the brain behind it was the infamous Mr. Moose. He must have given the thugs the order to bring Lloyd to him. Man, I would really have liked to know who Mr. Moose was. The genius behind hiring two idiots. And at least one littering idiot, just leaving that piece of fruit—

And then it dawned on me. Holy guacamole! It was right there in front of me. My heart rate went through the roof.

"I think I know where they're going," I said.

"What?" Edie asked. "What do you mean? Do you know something I don't?"

"I do now," I said and turned on the ignition.

I turned around and saw Gran was lightly snoring in the back seat. Actually, that wasn't that bad. I would wake her up in case I needed a good shooter.

"Where are we going?" Edie asked, totally sweating although the AC was on high.

"Look, I'm not one hundred percent sure I'm right, so we're just going to drive there and see for ourselves," I said.

"Could you make this more cryptic than it already is?" Edie asked.

"I could, but I'm just going to leave it at that," I said.

I made a quick U-turn and stepped on the gas. With Edie gripping the armrest, the only sound breaking the silence in the car while I drove back to the retirement complex, was Gran snoring even louder.

We entered through the gate, and I drove slower through the streets, looking left and right.

"Don't tell me we're looking for them here," Edie said. "This is our retirement complex. This is where we live."

"I know," I said. "Don't worry, we're in the right place."

"That's what's worrying me," Edie said.

I took a left and then a right and then I saw them. A silver Toyota Prius about one hundred yards away. It was the only car on the street, since it was already after ten thirty at night and the residents weren't out and about this late usually. I closed the distance just a bit and could make out a couple of people in the car. This was them. I just knew it.

I was on their tail, but still not super close. We drove to the southwest corner of the complex, when their car parked in the driveway of a pastel-blue house. I drove past the house, turned left, and parked the car by the curb one block over.

"Did they just park in front of . . .?" Edie asked. "I know that house! This can't be happening!"

"I'm afraid it is," I said.

Edie was speechless. Which didn't happen very often. I could tell she was trying to compute what was happening.

"Look, Edie," I said. "If it's true what I think is true, then I need to see it for myself first." Then I swallowed hard. "Before you call the cops."

"You serious?" Edie asked wide-eyed. "You're going back there?"

I nodded.

"Well, hell yes—then I'm coming with you," Edie said and already took off her seat belt.

I stopped her right there. "You are definitely not coming with me. You are seventy-five years old, and I don't care how brave you are; those guys will shoot you in a second."

Okay, I wasn't so sure about the shooting part. But the thugs did shoot Tammy Feldman without blinking, so Edie should take that into consideration. I needed to convince her somehow to stay in the car.

"If I don't come back in five minutes, call the cops," I pulled out my cell phone and reluctantly gave it to Edie.

"But . . . but . . ." Edie said.

"I don't want to hear another peep from you. It's either this way or no way. Got it?"

Edie looked disappointed that she wouldn't be in on the action but nodded. Clearly, I was a bad influence on her. She did have the "regular civilian" symptoms, like a tendency to call the cops, overreacting when faced with a dead body, and becoming alarmed when getting too close to illicit activities. But on the other hand, she couldn't stay away from danger. She wanted to be smack-dab in the middle of the action.

Edie and I both looked back and saw Gran was still snoring.

"How the heck can she sleep through a time like this?" Edie asked. "And what is she so tired about? It's not like she has a job."

I grinned. "I think this is just her way of not getting involved."

Edie wished me good luck and I got out of the car. The street was lit but there were no people around. Some houses had the light on. Other houses had the TV booming.

I walked along the sidewalk and tried to look casual. I turned the corner to where the car was still parked. I saw there was light inside, so I hid behind a hedge. I was so glad I wore my sneakers and not the flip-flops. I could still feel a bit of discomfort from my foot scrape, but I ignored it.

The front porch of the house was brightly lit, so I opted for peeking in through a window from the side of the house. Then I would report back to Edie what I saw, and I would drive us all back to our houses, and Edie could call the cops from her own phone. Giving Edie my own phone was just a safety net in case something happened to me.

I jumped out from behind the hedge and glued myself to the side of the house, right next to a window. From there, I peeked in. Lloyd was sitting on the couch, all tensed up, with a desperate look on his face, while Thug #1 was standing next to him, holding a gun to his head. Lloyd was almost crying. What a wuss.

Across from Lloyd was an older man with a wicked grin on his face. His whole vibe screamed *I am in charge*. So my suspicions were right. This was Mr. Moose.

My eyes searched for Thug #2, and I frowned because I couldn't see him anywhere.

"Well, well, well, what do we have here?" a voice behind me said.

Crap.

Now I knew where Thug #2 was.

I was about to whip around in a roundhouse kick and take him by surprise, but he was faster than me.

I felt a blow on the back of my head, and everything went black.

Chapter Nineteen

I OPENED MY EYES and let out a low groan. The first thing I felt was a big fat headache. Then I felt a pain in my upper shoulders. Where the hell was I? I looked around and tried to recognize the place. Was I in my home in Oregon? No, this didn't look like it. Where did I live now? Oh yes, I moved with my grandmother to Florida. It all came painfully back to me. But I knew Gran's house didn't look like this.

A couple of seconds later I realized I was sitting on a chair and my hands were tied behind my back and around the chair. My legs weren't tied to the chair, and I thought for a second, *why tie me at all if you're not going to do it right?* I tried to say something, but nothing came out. I had duct tape over my mouth. Was this really happening? A couple of weeks ago this was exactly how I found Edie when she was being held hostage in her own home.

I was in a living room. The last thing I remembered was . . . oh geez, now it dawned on me where I was. A few feet from me sat Lloyd Feldman, still on the couch, and Thug #1 was still pointing a gun to his head. Didn't his arm hurt? He must have been holding it like that for a while now. Lloyd looked all sweaty and frightened, and I wasn't even sure why anybody would point a gun at him. He was zero threat. In a fight, at least. His biggest advantage was he ran fast.

Thug #2 emerged from the bathroom and another man came out of the bedroom. They both stood and crossed their arms looking at me.

"She's finally awake," the older man said. "You hit her pretty hard on the head."

"Well, how are you supposed to hit someone on the head if not hard?" Thug #2 said.

Yes, exactly; and for that, you are going to pay.

The older man rolled his eyes then looked me in the eye. "I'm going to take that tape away and you're not going to scream, are you?"

I shook my head. He walked over and, in one fell swoop, ripped away the duct tape. I didn't even flinch. Pain meant nothing to me now, I was so pumped up with adrenaline. These guys had no idea what they were getting themselves into by taking me hostage. Hopefully Edie and Gran were somewhere outside. Hopefully they made a plan, realizing I didn't come back. Hopefully Edie could wake up Sleeping Beauty from her snoring coma.

"Why don't we start by you telling me why you were spying on me outside," the older man asked.

"Why do you think, Sherlock? I know it's you who was behind it all."

The older man had an evil grin plastered on his face. "And how did you figure that out?" he asked.

"Because you hired the most idiotic muscles out there," I said. "And you're not so bright either."

All three men sucked in some air. Lloyd almost fainted on the couch. I knew they didn't expect the person they tied up to speak to them like that. Theoretically, I was in no position to. But I didn't care. Especially since these nincompoops didn't even bother to tie up my legs too. All I needed to do was wait for the right moment to pounce.

I assessed my situation. I had to fight the two thugs and possibly the older man. Lloyd would be no opponent, but he ran fast. Still, he shouldn't be underestimated. Out of panic, even weaker ones such as Lloyd could do stupid extreme things, like pick up a gun and start shooting around aimlessly. Which brought me to the subject of guns. They only had one, as far as I could see, and Thug #1 was holding it. Nonetheless, Thug #2 could have a gun tucked in his jeans belt or anywhere else on his body.

FOOL ME ONCE

Same for the older man. I wished I had my knife with me.

"What did you just say?" Thug #2 said and his eyebrows shot right up. He took a few steps in my direction with steam coming out of his ears, but the older man stopped him.

"I ought to smack her right in her mouth," Thug #2 said.

"I dare you to," I said. "You can add more counts to your stupidities. Make it easier for me when I'm turning you in."

As if it only clicked now, Thug #1 came to life and said, shaking his head, "Idiotic muscles? That's really not cool."

"Who the hell are you?" the older man asked.

"You know very well who I am," I said. "I'm Edie's neighbor, and the one who's going to take you down."

The man stared at me, probably contemplating if I was full of bull or really meaning it. He must have decided not to take his chances. So he asked, "Are you a cop?"

I shook my head vehemently.

"Are you some kind of government agent?" he asked.

I shook my head even more frantically.

"Then I don't know who you are, but look around you," the older man said. "You're not really in the position to make threats now, are you?"

"That's what you think," I said.

If he only knew who he was dealing with, he would have just given up and turned himself in already without a fight.

"So when did you realize what was going on with Tammy and Lloyd?" I asked. I thought it wasn't such a bad idea to stall for time and to let Gran and Edie regroup. I also needed to figure out a plan. But first, I needed to study how the dynamics were between these fools here.

"How do you know I figured something out?" the older man said.

"Because that's the only explanation," I said. I glanced at Lloyd. "You realized he and his partner were scammers, and instead of turning them in, you thought you could cash in on it too. You threatened Tammy and Lloyd with exposing them. Then you collected your share of the money from them. But then you got greedy. That was your mistake. Greed will always get you, and that is when you realize that human nature is so basic and primitive."

"Is it, now?" The older man asked, evil grin back on his face.

"Yes, it is," I said and felt around the rope they tied me with. Unfortunately, the rope seemed solid and I didn't have anything on me to try to tear it or cut it. So I kept on talking. "Instead of getting a decent amount of incoming cash from them on a regular basis, you wanted more. And now look what you got on your hands. Tammy and Lloyd refused, so you shot Tammy, making Lloyd pay up. Now you have a murder and kidnapping on your rap sheet on top of extortion and being an accomplice to their scam."

The older man rolled his eyes. "Those two were lousy scammers. I used to work in a bank. I knew right away their investment schemes were a fraud. So I wanted in, obviously. It would have been easy too, if those two wouldn't have been so resistant."

Lloyd began whimpering on the couch and put his head in his hands.

The older man shook his head. "What a wuss."

"I have to agree with you on that one," I said.

Lloyd looked up and stared at me. "I don't know your story, but I thought you came here to help me."

"To help you?" I asked and almost jumped on him with the chair on my back. "I'm here to take you down as well. You jerk—you scammed all these people here out of their money. They're seniors!

DEANY RAY

That money was their nest egg! They counted on you. And you stole their money and now you think I came here to help you? Listen up, you moron, I will make sure you rot in jail, do you understand me? It's either that or put you six feet under. And believe you me, I don't have any problem with the latter."

I felt a wave of anger crashing over me. I wouldn't have cared in my old life what a scammer did. Moreover, I would look over their shoulder, see if I could learn a few more tricks. But the last three weeks had changed me. Okay, they'd *slightly* changed me. I found myself caring for the seniors and wanting to punish whoever did them harm.

I swear Lloyd almost started crying.

"You know what?" The older man said to Thug #1. "Maybe you should point the gun at her and not at him."

Thug #1 did as he was told.

"But guard the door," the older man said to Thug #1. "He's a runner."

Thug #1 moved in front of the door. He shook his arm, like it had fallen asleep. "Can I just point the gun at her if she moves? My arm kind of hurts."

The older man looked at him like he couldn't believe what he'd just asked.

"See?" I asked the older man. "I told you; you hired the stupidest out there."

Thug #2 jumped up at me again, but the older man yelled at him this time. "You're only moving if I say so."

Thug #2 didn't look happy, but he obeyed.

"So how did you figure this out?" the older man asked me while he took a seat on the couch next to Lloyd. He made himself comfortable by crossing one leg over the other. Lloyd scooched a couple of inches away from him.

"One of your henchmen ate your fruit," I said.

The older man raised an eyebrow.

I explained that I'd seen Thug #1 at Liberty Square munching on a fruit that looked an awful lot like a type I'd seen before. I knew that the older man was into cross-pollinating: oranges and limes. I also knew people thought they were too sourly. Thug #1 made exactly the same face Burt did after biting into the fruit. Burt was the resident dressed head to toe in green; hence, Green Man. I had seen him at the gathering in the rec hall, sitting next to the older man, trying out the fruit.

The older man looked stunned, and he turned his gaze to Thug #1. "You didn't like my orangelo?"

Thug #1 scratched the back of his head. "Sorry, boss, they're really not good."

"Then there was the thing with the name," I continued. I didn't have any patience for the rolling pins in Thug #1's brain.

"What thing?" the man asked.

"Mr. Moose," I said. "Your name is Earnest Reed. Reed spelled backward is deer. Moose, deer . . . you get it. Like I said before; you're not the brightest either."

Earnest Reed, resident of the Bitter End retirement complex, wearing his older man's cap with the orange and the lime as a logo, was sitting on the couch only a few feet from me and his grin disappeared.

"You better watch your mouth there, young lady, if you still want to live." Reed said.

"Why would I believe you would let me live?" I asked. "You're probably pondering what to do with me right now, since I messed up your plan. But like I've said before, you should be the one to worry about what happens. I really am going to take you down."

Reed let out a laugh. "I don't know if you're gutsy or just delusional." He paused. "I'm assuming you're the one these two talked to on the phone?"

"Yeah, that's her," Thug #2 said. He was now leaning on the kitchen counter with his arms crossed. "She was the cocky one. I wouldn't forget that voice."

"That was very clever," Reed said. "How did you get your hands on Feldman's phone?"

I told them about Lloyd dropping his phone at the paintball field and me taking it with me. That only reminded me of Sam and Ryker and the cops. Why weren't they here? Sam was tracking down Lloyd's phone. Then why weren't they at Liberty Square and why aren't they here now? The only explanation would be that Lloyd changed his phone.

"Yes, we thought something like that happened," Reed said. "I have to admit, we were thrown for a second when you proposed the deal. We had one already with Lloyd."

"Just out of curiosity," I asked. "How much money did Lloyd ask for in exchange for the audio file?"

Reed grinned again. "One hundred thousand."

I rolled my eyes and glanced at Lloyd. "Seriously? Only one hundred grand? How long would that have lasted you? You're really making me sick. How you managed to scam all these people here, I will never know."

Reed laughed. "Exactly. It was easy seeing through Lloyd."

"Was it also easy seeing through these other two?" I asked. "You stuck with the details of your deal, and that's how I found you at Liberty Square at ten p.m."

Reed went white and turned his look to Thug #1 and Thug #2. "How the heck does she know about that?"

I burst out laughing. This fool didn't even realize how I found them. He had no idea Thug #1 had told me the time for their exchange.

"You two are really worthless," Reed said to them. "I could have hired anyone else at that bar. Why the hell did I choose you?"

"Because we're the only ones who went along with it," Thug #2 said smugly. "It's not like your plan is so sophisticated. Why didn't you pull the trigger on the broad yourself, old man? You should be thanking us."

Thug #1 just nodded along.

This was awesome. They were turning against each other. So we had Lloyd, who was fighting for himself, we had the two thugs who were in the other corner, and then we had Earnest Reed. And then there was me. Who was going to take them down.

Could be that I was a bit rusty, considering I hadn't exercised properly in the last thirteen months and since I'd arrived in Florida. But I'd been in training for thirty-one years, up until I had to leave my old life behind me.

Lloyd was probably the easiest target. He was slim with barely any muscle tone. Reed was around eightyish, but still seemed to be sharp. Only his body wouldn't play along at his age. Thug #1 and Thug #2 were the ones I had to be careful of. They were literally no brain but a lot of muscle.

"Okay, okay, let's not get into a fight about this," Reed said to Thug #2. "Let's see how we can clean up this situation here."

Hmm. Interesting. Reed *did* possess an ounce of intelligence. He deescalated. He didn't get into a fight with Thug #2. He put his ego aside, because the current situation was more important. I had to give him props for thinking like that.

"Mr. Feldman," Reed said. "Tell us where you have the copy of the audio file."

"But I told you, I didn't make any copy," Lloyd said whimpering. "I gave you the flash drive and I deleted the audio file from my phone. There's no other copy. I just want to get this episode behind me. It's bad enough you killed Tammy." His voice trembled and he had to pause. "I don't want to lose *my* life too."

Oh, so this is what it was about. Reed and the thugs didn't trust that Lloyd would carry out his part of the deal, which was handing over the audio file. They believed Lloyd made a copy of it and therefore could blackmail them again. Lloyd couldn't even prove he didn't make a copy. How do you prove you didn't make a copy of something? So what did Reed have in mind for Lloyd? Was he going to kill Lloyd and then kill me too?

Frankly, I would believe Lloyd didn't make another copy, because he didn't come across as a mastermind. But again, the stupid ones were not to be underestimated. They were the most unpredictable.

Reed smiled at Lloyd. "Why would I believe you?" he asked. "You're a fraudster, you steal from seniors, you blackmailed us—so why would I believe you're not going to do it again?"

Lloyd threw his hands in the air. "Because I want to move on, and I want to live! The cops already think I shot Tammy, they've frozen my accounts, and they're after me. I only had the couple of hundred bucks in my pocket when I made a run for it, then I tried to lay low, but then I got shot at with paintballs by those stupid old people. Then she took the cell phone I had just bought, so I had to buy yet another one. Then I was being held at gunpoint in the middle of town. I did not sign up for this! I don't want to be part of this. I want you to give me my money so I can get the hell out of here and go to Guatemala or the Bahamas or wherever and just forget about everything that happened here."

Wow.

There was silence for a few beats. And I realized my arms had begun to hurt in their tied-up position behind my back.

The way Lloyd talked about himself and only himself, about saving his own butt . . . he didn't really talk about any love that he had for Tammy. Nor did he seem sad because she was dead, and that made me ask him, "Was Tammy even your wife?"

Lloyd looked in my direction. "Of course not. She was my business partner. And she got on my nerves every single day. I'm not that super sad she's gone, although we made a great team. I have to admit, I wouldn't have done this good without her. It's just that gullible older people buy into this whole married-couple-trying-to-make-a-living crap."

It was just like I had suspected. Business partners. Shamelessly scamming the seniors and knowing what buttons to push. I had to really control myself in that moment. I breathed in and out.

Reed stood and walked through the room. "You know what, Feldman? This is what we're going to do. There is one way you can prove you don't have a copy of the audio file. And that is if you're not going to blackmail us again. I'm going to let you go and I'm giving you zero money. If you call us again and blackmail us, we won't be this nice to you again."

I blinked twice. What kind of plan was this? I did not see this one coming. I thought about it. Okay, it wasn't that bad. It was really good, actually. Assuming Lloyd did have another copy, he wouldn't go to the cops with it, because he wouldn't have anything to gain. He only wanted money. If he blackmailed these guys again, then they would have to meet somehow again. And then Lloyd would be toast. I didn't think Lloyd was clever enough to set up an exchange with sophisticated details such as money drops in specific places, so that they wouldn't have to meet face-to-face.

Lloyd looked desperate. He whipped his head around from Reed to me to Thug #1 to Thug #2. "You're letting me go? But where's my money?

"Did you not understand what I just said?" Reed said. "You don't get any money. Now get up and get out of here."

Wow, this was getting unpredictable. If I were Lloyd, I would bail out of here and just save my skin as soon as possible. The money I could earn after that through other hustles.

Then I thought about the situation outside. We had a similar situation a couple of weeks ago. Man, these seniors had probably never seen this much action. And the cops were probably confused about this much action at a retirement complex. With the other hostage situation, the cops surrounded the house but arrived in silence. No sirens, no nothing. They had the element of surprise on their side. So I wondered now, could the cops already be outside? I honestly had no idea how much time had passed between the knock on my head and now.

If they were outside, they probably had to assign three officers to hold off Gran from bursting inside the house with her gun drawn.

I knew I was not a fan of the cops, and I probably would never be, but I had to admit, in a situation like this, where I was the one tied up and I didn't have the Oregon Falcons to save my butt, I wouldn't mind having the cops do that.

Lloyd got up and seemed to be confused. He probably wasn't sure if they would really let him go or shoot him right before he stepped outside.

"Go ahead, go," Reed said. "I'm a man of my word. What you do for money I don't care. You're not getting any from me, so you have to start a new scam. I don't care."

"If I were you, I'd skip right now," Thug #2 said in a disgusted way. "Just be happy you get to keep your life."

Lloyd's shoulders slouched. I could see defeat in his face. He knew he wasn't going to get any money and he just gave them the one thing he had as leverage over them. But I had to agree with Thug #2; he should be happy to just be alive.

Lloyd slowly took a few steps toward the door. Thug #1, with his constant dumb look on his face, moved out of the way. His gun-holding arm dangled next to his body. He wasn't alert at all.

Thug #2 moved in front of me, and I could feel his breath on my face. He said with a wicked grin, "Now let's see what to do about her."

I hoped so bad that it wasn't a mistake what I was about to do. If my calculations were right, Thug #1 had a gun, but Thug #2 still didn't seem to have any. If he wore it concealed, he still needed a couple of seconds to pull the gun out. Those were valuable seconds. Reed also didn't seem to have a gun at all.

So I kicked my leg high and it connected with Thug #2's crotch. His hands flew to his private area, and he crashed to the floor, screaming in pain. Just for good measure, I kicked his side as well. I knew the next move would be Thug #1 trying to shoot at me.

"What the . . .?" he said, raising his gun-holding arm.

In an instant, I jumped up and dived behind the couch while bullets flew into the cushions. I landed hard on my side. Possibly I broke a rib or two. But no time to think about that now. I was still tied up to the chair, for crying out loud.

That was when Lloyd probably thought it was a good idea to get out of there, especially since he got a free card. I was counting on that. He opened the door, ran outside, and two seconds later came back in a frenzy, shutting the door closed behind him.

"Oh, my freaking god, the place is swarming with cops!" Lloyd said wide-eyed.

Now it was my turn to grin evilly.

Reed asked, "What did you just say? The cops are here?"

Lloyd said, "I think every cop in town is here," In a split second, he jumped behind the couch next to me and assumed a fetal position.

I pondered if it was even worth it going after Lloyd. That was my plan all the last few days, to punch him in the face for what he did to Edie, but now . . . He was just too sad.

Reed and Thug #1 exchanged worried glances and they both bolted for the back, probably wanting to get out through the window in the bathroom. What idiots. If the cops were swarming the place, then obviously they were watching every exit point. There was no escape from any of them.

The only way they could have bought time or really get away clean, was to take me hostage. Which they kind of already had. I mean, Thug #1 had a gun, and I was still with my arms tied to the chair. It would have been so easy for them to use me for negotiating with the cops to get an escape car, a helicopter, whatever. It probably wouldn't have worked, but hey, at least they could have tried.

But no. The idiots opted for the brainless choice.

I looked next to me and saw Lloyd with his head between his hands, still in a fetal position. I rolled my eyes. He wasn't going anywhere.

I should, though. Just in case Reed and Thug #1 realized what they should have been doing instead of trying to bail, I decided it was time for me to get out of the house too. It was not that easy to get to a standing position when you had a chair strapped to your back and your arms and hands and the side of your body were searing with pain. Nevertheless, that didn't stop me getting up fast.

Just as I took the first steps toward the door, Thug #2 grabbed my ankle, and I crashed onto the floor again. *Way to collect more pain points.*

But he didn't have a firm grip on me. I kicked with my legs so hard, I probably broke his nose. I almost felt pity for him. He could have just waited for the cops to storm in, which they would do any second now. Then he at least would have avoided his injuries. But this way, I got some satisfaction as well.

I jumped up again and ran for the front door just as it burst open, and I crashed into a hard chest. Ryker's chest.

Oh, goody. Another broken rib.

I looked up and saw worry and relief in his eyes at the same time. Which was weird, because why should he be worried? His grandmother was safe.

I was glued to him when he swirled his hands behind me, saying in a soft voice, "Let me untie you."

DEANY RAY

I relaxed in his arms and pressed my forehead against his chest. Then I let him untie me.

Chapter Twenty

I STEPPED OUT OF THE bathroom after a refreshing shower and tripped over a gift basket, wrapped in pink cellophane.

Ugh. *Goddammit.*

My side hurt and I bent over.

"Gran, what the heck?" I asked. "I told you to put these somewhere else."

"Where do you want me to put them?" Gran yelled from the kitchen table. "I told you we should burn them."

"We can't burn them," I said, going to the kitchen area and straight to the coffeemaker. "We got them as a gift."

Gran let out a snort. "We got gift gift baskets. Just what I always wanted."

I poured some coffee into my mug and leaned on the kitchen counter. I scanned Gran's house. There were gift baskets everywhere. And I mean literally everywhere. Every corner and every surface of the floor was covered in spa gift baskets. Come to think of it, maybe this was a good thing. You couldn't see the ugly yellow carpet this way.

We now had foot powder until we died. As soon as word came out that we apprehended Lloyd and the other guys, the residents were ecstatic. They kept on coming to Gran's house to leave their gift basket as a thank-you for us busting Earnest Reed and the others.

I knew what they were actually doing. They were getting rid of their rash-giving foot powder. And what a lovely disguise they picked. As if we didn't know what was going on with that powder. Nonetheless, we accepted their gifts and kept up the pretenses. We couldn't prove that Sourpuss put something into the powder, although everybody kind of knew that. We couldn't even find out what it was that caused the rash, and by "we," I mean Edie and company: Gran and I stayed out of it as much as possible.

By the one hundredth gift basket, Gran almost lost it, though. I caught her Googling for house signs that read, "Visitors Not Welcome."

Every winner from the paintball game got rid of their basket. The ones that didn't win came by with pies, chicken casseroles, mac-and-cheese casseroles and whatnot. Gran's house was now littered with spa gift baskets, and our fridge and our cupboards had never been this full. I wouldn't even know when to finish all this food, especially since there was a dining hall here at the complex. Where residents expected to see us, I might add.

I convinced Gran to give up the Visitors Not Welcome sign, so she went for an improvised sign on a piece of paper she got from Edie, that read, "We are not taking food, just booze."

We also appointed Edie's house as gift basket central. Every basket that would come our way from now on would be diverted to her. That was another way of saying, "Edie, keep the baskets."

Today was Saturday and it had been two days since Lloyd and Reed and the thugs were busted.

After Ryker had untied me from that chair, I collapsed on the floor. I knew it was over and the adrenaline started to fade away instantly. I felt dizzy and I felt wobbly on my feet. Ryker had picked me up and carried me in his arms outside to the paramedics. From there, I made a short trip to the hospital.

I didn't plan on seeing the interior of the hospital only three weeks after moving here. But I was so out of it mentally, I just let it go. I didn't care what happened. I was absolutely exhausted. Dillon could have emerged out of nowhere and told me it was over and that Gran and I needed to move somewhere else or be out of the witness protection program; I wouldn't have cared. I was that drained. I did refuse staying overnight at the hospital, though. I had two broken ribs and a lot of bruises on my body. The raw skin on my wrist after being tied up, burned just a bit every time I washed my hands or took a shower. But hey, I almost had forgotten about my scrape on the sole of my foot. It was all relative when you put it in perspective.

Gran came with me to the hospital and then she drove me to the house. It could have been sometime in the middle of the night that we finally arrived home. Surprisingly, the couch that I slept on had never felt so good.

The next day, Gran let me sleep in. She usually whipped up a lot of commotion around the kitchen, so there was never any sleeping after Gran woke up, but she was somehow super silent and I woke up at almost noon.

I had the feeling Gran had contacted Edie and let her know that under no circumstances she should come knocking—or anybody else for that matter—or Gran would shoot them. Edie was smart and took that threat seriously. So it was not till afternoon when I texted Edie that she could come over.

FOOL ME ONCE

She brought a plum pie and the warmest hug ever, crushing my already wrecked ribs again. And then we talked about the night before and tried to get some closure.

As Lloyd had already confirmed, Tammy Feldman was not his wife. They were still looking into what other names those two had used for their other hustles. But Lloyd told the cops everything. He met Tammy about six years ago and realized how good they worked together. Since they both had good enough financial knowledge, they realized they could make a buttload of money by scamming people. Three years ago, they realized seniors were their most profitable target audience, so they went from state to state, scamming retirees out of their money. It was clever that they didn't stay for too long in only one place. It was harder to track down criminals if they were always on the move. That is, until they landed in Bitter End, Florida. I mean, the name already says it all.

Lloyd is facing enough charges to keep his butt in jail for a long time. Regarding Edie's money and the residents' money, the Federal Trade Commission was on Lloyd and Tammy's tail for a while now, and they were the ones that froze the accounts. A thorough investigation was underway and we heard it looked good for Edie and the others. They should be getting their money back soon.

Edie was so happy, she brought over a bottle of rum on top of the plum pie.

The residents were shocked to find out about Earnest Reed. Nobody would have thought he was capable of something like this. He never came across as someone engaged in any criminal activity. People said he enjoyed his retirement life and his hobby with the orange and lime thing. Which sounded very normal for everybody around here.

When Reed and Thug #1 jumped out of the bathroom window at Reed's house, they landed straight into the arms of the cops. Just as anticipated. Thug #1 and Thug #2 had been taken away along with Reed. But not before the paramedics took care of Thug #2's injuries. After Ryker untied me, he looked over my shoulder and probably saw a man in agony. Ryker then asked me, frowning, "Did you kick him in the nuts?"

I nodded. I was too tired to form any words.

Ryker winced but then nodded in agreement.

That was when I collapsed on the floor in exhaustion.

At the police station, Thug #1 and Thug #2 sang like two canaries. They spilled everything about

Reed. They had met in a seedy bar somewhere on the outskirts of Bitter End and Reed made the proposal to them and hired them on the spot. Their job was to collect the money from Tammy and Lloyd on a monthly basis. That is, until Reed wanted a bigger piece of the pie. And then we all knew what happened next. The good thing was that Reed couldn't escape the count of soliciting to murder.

The cops now also had the audio file. They found Lloyd's first phone in a ditch a couple of blocks from his office. What a dunce. That wasn't the way to discard a cell phone. But anyway, that was the phone Lloyd recorded the murder with. He knew then he had to get rid of the phone because the cops were after him. So he bought a new one with a prepaid card, sent the audio file to the new phone, turned off the old phone and threw it away. The prepaid phone was the one he dropped in that cabin and that I recovered.

With evidence like the recording, both thugs would accept a cooperating plea agreement, meaning they would get a reduction in the severity of the charge in exchange for providing information about other individuals involved. Hence, Mr. Moose.

Bottom line, they were all going down and I couldn't have been more satisfied.

When Ryker carried me out of Reed's house, Gran and Edie almost jumped on me. It had been only forty-five minutes since I had left them in the car. Recovering from that blow to the head didn't take too long apparently. Edie did as she was told and called the cops from my phone. It was only after the cops arrived that Edie woke up Gran. That was a good decision. Edie knew she couldn't have kept Gran from shooting her way into that house.

Edie then called Ryker, who arrived in record time at the retirement complex, as I was told afterward. Ryker, Sam, and the cops were all surveilling the Sunrise Peak Motel off the highway. That was where Sam had tracked down Lloyd's phone. And apparently the phone hadn't moved, so they all figured Lloyd was holed up in his motel room and the deal would take place there. So they took positions outside and waited for the other party to arrive.

Which they never did.

That was a good trick Lloyd pulled on them. He had the instinct to change his phone again. After Lloyd recovered his phone from Gran's sugar jar—a home invasion that we would never report to the cops and never admit to, no matter what Lloyd told the police in his statement—he bought another one.

FOOL ME ONCE

His third one. He left his second phone in his motel room before he departed for Liberty Square.

He wasn't sure about someone tracking his phone, but just knowing that I had the phone didn't sit well with him. On the off chance someone tinkered with his phone, he bought his third one from the money he had left, and could contact Reed and the thugs again.

Edie wanted to come to the hospital with me, but Ryker convinced her I was in good hands and Gran would be there. I sensed it took some convincing for Edie to really let me go without her. I only vaguely remember asking Gran on the way to the hospital how come she didn't burst into Reed's house with her gun drawn. Even with the cops there. Did they handcuff her?

Gran rolled her eyes and said it was Edie. Edie threatened Gran that if she pulled out her gun and started shooting, she would tell the cops it was Gran who shot at Lloyd in the back alley of his office. I remember trying to laugh but my aching body just hurt too much.

As I was standing in the kitchen now with a towel draped around my body and another one wrapped around my hair, I studied Gran at the kitchen table.

"What's wrong?" Gran asked.

"I'm just wondering," I said. "When you shot at Lloyd in that back alley, how come you missed? You're the best shooter there is and the distance was pretty close."

Gran grinned slightly. Then took another sip of her coffee.

"You missed on purpose, didn't you?" I asked. "At the last second you realized you couldn't just kill that person. So you missed."

"Well, if the rules around here were different, then I would have only needed one shot," Gran said.

I laughed and my hand flew to the spot where the ribs were broken. "This is the Gran that I know."

I realized I'd have to minimize laughing too. Same with taking deep breaths.

There was a loud knock on the door.

Gran threw her hands in the air. "That's it. I can't take it anymore. Edie may have held me back from shooting those guys in that house, but I swear, if anyone else comes by with one of those stinky gift baskets, I will shoot them dead."

"There's no need for that," I said and placed my mug on the kitchen counter. "I'll get the door, it's probably Edie anyhow."

FOOL ME ONCE

Without even looking through the peephole, I swung the door open and saw Ryker standing right in front of me. He looked taken aback for a second. Then he grinned and looked me up and down. Oh geez. I forgot I was only wrapped in towels. But it didn't matter, so I leaned with one hand on the doorway and put my other hand on my hip. Then *I* looked Ryker up and down in an very obvious way. That was one fine-looking man. His outfit resembled what Gran and I used to wear. Well, actually what Gran was still wearing. Ryker had on blue jeans, a tight black T-shirt, and his black aviators.

He saw me scanning him and said, "Touché." Then he took off his sunglasses and said, "Good morning."

"Good morning to you too," I said. "I'd invite you in, but as you can see, our house is ready to burst any minute now and it's going to rain foot powder."

Ryker laughed. "Yes, I heard about the foot powder. Never a dull moment around here, huh?"

I nodded. "Nope, kind of dangerous, actually." I rubbed the spot where my ribs were broken.

Ryker's eyes flew to where I applied pressure. "Speaking of dangerous, how are you feeling?"

I shrugged. "Fine, I guess. The doctor said I'm going to be as good as new in a couple of weeks. All I can do is put some ice packs on it and I have some medication for pain."

"Let me guess," Ryker said. "You're not using the medication. You're too tough for that."

I smiled. "You should work in profiling. You're very accurate." I paused. "Sometimes." Like I would ever admit to his face how good his assumptions were.

Ryker laughed. "I'll take that as a compliment. Anyway, I want to officially thank you again for taking down those guys. It wasn't so smart putting yourself in danger like that, but hey, that's your decision. I'm glad Grams was not inside that house."

"I'm not sure if you're really thanking me or if that was a scolding," I said.

"Well, I guess you could say it was a little bit of both," Ryker said. "If it weren't for you three, then we wouldn't have found those guys at Liberty Square. We were still watching the motel. But you already know I'm not a fan of your way of handling things. I have an idea how you got there, especially after what Sam told me."

"What did she tell you?" I asked, intrigued.

"She knew stuff but told me it was from a confidential source," Ryker said. "But I have a feeling I know what source she meant."

At least I knew Sam kept her word and didn't mention my name.

I just shrugged. I had zero interest in continuing the subject of was it or wasn't it me.

"Nevertheless, you got the job done and Grams is happy, and the other residents are happy, so I guess I should be happy."

"Glad to hear that," I said.

There was silence for a long moment.

"You know, Grams says we're making a good team and you should come work for me," Ryker said half-jokingly, but he kept studying me.

Ah. This was what it was all about. Instead of just coming right out and asking me, he found a roundabout way of doing it.

"Interesting," I said.

Ryker raised an eyebrow. "It is?"

"Your choice of words is interesting," I said. "'Team' and 'work for me' are not really the same things, are they? They're exactly the opposite."

Ryker grinned. "See? That's why Grams thinks we'd be good together."

Now I was the one who raised the eyebrow. "Does she now? Well, you can tell her I have to disappoint her. It's not going to happen."

I wasn't sure what Ryker's end game was. Did he really want me to work at his firm? Why? So he could command me around and tell me what I wasn't allowed to do? Or did he present me with this option so he could check out my background? I was guessing anybody who worked at a PI firm would have to have an impeccable past. Yeah, fat chance that would ever happen.

"That's too bad," Ryker said. "But I kind of already thought that would be your answer."

"Then why did you ask?" I said.

"I didn't ask," Ryker said. "I was just relaying what Gram's thoughts were."

Oh, come on. I didn't have time to play this game.

"Fine, you did," I said.

"I thought you were looking for a job," Ryker continued.

"I am," I said. "But I'm not that desperate yet."

Ouch, that hurt. I could see Ryker flinch just a bit.

There was silence again.

"Well, I guess I'll be on my way, then," Ryker said and smiled again. "I'll see you tonight, I guess."

"Oh, you'll be there?" I asked.

Ryker nodded. "Got my invitation too."

The seniors were throwing a party tonight in the rec hall for wrapping up the Lloyd mystery and the murder of Tammy. Edie told Gran and me it was actually a party in our honor. Great. Just what we needed. More attention to ourselves. I'd have to frisk Gran again before going to that party.

Ryker turned on his heel and headed for his bike. I tilted my head and enjoyed the view. Ryker's backside and the Harley. I wasn't sure which one was better.

I watched Ryker get on his bike and, with a nod, he drove away.

I was about to close the door when Edie exited her house. She looked up, saw me, and waved vigorously, making her white curls bounce with every wave. She held a gift basket in her other hand and headed over. She was practically skipping.

"Edie's coming over," I shouted to Gran from the doorway.

"Is she bringing another basket?" Gran shouted back.

I smiled. "Yes, she is."

"Okay, I'm getting my gun," Gran said.

DEANY RAY

About the Author

Born and raised in Romania (Transylvania, to be exact), Deany Ray moved to Germany when she was 21 years old and since then calls Cologne her home. She keeps hearing some mentions about vampires and Dracula and whatnot, but she thinks that's all just a bunch of hooey.

Just keep any wooden stakes far away from her, okay?

She's not a native English speaker, so her editor and proofreader make sure her books don't sound like baloney. You could come across some typos in her emails (this is a sneaky way of asking you to join her newsletter), but hey, she just wants to put some good, entertaining stories out there.

She hopes you enjoyed the 2nd Piper Harris mystery story.

DeanyRay.com (for that newsletter she mentioned)

Facebook.com/DeanyRayBooks

Made in United States
Orlando, FL
01 June 2025